CAPRICORN CHUCK'S
WORLD of PAIN

PALMETTO
PUBLISHING
Charleston, SC
www.PalmettoPublishing.com

Hardcover ISBN: 979-8-8229-4929-4
Paperback ISBN: 979-8-8229-4930-0
eBook ISBN: 979-8-8229-4931-7

CAPRICORN CHUCK'S WORLD OF PAIN

STEVE PENDELTON

For the loving memories of my grandparents,
Mark and Mary Dias
Maria Cavelier

Rita and Armand Lussier, (Gramp)who saved us all literally.
My gram who secretly told me that Im #1!
So important to have had them in my life growing up-forever and
truly grateful I am!

To my daughter Candie, who had one of the kindest hearts
I've ever known and deserved more and everything...

You only live twice:
Once when you're born
And once when you
look death in the face.

IAN FLEMING

PROLOGUE

AUGUST 2002

A SMALL, PRIVATE Eclipse 500 jet was flying back from Virginia, approximately just over the Chesapeake Bay area. Inside the cabin was an aisle running between five rows of two seats and two mahogany coffee tables. On the right, alone sat a Hispanic man in his thirties with an afro. His mouth was gagged with a cloth that tied behind his head and tears streamed from his eyes. His hands were bound in front of him.

The disheveled man looked down at his feet. A cinder block was duct-taped to each. He couldn't believe what was happening to him.

Four men in black suits filled the two rows in front of him while the seat across the aisle remained empty. At the very front of the plane, near the exit door, sat Silus Sin Kobol, a tall, thin well-dressed man with a generous head of hair and eyes that resembled a rabbit.

The cockpit door opened slightly and the pilot said to Silus, "Get ready. We're coming over the area in three minutes."

The door closed. Mr. Kobol looked at his men and signaled for them to bring Alfred up to the front.

A particularly ominous-looking man grabbed Alfred by the arm, dragged him up to the front, and sat him across from Silus. The gag was removed from his mouth.

"Please, Mr. Kobol, please," Alfred begged. "All this isn't necessary. Whatever you guys got going on is none of my business! I won't —"

"Shush now, Alfred. This is necessary, thanks to your boss. We need to send him a message, and unfortunately you are our little Huckleberry!" he smiled cruelly.

"A what?" Alfred asked.

Silus looked at one of his men. The thug opened the plane door slowly, the gust of wind that entered blowing everyone's hair wildly. Silus held more tightly onto the armrest of his chair as the men pulled Alfred up and edged him closer to the opened plane door.

The plane flew much lower than was customary and hovered above a body of water, which was visible from the gaping doorway.

Alfred began screaming as the henchman pushed him out into the open sky. He plummeted downward, speeding toward the waters below, the weight of the cinder blocks escalating his descent. His screams grew fainter as the plane door closed. Inside the cabin, it was as if nothing had ever happened.

Abby Taylor cruised down the highway as she headed to pick up her partner, Alfred Ford, from the airport. He was flying in from Virginia where he had met up with an informant who possessed information crucial to indicting members of The LoneStar Group. She was anxious and excited to nail them to the wall, and couldn't wait to share what she'd learn with her boss, Jed Ferrari.

She grabbed a pack of cigarettes from the center console to have a smoke on the way and thought to herself, I should really quit this bad habit. Abby knew Jed wasn't a smoker. She had to admit – at least to herself – that she was attracted to him and thought her habit might turn him off, if it was even possible he was interested in her. She deposited the pack back into the console and focused on getting to the airport on time.

TABEL OF CONTENTS

CHAPTER 1

IT WAS 1978

APRIL

IT WAS 11:45 pm. An orange 1975 Barracuda drove slowly through the town of Woodrow until it came across a side road off Aldo Drive. It slowed down and crept forward toward the end of the cul-de-sac. The tailpipe sputtered, but not quite loudly enough to wake anyone up. The two men in the front, dressed in black, looked at one another.

"Is this the house?" the driver questioned the passenger.

The mailbox on the left read "235 BARRETO".

"That's it. Pull the car into the woods up ahead."

The driver followed the passenger's direction and shut off the ignition. The men pulled black ski masks over their heads and retrieved handguns from underneath the seats. They looked at each other again as they attached silencers to their weapons.

"Ready?" asked the passenger.

"Yep, let's do this," responded the driver.

They quietly exited the car, looking around to make sure there were no witnesses. In sync, they snuck up the driveway in a crouch until they reached a double garage door. They stopped, backs pressed up against the wall.

"Let's go in through here," the passenger pointed to the standard door that led into the garage.

"Do you think they have a dog?" the driver asked.

"I dunno. If so, the dog goes too."

The driver prepared to jimmy the door while his partner turned the knob. The door opened.

"No need to break in. These idiots left the door unlocked. Score!"

The men walked inside the two-bay garage. In one bay was an old '55 Thunderbird with flat tires and in the other was a white 1974 Chevrolet minivan. The man who had been the passenger looked inside the minivan and saw something. He stopped.

"Hold on. I have a better idea," he whispered.

"What?" questioned the driver.

"Look, these jamokes left their car keys in the ignition. An unlocked garage door and now this. Boy, this guy's a beauty," he said, patting the hood of the Thunderbird.

"What do you have in mind?" asked the driver.

"We'll turn the vehicle engine on, then open the door over there leading into the house. They'll all be dead in the morning, and it will either look accidental or suicidal on Barreto's behalf."

"What if that doesn't work?"

"Don't worry. It will."

The driver opened the door leading into the house quietly, and his partner turned the vehicle on. Before leaving the garage, the passenger locked the outside door to the garage behind him.

They scurried back down the driveway to the orange Barracuda, breathing heavily from adrenaline, and removed their masks.

"Hey, my name is Karl Eiden," the driver said to the man with the strange-looking eyes sitting next to him.

"Silus Sin Kobol. What's Mr. Thorn having you do next?"

"I'm headed back to Chicago to do some work for him, you?"

"Believe it or not, he's sending me to law school," Silus smirked.

Gus Barreto's father-in-law, Armond Senior, was up early dressed in his usual plaid leisure suit with a white v-neck t-shirt underneath, looking like a buffed-up version of William Holden. He was heading to the garage to get in the brown and silver Pacer when he heard someone walk inside the house through the front door. In the living room, Armond met his youngest, Armond Junior, who was just strolling in late from drinking and doing who knows what with his hippie friends.

"Hey Meathead, where have you been?"

"Out bowling with the boys, Dad," said Armond Junior.

"This late?"

"Well, we went out to eat after at Big Boys."

"I'm headed to the auto body shop for an early coffee with Gus. You want to come?"

"No, Pops, got to get some sleep. We have a softball game later on today."

"Where is it? I'll come down to watch after Gary's soccer game," said Armond Senior.

"Over at the Chapin Street School."

"OK, I'll see you later then. Don't wake up your mother," Armond said.

Armond the old man he was often referred as, drove the bumble looking vehicle from his home for 3 miles casually until he pulled up to the aged AutoBody shop, he sensed something was off.

Gus's rusty old tow truck was missing from its usual parking spot on the side of the building. The man never missed a single day of work. It was his shop and he loved every second of being there.

When Armond walked into the shop, a senior man named George came out to greet him and also informed him that Gus hadn't yet arrived. George assumed Gus may have overslept, but Armond felt that was out of character for Gus and was unconvinced. He went over to the shop phone, which hung on a dirty wall next to metal shelving units stacked with old paint cans, picked it up, and punched in the phone number to his daughter's house. The phone rang and rang, and no one answered.

It was Saturday, and by now, his daughter Rita should be up with her kids, Chuck, Gary, and Stacey. Armond had an uneasy feeling.

"You could make a coffee and wait," George suggested, gesturing towards the dusty, old machine that spit mud down a chute into a paper cup. "I'm sure he'll be here soon."

"I think I'll take a drive on over to Gus's. I'll have a cup when we get back. Thanks, George," said Armond.

Ten minutes later, he pulled into the driveway of 235 Aldo Drive. Gus's tow truck was still parked by the back stairs.

Huh, Armond thought, he is still here.

He got out of his spotless Pacer and heard the minivan running inside the garage. As he exited his vehicle, he heard the family vehicle running loudly inside the garage. Hurriedly, he went over to the entry door and turned the knob, but it was locked.

Armond pressed his head against the window to see if anyone was inside the vehicle, but it was too hazy.

"Gus!" he began to yell. "Gus! GUS!"

He shook the door handle, then ran around the backside of the garage and up a flight of stairs to the cement patio.

Armond tried getting into the house through the back door, but that door was locked too.

I know, he thought. He walked up another small set of steps to where there was a sliding glass door on the backside of the house. It was locked tight, but upon looking through the glass, he saw Gus lying on the floor in the living room just past the fireplace. He was unconscious in his underwear, face down and slunk over the steps coming from the next room.

Carbon monoxide, he thought, putting together the running vehicle in a closed space and the unconscious man.

Armond sprang into action, relying on a combination of instinct and experience from time served in World War II. He looked around him and saw a couple of cinder blocks leaning against the house next to an old-fashioned Coca-Cola machine. He picked up one of the cement blocks like it was like a feather and heaved it at the door, shattering the glass.

He ran past Gus and into the bedroom where he found his daughter on the floor at the foot of the bed. He checked her pulse. She was unconscious, but thankfully still alive. While he worked diligently to rescue his family, he didn't stop to think about the lethal gasses entering his own body. Armond carried Rita out the front door and laid her on the grass. Gus, who was too heavy for him to carry, had to be dragged outside. He then ran up the spiral staircase to the children's bedrooms.

Armond got Stacey out first and then Chuck. Armond did not bother looking for Gary because he already knew he had spent the night at a friend's house, but he double checked his room quickly just in case.

Armond used the house phone to call 911. He carried out the dog, Misty, who was the only casualty of the day, and waited outside for the ambulances to arrive.

Chuck and Stacey were taken in one ambulance to the pediatric ER in Woodrow, while Rita and Gus were brought to the standard ER there.

Armond's older son, Richard, was waiting for Chuck and Stacey as they were rushed in through the rear. Stacey was stable, but Chuck was in critical condition and fading as they rushed him in on a stretcher.

As Chuck was being rolled down the narrow hallway, he floated on the ceiling, looking down at his own lifeless body. Uncle Richard walked quickly alongside him and the medics. He heard his uncle speaking soft, encouraging words to him.

"Chucky, it's your uncle. Come on, pal, you're going to be okay."

As Chuck was rolled into triage, he felt himself floating further away until he was surrounded by white, funnel clouds that rotated around him as he wore a white bathrobe and white hospital socks. He felt euphoric as he approached a darkness at the end of the tunnel.

After what seemed an eternity, he emerged from the tunnel onto a dimly-lit street. His robe and socks turned a dark green. He stood on a white street and saw that further ahead of him was a wide bridge that stood two hundred feet above a deep river. Directly in the center of the bridge, he saw a familiar figure. The individual came into full view in the middle, wearing a bright red shirt and jeans.

"Chuck, go back. Go back! Stay off the bridge!" Chuck's father, Gus Barreto, shouted before he turned around and walked out of sight.

Chuck thought of heeding his father's warning for a half-second, then walked faster to catch up with him.

He reached the middle of the bridge and saw a great city ahead. His father walked towards twin buildings that stretched into the sky.

Chuck ran after him and was almost to the end of the bridge when he heard a thunderous noise. He looked up into the black sky and saw two planes come roaring out of clouds. Seconds later, the planes flew directly into the towers. His father stood a hundred yards away from the buildings when they crumbled before Chuck's eyes.

Smolder and dust filled the air, swallowing Gus as the soot made its way rapidly towards Chuck until it surrounded him too. Chuck, frightened about what was happening, began to yell. "Dad! Dad, where are you?"

There was silence. The smoke cleared as fast as it came, and Chuck was no longer in the city. He looked around and found he was in a small, cement room. He looked down at himself and saw that he was a man in his thirties, dressed in a correctional officer uniform. He stood in a prison cell.

What the fuck? Chuck said to himself, Wait a minute. I must be dreaming. I'm at work. I must be searching in an inmate's cell for contraband.

Chuck was relieved because he would rather be doing that than be present in the vision he had come from. He began collecting his thoughts. Everything seemed surreal.

Chuck looked at the inmate's table and spotted an ID card. He picked it up and saw it belonged to inmate Larry Kevlin. Generally speaking, Chuck wouldn't go out of his way to bust balls on insignificant items, but this guy was a constant problem. He put the ID down and looked through the floor locker. Buried below some legal paperwork and magazines, Chuck found a homemade tattoo gun made from a small fan that had been taken apart. Chuck wrapped up the power cord, slung the altered device underneath his arm, and began to exit the cell.

Inmate Kevlin entered and began to confront Chuck about the item he was taking. Chuck took a military stance in anticipation of assault.

"CO, where you goin' with my fan?" demanded Kevlin.

"I'm taking it. It's contraband, and I think you know exactly why," Chuck said. He could see from Kevlin's body language that he was growing upset.

"That fan doesn't belong to me. It's someone else's."

"That's unfortunate for whoever owns it because it's going back to the property department, and you'll be the one receiving a disciplinary ticket for being in possession of it."

Lucky for Chuck, his observant partner, Jed Ferrari, had been watching him from the officer's podium when he entered cell number 53. Jed told officer Dave Loomis to watch the desk as he ran up to the cell to make sure Chuck was okay.

"You cocksucker!" yelled Kevlin who swung his right fist at Chuck. He stepped back just in time to barely feel the inmate's knuckles graze his nose.

Jed ran into the cell and yelled, "Kevlin!" and punched him square in his ugly jaw. Kevlin staggered backward into Chuck, who fell onto a metal bench welded to the wall. As Chuck's rear landed on the fixture, the back of his head hit the metal rungs covering the small window.

Chuck's vision went black and he heard music playing.

"No matter what you think you pull you'll find it's not enough/ No matter who you think you know you won't get through/ It's a given LA law/ No matter where you hide I'm coming after you, yeah."

Chuck felt a hand on his right shoulder, lightly shaking him. His eyes opened. He was in a dark room with his Uncle Richard who was sitting on the floor against a wall next to him.

CHAPTER 2
CHUCK'S PET PROJECT

FEBRUARY 2003

CHUCK TOOK HIS brand new pair of wireless headphones off so he could hear his uncle. Clipped to his belt was a small MP3 player that Samantha had downloaded music onto for him.

"Hey Chuck, where'd you go? You were out like a light!" said Uncle Richard.

They were in a dark room, sitting on the floor against the wall with Mike and Mitch. Mike Geller and Mitch Genpowski had been in the Army with Chuck in 1989 and now worked on Chuck's ranch in Woodrow, Massachusetts.

The four men were dressed in black tactical clothing and were armed with AR-15s and handguns as they waited on the fifth floor of an abandoned Coca-Cola building in Los Angeles. The old place was enormous. It was originally designed in the 1930s with cast-concrete doors. The structure was shaped like a ship with portholes on South

Central Avenue, catwalks and a bridge connecting the original five buildings, which had been built in 1939.

Uncle Richard was there to assist Chuck with a special task. He had experience from Vietnam, and besides, he wasn't taking no for an answer when his brother Armond told him what their nephew was up to. Chuck reluctantly agreed to let him come along.

"Whew!" Chuck awoke in a sweat. "Sorry, Unc. That was a nice toe-straightening break."

"A what?" Richard asked as Chuck pulled off his headphones.

"Ah, never mind," said Chuck.

Mitch looked over at Chuck with a mouth full of Funyuns. He whispered, "You ready, Rockstar?"

"You know it, Mitchell. Just like old times."

"Okay, ladies," Mike interjected. "It's go time. I just got a text from Allan. They're pulling in now. Everyone get into position and stay frosty."

Richard smiled. It made him feel alive again to be involved in a covert operation.

They rose off the floor quietly and got into their strategic positions.

Outside by the entrance, Detective Allan Miller stood in the sunshine posing as a realtor for a large corporation. He waited outside the building alone as a black stretch limo pulled up. Stealthily, he texted Mike about their target's arrival and put the flip-phone back in his jacket pocket.

It was early in the morning and the surrounding streets were somewhat barren; there were only a few other businesses in sight, operating or otherwise.

The limo driver's window rolled down, and the man said to Allan, "Are you the broker, Mr. Jones?"

"Yes sir, that's me," Allan responded.

"Is it okay to park right here?"

"That's perfectly fine."

The vehicle shut off. Allan waited patiently for a moment as four large men in black suits stepped out, looking like something from a scene of a Wyatt Earp movie. Allan – or Mr. Jones, as far as they knew – could tell the men were all fully armed underneath their expensive suit jackets.

One man went around back and opened the rear door for the boss man. The tall, well-dressed man with thick black hair and distinct eyes exited as if the world waited for him. Allan remembered him well. It wasn't all that long ago that he had hid in his car with the windows tinted, taking photos of the man with a high-powered Nikon at Chuck's fake funeral.

Oh yeah, finally, the detective thought to himself. Got you, you son of a bitch!

"Mr. Jones, what a nice day," said Silus Kobol with a devilish smile.

"Yes, sir, it is," replied Allan.

"Well, the outside structure has surely weathered some, but if the inside is still holding up, this will be quite suitable for a casino."

"Yes sir, it will. It's really a brilliant investment for a low price. Are the men with you your security, Mr. Kobol?"

"Let's just call them associates. Well, shall we take a tour?"

"Yes, sir. Let me grab my flashlight. The power is not on in the building as of yet."

"OK...," Kobol replied suspiciously as he looked at one of his henchmen.

Chuck could hear faint noise coming from five stories below him, echoing in the empty building. Mike signaled and whispered to be on point for what was about to come. Mike, Mitch, and Chuck felt as though they were back in Panama, only this time around it was more rewarding.

Allan's voice became more boisterous the nearer he came to their location. He was making up a bunch of bullshit to the intended target about property taxes, expenditures, profits, and the like.

Richard and the boys pulled their black ski masks over their faces.

Chuck whispered to himself, "OK, here we go. It's put up or shut up!"

Silus and his men were now only one room away.

Allan shut his flashlight off. Mike gave the green light, and he turned on the light attached to the barrel of his gun turret. Like a well-rehearsed dance, they ran out together, yelling, "GET THE FUCK DOWN! GET THE FUCK DOWN!"

They surrounded the men in black suits. Allan drew the handgun hidden underneath his blazer and put it directly to Silus's head. Silus put his hands up in the air and crouched slightly downward.

"Don't fucking breathe," Allan said coldly.

Two of the henchmen, unfortunately, also managed to get their weapons out and drawn as well. It was a stalemate.

"Who the fuck are you guys? We're not laying down shit!" yelled one henchman.

"Yes, you are!" Mike yelled back. "We're federal agents and we're bringing Mr. Kobol back to Massachusetts for murder and kidnapping."

"Fuck you guys. You're not agents, wearing those black masks."

Richard threw something hard smack dab in the middle of everyone, and the already dark room thickened with smoke, making it impossible to see. Gunfire erupted, as did more shouting.

Then the room grew quiet and Kobol's head guy shouted, "They're headed to the roof!"

He led the way up only to meet incoming gunfire from the end of the hallway.

"Get Kobol out of here!" Chuck yelled as he shot his AR-15. "I'll cover you!"

Just around the corner from where Chuck was holding up Silus's men was a small set of stairs that led to the roof. Chuck knelt down low, firing his weapon while using his peripherals to check that Mike and Mitch made it out.

One of Kobol's men was smart enough to run through the hallway to come up behind Chuck. Just in the nick of time, he heard the man approach and leapt out of the way towards the stairwell. He hit his head on a steel railing and recovered quickly, but not quickly enough, as the man was now hovering over Chuck with a glock pointed at his midsection.

Uncle Richard came out of nowhere and fired three shots. Pop, pop, pop! He hit the man in his torso and he fell. Richard grabbed Chuck's arm, pulling him up the stairwell.

"Let's get the hell out of here, Chucky," Uncle Richard said as they sprinted up the stairwell.

"I'm all for that, Rich," said Chuck.

Silus's men ran up to their comrade lying on the floor. He was still alive. He undid his jacket, revealing the body armor beneath. The henchmen shot at Chuck and Rich, but it was too late. The door swung behind them as they had already leapt through and onto the rooftop of the building.

A nervous Hispanic man with a pinstripe mustache smiled from inside the cockpit of an old Huey Cobra Frog helicopter built-in 1962. The machine had flown in Vietnam and was decommissioned in 1970 and refurbished for civilian use.

"Rock-o, Rock-o, Rock-o! Get the heck in here! Oh boy, oooh boy," he yelled and bounced in his seat, eager to take off before the police inevitably arrived.

The chopper blades spun as Chuck and Richard climbed aboard through the opening of the flying machine. You could hear the music coming through Chuck's headphones.

"No matter how the race is run it always ends up the same/ Another room without a view awaits downtown/ You can shake me for a while/ Live it up in style/ No matter what you do I'm going to take you down/ Shakedown/ Breakdown/ Takedown….."

In an instant, the helicopter levitated off the old, tar roof and quickly pulled away from the building with everyone still intact. The opposition came running out to the edge of the building, discharging their weapons at Chuck and his crew. Bullets blazed and ricocheted off – luckily nonessential – parts of the chopper as they flew out of sight.

On a bench seat in the back of the chopper sat the prize: Silus Sin Kobol. Mike and Mitch sat on either side of him and Uncle Richard was in the co-pilot's seat. Chuck and Allan sat on a rigged seat that backed against the pilot and co-pilot's seats, facing Silus.

Rich tapped his nephew on the shoulder. "You OK, Chucky?"

"Yeah, I'm fine. Thanks, Rich," Chuck said, though his lower back ached from the tumble he had taken.

"Goddamn, Rock-o. You had me worried there for a sec," Junior laughed. He always used colorful nicknames to show his love for Chuck.

"I'm good now, JuJu."

They all laughed except for Richard and Silus. Silus stared at Chuck with curiosity, for he was still wearing a black knit cap pulled over his face.

Chuck nudged Allan's shoulder, "Is this our guy?"

The detective pulled a crinkled, five-by-seven photo from inside his blazer and looked at it, then looking at Silus. "Oh, yeah. I never forget an asshole's face. You made a big mistake, pal, going to Mr. Barreto's funeral."

"Who are you?" Silus questioned. "You're certainly not federal agents. Or any kind of law enforcement, for that matter."

"Look, guys, this maggot has rabbit eyes!" said Mike, and they all snickered at the comment.

Chuck pulled off the cap, uncovering his face, and gave Silus the look that only few had seen. It even made the man with the odd, spooky eyes uncomfortable.

"I'm the guy turning you over to them. You kidnapped my ex-wife, tried stealing my land, and you murdered Wolford's corrupt Attorney General."

Silus smirked smugly, and Chuck so wanted to wipe it off his face.

"You have the wrong guy," Silus chuckled. "You look familiar. Who are you? Are you that famous rancher from Woodrow? Feels like I've been in your wheelhouse since you were just a youngling."

Chuck was confused and growing angrier. "You like to play games, huh, Kobol? Where's your boss, Thorn? And who is he exactly?"

Silus smirked nefariously. "You'll find out soon enough!"

"Great, I can't wait, '' Chuck replied.

Mitch was growing weary of listening to Silus and his anxiety was growing, so he took his glock into his hand, held the barrel tight, and smacked Silus in the back of the head with the butt of the gun.

"Lights out, asshole!"

CHAPTER 3
KELLY ANN GOES TO WASHINGTON

FEBRUARY 2003

CHIP HARRINGTON SAT at an L-shaped, Grigio-finished desk in his finely appointed state office. It was grand, and paid for by the almighty taxpayer's dollar. He was on the phone with his campaign manager, Alicia Stone.

"So Chip, we have to get to work immediately. No time to waste here on getting your approval rating up. The election will be upon us next year and our opponents will be announced soon. I have an idea of who we will be up against, and they are all well-established, tough adversaries."

"Alicia, I just got here. I have no intention of leaving Washington any time soon. Whatever needs to be done, we will get it done."

"OK, I also have to bring this up. I'm assuming that you're going to slide Jed Ferrari right into the Attorney General's spot until the next election."

"That is accurate, Alicia. It makes the most sense. He's already doing the job and that whole thing with LoneStar was a mess."

"We'll have Jed officially sworn in?"

"Yes, Miss Stone, we will."

"OK, then that's all for now. I will see you tomorrow afternoon."

Chip hung up the phone, took a sip of some expensive whiskey, and smiled. He thought to himself, Should I call my wife, Mellisa, who's at home alone in Massachusetts before my evening guest arrives? Nah, I'll call her tomorrow and tell her I got tied up.

Gary Barreto was nestled at home, sitting on his La-Z-Boy in his favorite Batman pajama bottoms and a baggy t-shirt. He smoked cheap Pall Mall cigarettes as he flipped through the bills that he and Lilly had accrued. They were trying to plan their wedding, which would be held in Woodrow because his mother, Rita, had offered to pay for most of it. It was an offer they couldn't refuse because they were severely in debt from living beyond their means.

Gary was pulling his graying hair out trying to figure out how to get out of their financial troubles. Since they had moved to Virginia, he had built separate respective houses for Lilly's divorced parents and another for themselves. He had also purchased a building in town large enough so Lilly could have her own yoga studio, but she didn't make enough to even cover the overhead on the place.

"Oh Gary, look at these dresses for my bridesmaids that I found," Lilly said. She was in the kitchen looking at wedding magazines and getting ideas that would put them further in debt. She had been drinking red wine and felt tipsy.

"I can't, Lilly. I'm busy trying to figure out how we're going to keep everything we already bought."

"Oh, honey, I'm sure you're just exaggerating," she waved her hand at him as if shooing the thought away.

He puffed harder on his burning cigarette. "No Lilly, we're in some serious trouble here. Three mortgages and a failing business."

"What about the rentals in Woodrow and the money your mother gave you from the land she sold in Portugal?"

"We spent it all on your fancy new vehicle and the overseas vacations you said we needed to go on so you could get good scenery pictures of you posing to promote your business."

"Gary, those photographs really helped with bringing in more customers."

"Clearly not enough because your business has cost us twice as much to keep it going than it has made."

"Well can't you just sell that land?"

"My brother and sister don't want to sell it. They're talking to me about building cottages and horse stables to extend Chuck's ranch. That's a long process and I wouldn't see any money from that for a while. We need quick cash now. Maybe your parents can move in with us for now and I can sell their houses. That would alleviate a lot of the burden."

Lilly's face shifted. "Oh no, Gary. My parents can't live together and they love their new homes. We can't do that to them. They'd never forgive me."

Gary was frazzled. "There's another possible option. I got a phone call from a land developer called The Devine Group. They made me a lucrative offer that could get us out of this mess. The only problem is they would also need Chuck and Stacey's land too."

"Well, that's the answer then. You have to convince them somehow."

"Lilly, you know my pigheaded brother. He's one stubborn asshole."

"Yeah, yeah. Speaking of which, isn't the television mini-series of his book airing tonight?"

"Oh, yeah. I guess that is tonight."

"Are we going to watch it?"

"No, there's a new episode of Two and a Half Men on. We'll just lie and say we did."

Chuck and the boys flew over Wolford City on their way back from their week-long journey to California. They made some stops at multiple military bases along the way that Junior had access to for refueling. In a cargo spot behind the passenger's seat in Junior's old but sturdy helicopter, Silus remained gagged and awake, listening attentively to what was being said. He could just hear them talking through the wind and noise of the engine.

"Hey guys, we're finally getting close to the SkyTower," said Junior.

Richard turned his head. "Hey Chucky, what's the CB frequency in your car?"

"27.402," replied Chuck.

His uncle adjusted the dial and picked up the mic to transmit a message.

"Ah, Capricorn One to Nightrider, come in!" said Richard. He waited a minute, heard no response, and repeated the message.

"Nightrider to Capricorn One, I read you," a voice answered. It was Chuck's friend and ranch hand, Dave Loomis. Chuck, Mitch, and Mike smiled when they heard his familiar cadence.

Dave was sitting inside Chuck's midnight blue 1972 Dodge Charger in an upper-level of the SkyTower parking garage. It was the same building where Chuck's ex-wife, Kelly Ann Texeira, had a penthouse apartment and an office for her realty company, The Silver Bell.

"So good to hear you, Nightrider. Prepare, for the Eagle will be landing shortly."

"Roger that, Capricorn One. We are ready to receive, over."

"Roger, see you on the dark side of the moon, over and out."

Uncle Richard put the mic back on the clip as Junior prepared to land in the frosty night air atop the tallest building in the city.

Nearby in a modest townhouse apartment, soft music played in a bedroom lit with candles. Smoothe, silk sheets moved up and down on a queen-size bed as moans came from underneath them. A cell phone on top of the white nightstand next to the bed rang.

"I'm sorry, just one second," a man whispered. A hand reached over to the phone to pick it up. "Shoot. I'm sorry, Abb. I have to take this."

The man rose, uncovering their bodies to the waist, to answer his phone. Abby slid over, one hand resting on Jed's arm.

"Jack! What can I do for you?" Jed answered. He listened and then responded. "OK, Jack. I'll meet you in fifteen minutes. I'll see you there."

Jed hung up the phone and looked at his lover in disbelief.

"What's going on?" Abby asked.

"That was Jack Bufford. He wants me to meet him at the Wolford Police Station. He said they got Silus Kobol and that he can't tell me anything more until I get there."

"Holy shit, Jed. That's fantastic! Want me to drive you? I'd love to get a look at the scumbag."

"I would really love that, but it would look suspicious. We can't let anyone find out about us, not yet," he said and kissed her.

"I suppose you're right. You're probably going to be sworn in soon, and you did just give me a promotion. Well, I'll be waiting for you when you get back."

Chip Karrington was thinking about his success when an intercom buzzed. He pressed the red button to answer.

"Your guest has arrived," said a deep voice.

"Send her up, Pete," Chip answered.

"Yes sir, right away."

Chip reached for the radio next to the intercom and turned the knob up just enough to hear the music. Wearing a red silk bathrobe, he stood to let his visitor into the room. He heard a quiet knock and opened the door with a smile.

Kelly Ann Texeira stood in front of him smiling from ear to ear, her hair and makeup done up as if she was ready for an extravagant New Year's Eve party. She wore a long fur coat, a black studded collar around her neck, and shiny, black heels to add height to her small stature. Kelly held a small suitcase in her right hand and had a single rose between her teeth. She was just as stunning as ever.

Kelly gently placed the luggage on the floor and took the rose out of her mouth.

"Bonjour, Mr. Senator!" she said and opened her arms to embrace Chip, who planted a sensuous kiss on her cherry-red lips.

"Get in here. God, you're beautiful," said Chip. "How have you been?"

"Well, you probably heard that Chuck left me," Kelly said, a hint of sadness in her eyes. "They granted us an annulment. I didn't contest it and everyone agreed to drop the charges against me. My little sister is sleeping with him, and I'm back where I started. But on the bright side, I have my favorite senator finally in D.C."

"What a fool he is, Kell. If you were mine, I'd never give you up," Chip said as he made her a drink.

"Well lucky for you, Mr. Senator, I'm all yours tonight."

She slowly took off her coat and, to Chip's surprise, she wore nothing underneath except barely-there, black lace lingerie.

* * *

Jed walked into the Wolford City police station lobby after parking his vehicle, excited to hear more about the long-awaited capture. The officer at the desk knew Jed very well and greeted him as Jack Bufford came walking out from behind the secured area of the station.

"Wow! That was fast, Jed. Don't you live on the other end of the city?"

"I do, but I was visiting a friend nearby."

"Gotcha. Well, let's step over here so we can talk privately," Jack said and led Jed to a nearby room.

"Everything okay?" asked Jed.

"I'm not sure. In regards to finally having custody of Kobol, we have quite a situation on our hands as to how he was detained. Did you know that Chuck Barreto was in California?"

"Yes..." Jed began slowly. "I knew. He was heading out there to turn in another manuscript and attend a couple of final meetings about the miniseries that's coming out tonight."

Jed tried to keep a flat affect, though he was thinking to himself, Jesus, Chuck. What the hell have you done now?

He recalled the moment when his old boss, Nick Colombo, lay dying, and Chuck proclaimed that it would be his mission to hunt down the culprits who had upended his life.

The look on Jack's face answered any questions Jed had about Chuck's involvement in Kobol's detainment.

"While Chuck was in California with his friends, they somehow found out where this guy was, abducted him, and flew him back in an old Army helicopter."

"Great Caesar's ghost! Jack, are they in any trouble? Can we keep Kobol incarcerated?" Jed asked, bewildered.

"Possibly. You and I will have to work fast to get something to stick on this guy. Our overall goal is to squeeze him until he gives up this alleged Thorn character that runs the LoneStar Group. We also have Kelly to testify that Kobol was in the house and gave the command to have Columbo murdered. They held Mrs. Texeira hostage, blew up the Holiday Inn parking lot, and fired weapons at us, endangering the public. I'll make it stick, somehow."

"How did you learn that Chuck was involved?"

"A man named Dave called me a few hours ago to tell me he and Allan Miller had Kobol and that they were bringing him into the station. Allan explained to me what happened. I may be able to finesse some background checks and predate them to say Allan was working for the FBI in a limited capacity."

"You can do that? Is that legal?"

"We can do anything, Jed. We're the FBI. But if you repeat it, I'll deny it," he said, pointing a finger and smiling. "Don't thank me yet. I'll do my best. And tell Chuck – if I don't see him before you – that his favors from me are running on empty. Last year he stole a helicopter, now this. If I didn't like him so much… he's a hard guy not to like, but he's a pain in the ass."

Jed shook his head. "Believe me, Jack, I know."

You could hear the helicopter blades touring the night sky as they finally hovered over Chuck's homestead, music blaring on the radio inside the cabin.

"Times have changed and times are strange/ Here I come, but I ain't the same/ Mama, I'm coming home/ Time's gone by, it seems to be/ You could have been a better friend to me/ Mama, I'm coming home."

Mike was singing loudly and passionately, and everyone laughed at how well he actually carried the tune. They had lost Allan and Silus, who had been dropped off on top of the SkyTower building and retrieved by Dave Loomis.

Chuck looked at his phone to read the text he had just received from Allan and then relayed it to everyone else. "Hey guys, it all went great. Allan and Dave dropped that shitbag off at the Wolford City PD. He's in custody, and I'm sure Jed and Jack are there now, getting ready to interrogate him."

"Let's hope they can keep us out of trouble for the way we pulled this off," said Uncle Rich.

"I'm sure they probably wanted this asshole as much as Rockstar here. Almost as much," said Mitch.

Junior carefully maneuvered the chopper onto the well-lit helipad that Chuck had Chad build for them. There was about three feet of snow on the ground, but the pad had been cleared. The chopper's bear claws hit the cement, blowing the surrounding snow. The blades and engine began winding down, and the boys were glad to finally be back in their own territory.

As they got ready to dismount, Rich asked Chuck, "Oh nephew of mine, what made you build the pad here anyway?"

"This location has a certain… sentimental value, Rich," Chuck said, smiling.

"Yeah, this is where he killed the landscaper," Mitch blurted.

"Mitchell!" exclaimed Chuck, feigning outrage.

They walked back to the house on the snow-covered pathway, their vehicles parked in the driveway exactly where they were left.

Chuck held his lower right back.

Mitch noticed. "You okay, Rockstar?"

"Yeah, buddy, I'm fine. Just a little stiff from the long ride home."

Chuck was lying. He hadn't felt right since he fell during the gunfight back in Los Angeles.

Chuck said goodbye to Mitch and Mike until the morning when they would be back to work on the ranch, and Rich wandered off into the house.

"Hey, JuJu? I owe you big time," Chuck said to Junior.

"Hell no, Rock-o, you don't. We're friends and brothers, for life. You remember that! And don't forget your lesson we got next week. You'll finally be getting that pilot's license soon."

"Roger that, brother. I won't," Chuck smiled again and gave him a hug.

Junior piled his large frame into his car and Chuck waved, feeling more at peace than he had in a long time.

CHAPTER 4

SWEET HOME

FEBRUARY 2003

CHUCK OPENED THE front door to his warm home and the aroma of apple-scented candles wafted towards him. He observed they had been lit throughout the house, the dim light setting the mood. As he stood in the kitchen, he looked over into the living room and saw what he had so missed during the long, hard week: his gorgeous lady, Samantha Dixon, cuddled on the couch with their dog, Rupert.

The little dog started barking with joy and jumped off the couch, energetically running over to Chuck. Samantha followed closely behind. As she hugged and kissed him in welcome, she sensed something was off.

"You okay? What's wrong?" Sam asked.

"Nothing at all, now that I'm home with you. I'm just a little stiff from the long flight back is all."

She smiled. "You better slow down in your old age. You're no spring chicken anymore."

"I'm fine, really, Sammy. Just need a good night's rest."

"You mean after we watch your show, which is coming on in 10 minutes. I got the living room all set up and some snacks are ready to go in the fridge," she said. "Come on, let's go sit down. I can't wait to watch."

Samantha cozied up next to Chuck and Rupert jumped up too. A bottle of chilled wine sat on the coffee table next to two glasses, one of which was already half-filled.

"Your aunt is at your mother's house. They're all excited about the premiere. She's been calling me all night, asking if you were home yet," said Sam.

In addition to Uncle Armond, Chuck's aunt Joanne was also temporarily living with him. She had sold her home in New York and Rita was helping her shop for a new house in Woodrow.

"So how was your trip?" continued Sam. "Did the producers like your new manuscript?"

"Surprisingly, they said they loved it at first glance."

"It doesn't surprise me, Chuck. You're a talented writer… amongst other things," she giggled, teasing.

"Ho, ho, ho, you're a funny girl. The boys were star-struck, being able to meet a bunch of people on the set."

"Wow! Who was there?"

"The great Keanu Reeves," said Chuck.

"You mean Neo, Mr. Anderson!"

Chuck laughed. "Yep, that's the man, the one and only. And of course our producer, Kenneth Carlson."

"Dave was bummed out he couldn't go with you guys."

"I'll take him on my next trip out there."

"I went with you on your first trip there," she said and pinched his arm gently.

"How could I forget? It was special. And we also got to meet Captain Kirk."

She smiled at him. "It was special for me too. Oh, before I forget again, is it okay that Dave borrowed your car? I know you don't let anyone go near it, let alone use it."

"Yeah, I told him he could borrow it. He'll bring it back in the morning. His car was in the shop."

Their attention was then alerted to the television as the introduction to Chuck's show played through the speakers. Chuck grabbed the bowl of popcorn off the table.

"Tonight is the first of the two-night ABC special for the best-selling book, How Booze, Women, and Corrections Ruined My Life," came the announcer's voice over jazzy music. "Starring Edward Albert as Steve Burnett and David Hasselhoff as Teddy Manero. Don't miss the murder, the backstabbing, the lies, the intrigue, the friendships, the loss, the love affairs of these working-class heroes."

The introductory song began. "Push it to the limit/ Walk along the razor's edge/ But don't look down just keep your head, or you'll be finished/ Open up the limit/ Past the point of no return/ Reached the top, but still you got to learn how to keep it."

The scene opened with the actor playing Steve blow-drying his hair as he listened to some old music on a record player. It cuts to Hasselhoff doing a few sets of push-ups before putting his tight-fitting uniform on, and then to a female officer, played by the actress Veronica Cartwright, getting pulled over for speeding on her way to work. She stabbed her leg with a pin so she would be crying actual tears when the police officer approached her rolled-down window.

Then the superintendent of the fictional jail, played by Harry Dean Stanton, blows into his ignition to start his vehicle.

Samantha laughed aloud.

"Chuck, is that a blow-and-go ignition for getting a DUI?"

"Yeah, we had a superintendent who was charged with drinking and driving. That's where I got the idea from."

"Wild. What's that intro song they're playing? It sounds so familiar."

"Push It to the Limit by Paul Ingemann. That song was also used in the movie Scarface."

"Interesting. I was wondering… how come they didn't ask you for your input on the actors they used?"

"Not sure, Sam, this is all new to me. They just usually brief me on what they're doing. When I gave them the new story, they handed me a check. Then they'll polish it to their liking and tell me about it later. They actually already asked me for a third manuscript."

"Is Hasselhoff supposed to be Jed?" Sam laughed.

"Well, it's all loosely based, but yeah, basically. You know, Mr. Hasselhoff is pretty big in Europe."

Samantha smirked. "I didn't know that."

They continued watching the show. Chuck's flip phone buzzed on the end table next to the couch. He opened it up and looked at Samantha.

"Speaking of, it's Jed texting me saying he's watching the show now and loving it."

"Tell him I said 'hey'."

It was Jed, but Chuck wasn't telling her the truth. He didn't enjoy lying to her.

The text really said, Hey partner, guess what I'm not watching tonight? Thanks for the mess you left me!

Chuck quickly and nervously typed a reply. Sorry, bro, I'll make it up to you.

He flipped the phone shut and cuddled closer to Samantha.

At the station, Jed and Jack were dealing with Silus Sin Kobol. They had been grilling him for a while, and Jed stood outside the interrogation room as he read Chuck's reply. He frowned and closed his phone before putting it back into his pocket.

The shift sergeant came out of the room that Silus was in.

"You guys have got to give him his phone call and the attorney he has requested. I'm sorry, there's nothing I can do. It's the law," he said.

"OK, let him have it," said Jack, looking at Jed. "Sorry, Jed, he's not going to talk. This mutt's been schooling us big time and knows the drill all too well."

Jed was frustrated, to say the least. He finally had the devil in the palm of his hands. These guys had eluded him for long enough. He felt so close…yet maybe not close enough.

"This scoundrel is not beating me…darn it all! OK, yeah, give him the call," Jed said, hands on his hips.

"Stay the course, Jed. We'll squeeze this guy until the dominoes fall."

Jed and Jack continued to discuss their dilemma in a room adjacent to Silus that had a one-way mirror. The shift sergeant and another officer handcuffed Silus's wrists in front of him and brought him down a hallway to a payphone.

"Let me know when he's done. Then we'll bring him to his cell for the night until his arraignment in the morning," the sergeant told the officer.

"Yes, sir," the officer replied.

He gave Silus a dollar in change and the sergeant left the assisting officer with him to monitor the call. He stood five feet away as Silus dialed.

Silus knew he had to make his phone call count, but he was already regretting the conversation he was about to have. He had let down the one person he did not want to let down. The man who took him in when he was a young, homeless thug on the streets. The man who helped mold him and bring him to a place in life his younger self only could have dreamed of.

Wooden Venetian blinds shed moonlight inside a dark office. A slender man in his early sixties wearing a Desmond Marion suit and sporting a head tufted with thick hair had both feet up on an old oak desk. He drank a glass of whiskey on ice. At the end of the room, a small television displayed a show about how booze, women, and corrections ruin the character's life.

The man chuckled aloud, fully enjoying the show, and a young lady entered the room wearing a black nightie, her long, blonde hair flowing. She wrapped her arms around him.

"Can I get you another?" she says, gesturing to his glass.

"No, I'm good right now."

"You coming to bed soon?" she kissed his leathery, tan cheek.

"I'll be in soon. I'm just finishing this show."

"OK, dear, don't be too long," she said and strutted out of the room, closing the door behind her.

The man jingled the ice in his glass and continued to enjoy the show. A cell phone rang. The man looked to his right at a collection of burner phones. Most of them were black or silver, but one glimmered a metallic red, which was the very phone that was ringing.

The man reached over, picked it up, and looked at the small screen to view the number of the incoming caller. He did not recognize it. "This better be good," he muttered to himself and flipped the phone open. "Yes, who is this?"

"Sir, I'm sorry to call this number. It's Silus. I'm in a bit of trouble. I was abducted in California when I went to that land deal in L.A. and was flown back to Wolford City. I'm being held at the police department for murder and kidnapping."

"It must be pretty serious for you to be calling me on this phone."

"Yes, sir, I believe it is."

He paused for a second, and then the older man replied, "Voices callin', voices cryin'/ Some are born and some are dyin'."

Silus was confused and somewhat disturbed by the overt mention of death. "Sorry?"

"It's just a song, Silus. So tell me, who exactly extracted you from California, and how was it possible with your security?"

"I believe the realtor I met was really an undercover FBI agent. But sir, we were ambushed by four men dressed in black. And guess who one of those four men was?"

"Who?"

"None other than Chuck Barreto."

The man paused and smiled to himself in the low-lit room. His extensive set of white teeth shone. "Interesting!" He paused again. "Silus, my boy, I told you to handle this guy a month ago, and this is what happens because of your failure."

Silus felt choked, his lips dry as he struggled for words. "I apologize, sir. I will not fail you again, if I get another opportunity."

"No, I will have to handle this another way. We tried destroying the Barreto and family once long ago and the results of that defeat have cost me a small fortune. I'm done playing with this fucked-up family."

"Sir?"

"How did they get you back to the East Coast? You said they flew you back."

"Some sort of old helicopter. They flew it to the helipad atop the SkyTower. There was a guy waiting in the parking garage in a classic Dodge Charger. They were communicating with a CB radio system. The driver mentioned to Barreto that he didn't get a scratch on his car."

"So the car obviously belongs to Barreto," he stated sternly.

"Yes sir, that is my assumption," Silus replied nervously.

"Did you happen to catch the frequency they were using?"

"Actually, yes sir. I did."

"Time for a change in our strategy. I'm going to destroy them from within and be rid of this virus once and for all."

"Very well. What shall I do now?"

"You just sit tight. I'll get you out somehow. When's your arraignment?"

"I'm guessing tomorrow."

"I'll get to work. One way or another, if I have my way you will be back out and in the free world soon, Silus?" the man said, still sounding ominous.

"Yes, sir. Thank you, sir."

After Silus hung up the phone, he was taken to a holding cell somewhere in the station.

When Silus was a young punk – before Mr. Thorn scooped him up and took him under his wing – he committed petty crimes. But he had never been caught.

Was he smarter than others, or just luckier? He had been a criminal of sorts his whole life, but this was his first time being incarcerated. If not for Mr. Thorn and his talented recruiters at that time, Silus was pretty sure he would have wound up dead or in prison a long time ago.

Maybe my luck is running out, he thought.

Thorn put the red emergency phone back in its place and picked up his desk phone. He dialed a programmed number, put it on speaker, and waited for an answer. After several rings, someone finally did.

"Mr. Thorn! What can I do for you?" someone replies.

"Good to hear your voice, Mr. Logan. How is everything going in our city?"

"Wolford is doing well. We're getting ready to start construction on the casino and hotel in the south end. I've, of course, been selling a lot of product as well. Have you decided what to do about our issue with Indians Leap?"

"I'm working on it, Mr. Logan, but I'm going to require your very useful expertise."

"Anything, anytime, Mr. Thorn. You know that."

"I'm actually also calling about one of my assets that got arrested out there tonight. He's in the police station right now. Tomorrow he'll most likely be arraigned. If our attorneys can't get him out on bail, he'll be sent to one of the prisons out there to await pretrial. You know the game. They'll try to squeeze this guy until he sings."

"Has he ever done time?"

"No. That's the problem."

"Do you want me to cancel his contract?"

"If you can't get him out... yes, absolutely."

"How important is this asset to you, Mr. Thorn?"

"Let's just put it this way. I've spent an abundance of time and money training him. If he has to go, I have one more very important job for him to do in order for me to execute my plans for Wolford City."

"Say no more, Mr. Thorn. If he doesn't make bail, I'll get him out, sir. What is the asset's name?"

"Silus Sin Kobol. Thank you, Mr. Logan."

"Not a problem, sir."

Mr. Thorn pressed the button on the phone and put it down. He took another sip of his whiskey before placing it back onto the glossy desk. Getting out of his chair slowly, he walked over to the moonlit window and stared outside, deep in thought. He looked out at the beautiful view of Washington D.C. on the snow-covered evening, The Capitol building stood solidly in the distance.

CHAPTER 5
A DRIVE IN THE WINTER

FEBRUARY 2003

"**THEY SAY WE'RE** young and we don't know/ We won't find out until we grow/ Well I don't know if that's all true/ 'Cause you got me, and baby, I got you/ Babe/ I got you babe, I got you babe/ They say our love won't pay the rent/ Before it's earned, our money's all been spent/ I guess that's so, we don't have a pot/ But at least I'm sure of all the things we got/ Babe/ I got you babe, I got you babe."

Chuck awoke and heard the song playing from the radio on the nightstand. His eyes were still crusty with sleep, and he was trying to remember why he had crashed so hard. Then it hit him. I'm home, thank the Lord.

He looked over at the left side of the bed and saw Samantha and Rupert were gone, so he reached over to the alarm and shut it off. The song stopped.

A pink Post-it note was stuck to the lampshade that hung above the clock. He unstuck it and brought it in close, his vision still blurred.

Written in Samantha's hand, it said, I'll see you down at the barn, Chucky :)

He grabbed the edge of the bed to roll out and felt a sharp twinge in his lower back. The pain surged straight down the side of his right leg, all the way to the ankle. Ah fuck, he said to himself. This is not good. All I've been through…now this!

Chuck hobbled to the bathroom, opened the medicine cabinet, and gobbled down a couple of aspirin with water before brushing his teeth. Downstairs, his uncles were talking and laughing with his aunt. Chuck's discomfort had grown to the point where it was hard for him to get down the stairs without help, but he attempted it anyway. Slowly, he inched downstairs and around the corner into the kitchen where Uncle Armond, Uncle Richard, and Aunt Joanne sat at the table by the window.

"Welcome home there, mister movie executive," smiled his aunt.

"Thank you, Aunt Joanne," said Chuck.

Richard could see his nephew was in pain, but he and Armond were sworn to secrecy about their mission, so he kept tight-lipped.

"Come on, old man. Sit down with us before you take off for the day," said Uncle Armond.

"Mmmm, OK. For a few anyway," he said, limping over to the freshly-brewed coffee pot to pour himself one. "Anyone need a refill?"

They shook their heads, so he sat next to Armond and looked out the window. To his surprise, his mother's car sat in the driveway alongside the Charger.

"Oh, my mother's here?" he asked.

"Yeah, she brought your sister too. They're all down at the barn with Samantha."

Chuck looked bewildered.

"My sister has been doing a lot of bonding with Samantha while you were away," commented Uncle Armond pointedly.

"Really? About what?"

"Well, for one, we were talking about the weekend Gussy came out to New York before the attack. I wasn't sure if you'd be bothered by it."

"I'm fine with it, but thank you for the thought."

"Did your Dad ever tell you that we received a phone call from your uncle Charlie a week before that awful day?" she asked delicately.

Chuck was confused. "My father's long-lost brother who disappeared with Gus Senior shortly after coming to America?"

He knew the family story well having grown up hearing about it from his dad and grandmother. Shortly after they settled in the United States, Gus Senior had taken little Charlie in the middle of the night and vanished. He left his wife and other son – Chuck's father – with a substantial amount of money and land. When Gus Junior was older, his mother remarried and had Joanne.

"That's the one," said Joanne. "I was in shock, too. He told my mother over the phone that he was going to meet us at the Del Frisco Grille the day of the attack in New York City. That's where we were, waiting for his arrival, when the planes struck the Twin Towers."

Chuck's facial expression was one of shock. "No, he never told me he was going down there to meet with his brother. He just asked me if I wanted to visit Vovo for the weekend, but I had to work at the prison. After that day, did you ever hear from Charlie?"

"No, we assumed he may have also perished that day, and the phone number he had called from came up unknown."

Chuck took a sip of his coffee. What if the Towers never fell? His father would still be here today, and he would have probably met his long-lost uncle.

Uncle Armond changed the subject to how much he enjoyed Chuck's television show. They asked him about his time in California, and then Chuck looked at the clock on the wall.

"Well, I gotta get down to the barn to check on the new winter coats they were putting on the horses. The boys are also supposed to be working on electrical heaters for the water troughs."

Chuck stood up and gingerly walked over to the door to slip into his snowsuit and boots.

"Hey nephew, maybe you should take it easy today. Possibly get that back looked at?" Uncle Richard suggested.

"Uh, no thanks, Rich. I took a couple of aspirins. I'll be alright."

"Hey Meathead, aren't you gonna put on a pair of pants first before going outside?" Uncle Armond asked.

Chuck was already stepping into the heavy-duty, quilted suit. "No need, Unc. This thing is so damn warm, you wouldn't believe it."

He stuck his feet into the rubber boots and opened the door to the blustery air. From the porch, he saw the heaping white snow drifts of unfettered crystals. Plowed paths for the ranch hands, clients, and horses to walk on scattered the landscape. Since Chuck had killed his landscaper, Andy had temporarily taken over the duties and was doing a hell of a job.

Chuck held onto the railing to get down to the driveway and walked over to his car to inspect it and ensure Dave hadn't left any scratches on the immaculate facade.

Several of the four-wheelers had been fitted with snow tires, but he decided to fire up the CAT snowmobile to get down to the barn. After removing the tarp, he carefully hit the automatic start button.

Chuck smiled as he drove out onto the beautiful snow-covered ranch. Junior's helicopter was sitting quietly on the helipad. Chuck still couldn't believe what they had pulled off. He knew he was going to have to do some damage control with Jed later on and hoped the charges against Kobol would stick in court.

He hit the throttle on the snowmobile and glided across the powdery snow. As soon as he started hitting bumps, the pain in his back and leg felt worse so he eased off the accelerator. Chuck got close to the small bridge that crossed over a ravine, steered the vehicle onto the plowed path, and drove over it.

He could see the snow-covered barn and stables getting closer. There were a couple of horses outside in the corral, enjoying the winter morning. The snowmobile pulled up to the entrance of the barn. He shut the machine off and parked it on the side of the barn, noticing how quiet it seemed to be inside. Chuck opened the door and felt the gust of warm air from the heating turbines. Chuck heard noises coming from one of the stalls.

"Hello, anyone here?" he called.

Suddenly, Dave Loomis and Candie stumbled out of stall number seven.

"Oh, hey dude. We were just fixing Lucky's winter coat," said Dave Loomis guiltily. Candie's face was flushed. Chuck looked at them suspiciously and smirked, but decided to keep his comments to himself. Dave closed the gate behind them.

"Well, Mr. Barreto, I'm going to tend to the horses outside," said Candie awkwardly.

"Candie, after all we've been through in the last year, please call me Chuck."

Candie smiled back at him. "Okay...Chuck."

"Thank you. That's much better."

"Oh Chuck, I loved your show last night, by the way. I can't wait to see the second half."

"Yeah, good stuff, dude," agreed Dave.

Chuck thanked them and Candie left to get to work.

"So, how are the new electrical heating units working in the troughs?" asked Chuck.

"Fantastic."

"Hey Dave, thank you so much for all your help last night."

"No problem. I felt honored to be a part of it. Felt like the old days."

Chuck laughed out loud. "It sure did."

"What about our boy Jed? Is he going to be upset?"

"Ah, don't worry about it, Dave. I'll smooth it over with him somehow. In fact, I think I'll reach out to him this morning."

"Oh shoot! I forgot to tell you I had a problem with the passenger door on the Charger. It wouldn't stay locked in place. The latch must be frozen in the open position or something. Allan had to hold it shut the entire drive back from the police station."

"Hmmm, that's strange. I'll take care of it, thanks." He looked around and realized it was still oddly quieter than it should be. "Hey, where is everyone else?"

"Your mom and sister took off with Samantha and Mike over to the gun range, and Mitch and the rest of the ranchers are down further out by area nine walking horses."

Chuck gave Dave a funny look. "The range?"

Dave shrugged his shoulders. "Yeah, you got me, dude. I didn't ask questions."

Chuck nodded. "OK, well I will catch up with you later then."

"Tell Jed I said hello when you talk to him."

Chuck walked out of the barn to get back on the snowmobile, waving to Candie in the corral fixing the other horses' winter coats.

Kelly woke up in a luxurious bed with the feel of fine silk sheets caressing her skin. She looked over at Chip who was now fully dressed in an expensive suit, fixing his cufflinks and looking at his hair in the mirror. He heard her groan as she stretched.

"Hey, gorgeous. You're up."

"I'm getting there slowly... especially slowly after last night, Mr. President," she said with a sexy smile.

"Mr. President? I have to keep my Senate seat first, Kell."

"You're going to destroy whoever your opponent ends up being next year. I have no doubts."

He smiled back. "Why, thank you, Miss Texeira."

Kelly stood up to give him a kiss, wrapping the sheets around her nude body.

"You going to be here tonight when I get back? We could go out for a nice dinner."

She made a pouty face as he wrapped his arms around her. "I'd love to, you know that, but what a scandal that would be."

"I've got connections."

She chuckled. "Yeah, I hear that, but the truth is I have to catch a flight later today. I'm going to Texas to visit Daddy."

"I see. I remember meeting Vic. He was a great guy. Well, I'm going to miss you. When will I get to see you again?"

"Soon. Sooner if you come to Massachusetts."

"Sure, I'll be back there in the springtime."

"That's a long time from now. Mellisa doesn't mind?"

"She's going to be making some weekend trips here until then."

Kelly, feeling uncomfortable, changed the subject. "Before you leave, I was wondering if you could help me out with something?"

Chip thought to himself, Just when I thought I had a clean getaway. There's nothing free in life. I knew her trip here wasn't just to spend the night with me.

"Sure, if I can."

Kelly skipped to the desk where her purse was, holding the sheet around her body with one hand, and pulled out some papers. "I'm doing a favor for a land developer in Wolford City. They bought land next to the new casino and hotel going up there. They're looking to build a small retirement community. They need some help with zoning. I was wondering if you could make a few phone calls for me?"

"Kell, I hope this isn't like the LoneStar group."

"Oh, God no! These guys are small potatoes. Well known and honest, from what I hear."

"Who are they?"

"They're called The Birch Group."

"Hmm, yeah, Elliot Birch. I've heard of him."

"Like I said, he is legit and has bought into the project for some shares. I'm giving them a hand. I thought it would be nice to be involved in a community for the elderly."

"I'll see what I can do," said Chip.

She bounced on her feet and gave him a kiss on the cheek.

Chuck pulled up to the gun range and could see that everyone was gathered around the bonfire Mike and Samantha had built to keep warm. He couldn't believe the sight he saw as he pulled up: Rita, his mother, had a shotgun slung up snug to her shoulder and the right side of her face.

BOOM! The bullet from Rita's gun hit the center of a paper silhouette target tacked down to a bale of hay about 100 yards out. Stacey had a handgun in her right hand. Rupert was sitting by the fire attentively, wearing a red winter vest and snow boots on his four little paws. He saw Chuck and started barking at him, but wisely stayed close to the warmth. Everyone turned their heads as Chuck got off the snowmobile.

"Hey there, Steve Burnett!" said Mike, referring to the main character on his show.

"Ho, ho, ho, ho. Full of jokes this morning. OK, let's get them all out of the way."

"I loved it, Chuck. Congratulations, big brother," said Stacey.

"Thanks, Stace."

"Wow, my son, the big movie mogul. Who would have thought?"

Chuck blushed. "Ma, what are you doing out here firing a shotgun? And Stace, why do you have a glock in your hand?"

"Samantha and Mike were giving us some lessons," replied Rita. "Looks like you're not the only one who can shoot in this family."

"Apparently not!"

"Your mom's a natural, Rockstar, and Stacey's not too bad either."

Chuck couldn't believe it. The women in his life never ceased to astound him. He often thought that they were much stronger than men.

"Where'd you get the shotgun? That's not one of mine."

"Oh, this was your dad's. It was in storage and I had been meaning to give it to you."

"Well, you keep it for now, Ma. Oddly enough, it seems to suit you."

"I'll hang onto it, but it will always belong to you. I don't think your brother would have any interest. He doesn't like guns."

Chuck and Stacey shared a glance.

"Okay then," said Chuck, brightening. "Mike, you got one for me? Let's shoot."

"Absolutely!" He pulled out another Glock and handed it to Chuck.

Rita noticed Chuck had a limp as they were shooting at targets. "What's wrong with your leg?"

"Nothing much, just a little sore. Nothing serious."

"You know Becky Clementine, one of our clients? Her husband is a chiropractor in town. I'm going to see her today. I could make you an appointment," said Samantha.

"Thanks, Sam. That would be great," said Rita, responding to Chuck.

"Really, ladies, that's not necessary." Chuck attempted to brush them off, but Stacey gave him a pointed look. "Okay, okay. I'll go see him."

"That's more like it," said Rita.

While they were practicing, Rita mentioned Gary's upcoming wedding. She began talking about the venue and then had some surprising news for Chuck. "I called up your old bandmates."

"What? The band is together?"

"Oh, yes they are, and they have a new female singer. I'd like to hire them to play at the wedding. If that's alright with you, that is."

"Sure, why not?" Chuck responded, somewhat shocked.

"And Bob said to say he misses you and wants you to give him a call," Rita finished.

"Yeah, yeah sure. I'll do that Mom," said Chuck.

Samantha could see in his face that it disturbed him, that he was probably now lost in memories of Shandi. While Chuck was clearly conflicted, she didn't know how to feel about it herself.

CHAPTER 6

A MAN COMES AROUND

FEBRUARY 2003

AFTER LEAVING KELLY, Chip got into a black stretch limo to head to the Capitol building to get to work for his voters. The chauffeur opened the rear door for him to get inside, and his two assigned Capitol Police officers, Hamil and Waters, got in as well. One sat in front with the driver and the other sat in the back with Chip.

First thing's first, he thought as the vehicle pulled out. Chip called the governor of Massachusetts. There was no answer, so he left a message saying he needed to get some zoning issues taken care of for the Birch Group and to call him back when the governor had a chance. Chip owed Kelly big time; she knew many of his secrets. Hell, she was one of his secrets. He certainly would not want the public to know about any of them. In the world of politics, you never really knew how long you would be able to trust someone, but he wasn't quite ready to find out.

On to new business.

Chip looked at the fully stocked minibar. He reached over and pulled the handle on the door. It opened and revealed several bottles of the finest scotch, whiskey, and vodka, as well as a small bucket of ice. Waterford Heritage tumbler glasses sat in a side console. He reached over and used the small metal scoop to put ice into a glass and then poured some Scotch.

Chip looked over at Officer Waters and raised his glass. "Cheers."

As they drove down Pennsylvania Avenue, Waters said, "Starting early, sir?"

"The breakfast of champions, Officer Waters, the breakfast of champions." He grinned, then turned the volume up on the radio and put his alligator skin boots up on the seat, closed his eyes, and enjoyed the song.

"Risk my soul/ Test my life/ For my bread/ Spend my time lost in space/ Am I dead?/ Let the river flow/ Through my calloused hands/ And take me from my own/ The eyes of the damned."

The driver yelled over the din, "Sir, would you prefer to go in through the rear entrance? There will be a lot of reporters out front. They can be annoying."

"No, that's alright. Drop us off in front, please."

The song continued.

"It makes my stomach churn/ And it tears my flesh from bone/ How we turn a dream to stone/ And we all die young."

The limo arrived at the front steps of the Capitol, and Chip put his glass away and buttoned his overcoat, pulling his scarf tight against the February air. He popped a couple of breath mints that he had in a tin case in his inside pocket and got out.

Chip and his officers walked up the long stairs until they reached the landing outside the door. A group of reporters approached them and began blurting out questions.

"Let's get inside the lobby and then I'll take a few questions, everyone," Chip said jovially. After they got situated inside, Chip removed his scarf and he took his first question.

"Mr. Karrington, congratulations on your victory. How does it feel to win over the long-established Senator Lee?"

"First of all, thank you, Shannon. I think the voters were ready for some real change in Massachusetts. I've come here to do exactly that."

"Mr. Karrington, just after the election you made a statement about a developer called the Lone Star Group. Is the company involved in any corrupt activity, and what is your affiliation with them?"

Chip knew he was in trouble with that one, but thankfully one of his aides, Miss Winters, walked up to him at just that moment and told him he had to wrap it up. Chip quickly deflected the question.

"I believe the company is being looked at, and I'm sorry to cut this short, but it appears I am needed. You all have a good day."

Chip spun on his heel and walked away as reporters fired off additional questions at his back. When he approached the office door, Miss Winters pointed to his name that maintenance had recently affixed to the door.

"Looks good, doesn't it?" He smiled at her.

They walked into his office and the officers waited outside. Chip sat comfortably behind his desk.

"Would you like to go over today's schedule now?" Miss Winters asked.

There was a copy on his desk. He looked down and skimmed it over quickly. "No, I think I'm good for now, Miss Winters."

"Yes, Mr. Karrington. Oh, don't forget your first appointment this morning with—"

"Yes, I know about that one," he interrupted her. "How could I forget him?"

"Very good, sir. I'll leave you to it. If you need anything further, please let me know."

Chip gave his wife a quick phone call before he started what was sure to be a busy day. He told Mellisa how much he missed her and couldn't wait to see her. That wasn't altogether true. He was in the middle of telling her how much he was working on getting done for the people of Massachusetts – that wasn't altogether true, either – when there was a knock at the door. After a brief goodbye, he hung up the phone.

"Yes, come in," he called.

Officer Waters cracked open the door. "Yes sir, Mr. –"

Chip cut him off. "Yes, yes, send him in right away."

The door opened and a well-dressed man, about five-foot-eight, entered. The navy suit with gray pinstripes that he wore was even more expensive than the one that adorned Chip, but what was most noticeable about the man was his thick, flowing salt-and-pepper hair. For a man of his age, he still had a full head, and he was sporting an enormous pair of Ray-Ban sunglasses even though they were inside. There was a large gold ring on his left index finger and he walked with a dark wooden cane.

"Gentlemen, please wait outside with these fine officers. I have business to discuss with the Senator…alone," the man said to his own security detail through a glistening smile. There was an aura about him that suggested a certain charm and lifelong chain of successes. Still smiling, he said to Chip, "At last we meet, Senator Karrington."

Chip rushed around his desk to shake the man's hand. "Mr. Thorn, the pleasure is all mine. With your help, I am humbly sitting here today to serve."

Chip noticed his hand felt warm but firm in his grip.

"Everybody won't be treated all the same/ There'll be a golden ladder reachin' down!" Mr Thorn quipped.

"I'm sorry, Mr. Thorn?"

"Just a lyric, son. Just a lyric."

"I'm not familiar with that one. I'm surprised by your visit today. I wasn't sure if we would ever formally meet," said Chip as he sat and gestured for Thorn to do the same.

Thorn sat across from Chip and rested his chin atop his cane, still wearing that exuberant smile. "Well, I did come here today in part to thank you for the loan of your yacht last year to get one of my associates out of trouble."

Chip's throat suddenly felt as though it was closing up as he sensed where the conversation was headed.

"Mhm, yes. Well, you know, it was a risk, for sure. That may have cost us everything if they caught him, but I felt I had to do something. I apologize for disavowing the LoneStar Group on television the way I did."

"No need. It was a wise move, Chip, and you need not worry any further about them."

"How's that sir?"

"The group is being dissolved as we speak. All shares are being sold, liquidated out into smaller groups. We have let all the partners go with equitable severance packages."

"So you no longer have attachments linking you to them?"

Still smiling with his chin on his cane, Thorn said, "Very good, Chip. I am well-insulated from anyone's investigations, including your Attorney General."

Chips noticed Thorn's expression change ever so slightly.

"Look, Mr. Thorn, I figure it's safer to keep Ferrari close. He's proved to be more dangerous and unpredictable than I would have thought."

"A calculated risk," said Thorn. "I hope you're right because Ferrari and his buddy, Barreto, are costing me a fortune. I have all that land on the south side of Wolford City being developed, but its worth is halved unless we take down a section of Indians Leap and develop Gussy's Pitts along with it."

"I understand that, sir. Really, I do. It's a problem I've been trying to resolve for you. When I tried pleading my case to Barreto last year, it didn't go so well. And we all know what happened after that."

"There could be another way," began Thorn, "if you are a man who is willing to take calculated risks." He paused and Chip waited for him to continue. "When's the last time the Wolford City bridge underwent any major repairs? If you had an inspector deem the bridge in need of them, if any of this could be pulled off, you may order the governor to sign an executive order giving us passage through Indians Leap and Gussy's Pitts. This kind of pressure may force the Barretos to think twice about selling. If the state is able to take it by executive orders, the Barretos would only get what the land is valued at. Certainly, they would want to get a developer's price, above book value."

"You could be on to something," said Chip as he stroked his chin. "I know it's been a while since the bridge has had any serious main-tenance. Let me see by way of locating an inspector that would… fit the mold."

"Yes, please let me know how you fare."

Chip nodded. He was only a few feet from a real-life powerful gangster. He knew he had paid a price to get to the top, but he did not get this far just to end up in political ruin.

Thorn got up and caught the Senator off guard with another zinger. "Do you know the woman from Wolford City who owns the Silver Bell?"

Chip knew he had to be careful with the answer to this one. "Yeah sure, of course. Her name was Texeira before she married Barreto. Why?"

"Well, she accused my associate of being involved in the murder of Nick Columbo, and now to complicate matters, the associate was abducted by Barreto and some of his pals."

Chip's jaw dropped. "What?"

"Yes indeed, and it gets worse. They turned him over to the Wolford City Police yesterday and Ferrari is attending his arraignment as we speak. Miss Texeria is the only witness that could put him away, and he could sing on you too. If she somehow doesn't testify, he'll remain quiet and I can work on getting him out. So Chip, to sum it up, Silus Kobol is a major potential problem right now."

Chip's head began to perspire. "What can I do about it, Mr. Thorn?"

"Do you know where Miss Texeria is? Will she be a witness?"

Chip thought really hard before answering, wondering if Thorn knew she was with him in his room last night. No, there was no way he could know any of that. He decided to lie.

"I'm sure she's at her office in the city. I don't have the faintest if she's going to testify. I'll give Ferrari a call to see what he's up to with that."

"Exactly, Chip, which brings us back to our problem with Ferrari."

Chip sank into his chair. He felt fairly certain Thorn didn't play with problems. He got rid of them, and that would only cause additional problems for Chip.

"Let me see what I can do, Mr. Thorn."

"Don't worry yourself too much, Chip. If all else fails, there is a contingency plan for my associate, Silus," said Thorn.

"Contingency?" Chip asked.

"For everything, Chip. There's always a contingency. Anyway, I've taken up enough of your time. I'm sure you have many other appointments today."

Mr. Thorn rose using his cane and pulled an envelope out of the inside of the jacket he was wearing and put it on Chip's desk.

"There's a check inside for your continued success. And for some bills that I'd like to be passed. We need these votes on the hill to meet our constituent's requirements."

Chip stood and shook the man's free hand before Thorn exited leaving Chip wondering what the hell he was going to do now.

CHAPTER 7

GUARDIAN ANGEL

FEBRUARY 2003

CHUCK WOKE UP late to the alarm clock going off, still in agony. His eyes opened. Damn, when's this pain going to go away? He looked over to his left and again the bed was already empty. Samantha had left another pink Post-it note, this time next to the clock. He shut the alarm off and read her flowing handwriting.

Chucky, either before or after you run your errands, remember you promised to go see Paul Clementine, the chiropractor, on Elm Street.

Chuck was in such pain that he figured he had nothing to lose, even though he wasn't quite sure he believed in chiropractics. He also had to get his ass into town to discreetly meet with Jed and Allan to discuss what happened at Silus's arraignment. And though he was reluctant, he also wanted to send Kelly a message to acknowledge her role in the capture of Silus. He hated all this cloak and dagger stuff, keeping everyone in the dark, especially Samantha. Maybe he should have included her in his plans, but what was done was done. He had his reasons.

His grandfather's words came to the forefront in his mind.

Chuck, once you start lying to people, you'll dig yourself a hole so deep that you can't get out of it.

He just wanted to put it all to rest, once and for all. When Kobol was convicted, it would finally be over and he never would have to worry about it again.

Chuck slowly put on jeans and a fresh shirt. After using the bathroom, he hobbled downstairs. To his surprise, the house seemed to be empty. He assumed his aunt and uncles must have gone into town. Hopefully not anywhere near the location where he'd be meeting Jed and Allan.

Rupert was in the living room watching television comfortably from the couch. He heard his master and sauntered into the kitchen to greet him. Chuck bent down to pet him, wincing.

"Hey boy, where is everyone? They leave you all alone?"

Rupert barked repeatedly in response.

After playing with the dog for a short time, Chuck headed out into the sunny, frosty morning. He thought about inspecting the Charger more extensively, but he was not in any condition to do so. He pulled himself into his trusty Jeep, fired her up, threw it into four-wheel-drive in case the driveway was icy, and drove down the road to get into town.

A brand new black Hummer was slowing on the main road to take a left into Gussy's Pitts. Even though the snow was deep, the vehicle plowed through it, spitting up snow. Inside were four middle-aged men dressed in black and wearing snow boots. They sat in an uncomfortable silence, looking at one another with curiosity, wondering where the driver was taking them.

The driver himself was unique. He was a tall, thin African-American man with a wooly beard and wearing a long, cashmere trench coat and an oversized, brown cowboy hat. The red winter scarf around his neck was in sharp contrast to the bright yellow leather gloves on his hands. He was known in the criminal circuit as "The Cowboy", and his choice of attire was a mystery to everyone but him. He was humming an unknown melody that made his passengers antsy.

One of them finally broke the silence. "So, Mr. Logan, why are we driving out here in the middle of nowhere?"

Mr. Logan turned his head and smiled, exposing one gold molar.

"The boss wants me to show you guys something before you get your new assignments, Lewis."

"Mr. Logan, shouldn't we be searching for who took Mr. Kobol?" Lewis asked nervously.

"Oh, we know who took him and we know his whereabouts," said Logan.

"We do?"

"We do, Lewis, most certainly!"

"Mr. Logan, where is he? Is Mr. Kobol alright?"

"He is in the Wolford City Jail, probably being transported to the Pocomtuc facility soon."

Lewis was surprised by the development and wanted to redeem himself and his men. "Mr. Logan, I'm sorry this happened. Give us a chance. We'll break him out of the PD before he's taken out of there. Please!"

"Nah, don't worry about Silus for now. We have other plans for him, boys, not to worry. Lewis, can you reach into my glove box and grab the map that's on top of my gun?"

"Yes sir, Mr. Logan."

Logan took his foot off the gas and came to a stop. "I have a diagram of a sidewinder section of Indians Leap that we need to find. It will be an easier walk if we go up on that side of the mountain."

"Side of the mountain, Mr. Logan?"

"You'll see. Oh, by the way, are all you boys packing?"

They looked at one another, confused, and Lewis spoke on behalf of them again. "Yes, sir, we are. Are we going to be needing them?"

"You never know," said Logan with a cryptic smile.

Chuck limped into the little cafe in the Belchertown Plaza, which his mother still owned. Thankfully, he didn't see his family when he scanned the room. He opened the door and a bell jingled as a stiff wind followed Chuck in.

A server approached. "Is it just you, sir? Would you like smoking or non-?"

Chuck spotted Allan and Jed waving to him from a corner booth.

"Actually, ma'am, I see my friends over there."

She smiled and Chuck began walking, pain shooting down his leg. He slid in the booth next to Allan.

"You alright there, old boy?"

"Oh yeah, just a little sore right now." Chuck didn't want to tell them he was going to the chiropractor after their meeting.

"Don't worry about this guy, Al. He's like a Duracell battery," said Jed, clapping Chuck on the shoulder. "So you couldn't find anyone better than Hasselhoff to play Ted?"

Chuck laughed. "What? He's a great actor!"

Jed made a face at Chuck.

"Sorry, bro, I'm not in charge of casting."

"Well, I'll tell ya, Chuck…you never cease to amaze me!"

Allan laughed.

"Nor myself!" said Chuck.

Jed shook his head like Chuck's father used to do at all the foolish stunts he pulled. "What is it with you, Chuck, and helicopters?"

"At least he didn't steal it this time," Allan pointed out.

"You going to leave me in suspense? You told me to stay away from the courthouse yesterday for this guy's arraignment. What happened with the creep?" asked Chuck.

"I'm still trying to wrap my head around it all. His lawyer was awful," said Jed.

"What? Really?"

"Yeah, it was almost as if he messed it all up on purpose. Kobol's pre-trial will be held in May, and then we'll see if it actually goes to trial."

"What was bail set for?"

"That's another factor that stunned me. The judge said no bail and his attorney didn't argue it."

"Is that normal?"

"No, not by any means."

"Did his attorney bring up how he was captured? Or did they bring me up?"

"That's another suspicious thing…no."

"Do you think they have a strategy? Maybe they'll bring it all up at pre-trial."

"Who knows. It is possible. But we now have time to try to get Kobol to do some singing on his boss. Jail time could soften him up."

Chuck smirked at that thought. "Where is he being incarcerated?"

"Our old stomping grounds. Imagine that?"

"Hot damn. I'm going to have to make a few phone calls, see if I can make his stay even cozier."

Jed's face turned stern. "Chuck, no. I got this, okay?"

"OK, but when you go to see him, I'm going with you."

"We'll see," said Jed shortly. Chuck was anxious to get back at the guys who had caused him so many problems, but Jed knew how the wheel of justice worked.

Allan took the opportunity to change the subject. "Jed, you should have seen Kobol's men standing on that building with their dicks in their hands as we flew away with their boss!"

Chuck wasn't going to let the conversation drift that easily. "So what about LoneStar and this guy, Thorn?"

"We still have no proof Thorn even exists, and LoneStar got spooked and sold all of their shares to other companies. Jack and Abby are working hard to find out who the companies are," said Jed calmly.

"Who bought all that land on the other side of Indians Leap?"

"A smaller fish. A builder called The Birch Group."

"Is this builder linked to LoneStar in any way?" Chuck asked.

Jed gave his buddy a funny look. "We're on it, Chuck."

Logan parked his vehicle halfway up the sidewinder off of Indians Leap, and he and Kobol's men trudged the rest of the way to the top on foot. They walked along the peak of the ridge in the heavy snow for about a half-mile with Logan leading them, until he stopped. He was standing about ten feet from Lewis and the others when he turned to face them.

"Well, this is it."

"Mr. Logan?"

"This is far as we go. Mr. Thorn wanted me to show you this."

They looked at one another, not knowing if he meant that was as far as they were walking, or as far as they were going to go in life.

"Boys," Logan began boisterously, "you're standing on top of the great Indians Leap. If you look down this side, the drop is almost 1,200 feet. Down below is all the land owned by Mr. Thorn. Hotels and a casino will be going up this spring. Kobol was helping us to get a section of this mountain removed so that Mr. Thorn could expand. Now he is in jail, thanks to you knuckleheads!" Logan's voice grew louder. "You had one job. and you all failed!"

Lewis and the other three looked at one another, abashedly.

"Mr. Logan…." Lewis began.

"No excuses. Look down there!" he said as he pointed to the steep drop below. "Do you guys know why they call this place Indians Leap?"

They shook their heads.

"Because an Indian was being pursued and leapt from here to escape his captors. I'm going to give you gentlemen the same opportunity."

The men stared at him blankly.

"Yeah, you have two options right now. Draw your weapons and try to gun me down, or you can jump."

"No, please, Mr. Logan! We will make ourselves useful."

"OK then, I guess we're going to do this the hard way."

Two of Lewis's associates went for their guns. Lewis himself put his hands up, but Logan was too darn fast. He drew a Colt AR-15 with a specialized handle from underneath his trenchcoat and blew them all away.

Logan looked at their lifeless bodies with joy and he screamed. "Wooooooo-hoo! Yeah!"

His breath was visible as it left his mouth in puffs of exhilaration. He walked over to the bodies, blood seeping into the pure white snow, and emptied their pockets.

"Sorry, you pukes, you lose. Too slow." Logan dragged the bodies to the edge and pushed each over the steep ledge, sending them sailing downward. They hit the ground with thuds, which were lessened by the snow.

After the last body hit the ravine, Logan said, "With any luck, maybe you boys will be discovered by the springtime. If the animals don't get ya first."

He walked back to his vehicle, took out a cellphone, and dialed a number. A few seconds passed by and then he said, "Sir, mission accomplished."

CHAPTER 8

SIGNS

FEBRUARY 2003

CHUCK LEFT JED and Allan feeling frustrated by their discussion, and his sour mood was enhanced by his search for the chiropractor's office. Stacey had given him directions. He knew it was on the main road in town, though he had never noticed it before, and slowed his Jeep down by an old factory called The Mills.

He noticed a large green sign in the front yard of a nearby three-story house that denoted the Clementine name. Chuck put his blinker on and shifted to four-wheel drive to better navigate the icy driveway. He pulled around the back of the house to a small parking lot. There was a back door with another sign in the window door that said, "Open". A small set of steps led up to the doorway, flanked by a handicap accessible ramp.

Chuck remained skeptical, but the pain had him desperate. He threw the emergency brake on before he slowly climbed out and walked over to the stairs. The door opened into a very narrow, carpeted hallway. Further down, he reached a small lobby with a reception station on the left and a few chairs against the wall on the right that served as a waiting area.

A gray-haired gentleman in his mid-forties that seemed to be seven feet tall greeted Chuck exuberantly.

"Hello there! Good morning! My name is Bill. Are you Chuck?"

Chuck could hear Creedence Clearwater playing on the radio. Bill was bobbing along to the rhythm.

"Yes, sir. Are you the doctor?"

"No, no, not me. You will be seeing the doc after I have you fill out some forms right here."

Bill handed Chuck a clipboard and continued making smalltalk as Chuck wrote. One form had a diagram of the human body and he was to circle his problem areas on it. The others required the usual personal information, health insurance, and medical history. After he was done, Chuck gave Bill the paperwork and his insurance card, who in turn entered and filed the information.

"Before the doc talks to you, would you like some stem therapy?"- Bill asked, smiling as he handed him the card back.

Chuck had no clue what that meant. "Stem therapy?"

"Oh, we hook up some rubber pads to the problem areas and it sends a vibration to those muscles to loosen them up before you see the doc."

Chuck thought for a second. "Uh, sure. Why not?"

He got out of his chair and followed Bill down another short hallway into a room with two small beds covered in padded leather. On the side of each bed was a machine with a small tank of water on top.

Bill cleaned one bed, then put some wax paper down on the headrest.

"OK, you lay face down here," said Bill, pointing. Chuck gingerly lowered himself onto the bed, face-down. Bill pulled four five-inch round rubber pads from the warm water tank. The pads had wires attached going back to the machine. Bill lifted Chuck's shirt slightly to attach the pads to his skin on the areas he had indicated on the form. He explained that he was going to turn the machine on and adjust the shock to Chuck's comfort zone.

Bill began to turn the knobs up. "Tell me when to stop."

As he turned the knob slowly, Chuck felt a shock running through his lower back and his muscles tightened. The pain running down his right leg became more intense and Chuck gestured to Bill to stop.

"OK, just relax and I'll be back," said Bill as he exited the room.

This is an odd sensation, thought Chuck. It hurts so good.

He looked through the opening of the table and stared at the old, shiny hardwood floors. He closed his eyes. It seemed an eternity had passed since he felt good, even though it hadn't been that long that he had been in pain. Fifteen minutes later, a quiet alarm sounded and the pads stopped vibrating. Chuck felt a lot looser and more relaxed than he had before.

Bill returned and removed the cooled pads.

"OK Chuck, come this way to see the doctor now."

Chuck slowly got up, disappointed to find that the pain was still there. Well, it wasn't going to be that easy, Chucky, was it?

He followed Bill into another small room with a desk and chairs. Bill said to the man sitting in the room behind the desk, "Paul, this is Chuck Barreto," and then left.

The doctor shook Chuck's hand and gestured towards a chair. "Please, sit down."

Chuck noticed that the guy seemed a few years younger than him, and he wasn't sure how to feel about that. The doctor was clean cut and a little shorter than him, built like a powerlifter.

"You went to Woodrow High?" the doctor asked.

"Yeah, I did. Did you?"

"Yes, I was in your brother's grade. Gary and I were on the same soccer team. I used to see you when you worked out at the gym in Woodrow. I don't see you there too much anymore."

"Yeah, I built my own gym down in my basement, so that's where I work out now." Now that Paul mentioned it, Chuck did vaguely recognize his face. "You and my brother, on the same soccer team. What a small world."

"How is your brother doing?"

Chuck made a general comment about him doing well that wasn't altogether true, and then they talked about small-town life in Woodrow before getting into Chuck's back problems. He had to chalk it up to issues that had arisen from working around the ranch and lifting weights, as he couldn't exactly admit how it had actually occurred.

"OK, Chuck, follow me," said Paul.

In the next room was a light green, padded chiropractic table that had a multi-directional headpiece. There were caulking pedals on both sides, as well as other gadgets of which Chuck couldn't identify the purpose. Paul sanitized everything in front of him, then had Chuck lay face down, resting his arms over the edge. His legs were straight behind him, his toes pointing towards the wall.

Paul pushed down on the area of his lower back where Chuck had indicated the pain was located, and then walked around to his feet and pulled on each one.

"Chuck, do you run or jog?" he asked.

"Yeah, outside when it's nice enough or on my treadmill during the winter. Why?"

"Hmmm, did you ever injure your right leg?"

"Actually, yeah. How did you know?"

"I can see that something is off. What happened? If you don't mind me asking."

"I got shot back in '89 when I was in the Army," said Chuck.

"Wow, the Army!"

"Yeah, I was in Panama."

"I knew it was something. Maybe over a period of time it just took a toll on your back as well. I'm going to try a few things here." He walked over to the middle of the table. "OK, breathe in deep." As Chuck filled his lungs with oxygen, Paul pressed downward on the middle of his back, and he heard a loud crunch that came with a strange feeling, like gas releasing from the pores in his back.

"Holy shit! What was that?" asked Chuck, feeling strange but good.

"Your body's releasing toxins," Paul replied.

At that point, he could not tell if the pain was still there or not.

"Now lie on your left side with your right knee bent over this side of the table."

Paul helped Chuck readjust. It was an awkward position. Once he was ready, Paul put his knee on Chuck's leg while holding his body in place, and, without warning, he pushed down on the leg with force. Chuck heard another large crunch coming from his right hip.

Holy shit, he thought again.

"OK, now I'm going to have you lie down on your back with your legs out straight."

The doctor made sure that Chuck had his head aligned in the tilted headpiece perfectly. Paul told Chuck to relax and then picked his head up from the back a few inches with both hands. Chuck was looking up at the white stucco ceiling.

"Stay loose," said Paul, as he moved Chuck's head back and forth slowly. Chuck couldn't help but tense up a little. "Relax, Chuck," Paul repeated, and then twisted Chuck's head sharply to the right. Snap!

It was like nothing Chuck had ever felt before. His vision flared bright white once, and then again, like a camera flash going off.

He opened his eyes and moonlight beamed down onto his body from a skylight window of a very familiar room. What the fuck am I doing here?

Chuck was in the middle of the king-size bed in the old house he sold last year with the help of Kelly. He looked around the room and listened. He heard no sounds. No Rupert. Nothing. He stood up expecting the surging pain to run down his leg, but it was completely gone.

Chuck then noticed that the bedroom was exactly the same as when he had lived there with Shandi. There were pictures of them together, as well as Rupert as a puppy. Shandi's personal belongings were all over, which was odd because he had gotten rid of them long ago when he was trying to dull the pain of her death.

Well, he thought, I might as well go downstairs to see who's home.

As he walked down the flight of stairs to his old living room, it was as if he had stepped back in time. Before he joined the Army, worked for his father or the Department of Corrections, lost his dad, bought and built the ranch, and married Kelly Ann. Maybe I'm back. Maybe, just maybe, all that was a bad dream.

He reached the bottom of the stairs and was still without pain. In fact, he was feeling pretty good. He turned the corner and walked into the living room where the natural light from the moon came streaming in through the oak-framed bay window. The ambient light bounced off the hardwood floors, smelling of fresh Pine-Sol. Candles were lit around the room, and the windows were wide open to the summer breeze which carried the sweet smell of flowers.

Chuck heard the music of a keyboard playing a vaguely familiar melody, and then a lovely voice singing the lyrics delicately. My God, he thought, it's Shandi. Lord, I really am home in my protective bubble with my girl.

Chuck walked happily to the basement door which was slightly ajar, the sound of Shandi's voice growing louder. He was so excited to see her but didn't want to interrupt what she was working on, so he tiptoed down the carpeted basement stairs. They could be creaky at times, and he hoped they wouldn't betray him just yet.

At the bottom, there was a bar area on the right with knickknacks and all of their favorite albums. He walked to the wide open studio door, anticipating the moment when he would look in the room and see her. Chuck wasn't disappointed; Shandi was more beautiful than ever, sitting at the keyboard, her long, wavy chocolate hair falling over her shoulders. Her face was tilted down at the instrument and her Dylan Thomas poetry book sat next to it.

"Waiting for me with flowers in hand/ Poetry in every word/ He won't call me by name, only babe/ I need less when you give more/ I look happy to everyone/ Feels right when it doesn't/ You know that I am wrong for you/ On the day I leave, I'll wish we never met."

Shandi hadn't noticed Chuck as he watched her in awe from the doorway. It was such a dark, bittersweet song she was working on for their new album.

"... I made you kneel before me/ It's said that misery will love company/ I ruined everything, not you/ It's not your fault, I'm not what you need/ Baby angels like you can't go to hell like I can/ I'm everything they told you I am/ So please, don't follow me over that bridge!"

Chuck got a little choked up as she sang the last line and saw him. Shandi stopped playing and a radiant smile appeared on her angelic face. Her big blue eyes lit up the room.

"Hey there, you! I didn't hear you come in. What do you think so far? It's called, "An Angel in Hell.""

He was so glad to see her again, he wanted to run over and kiss her.

"It's going to blow their minds, Shandi," he said.

"Well, we'll see. It's getting there, anyway," said Shandi. She could see something was different in his face. "What's wrong, Chucky? You look like you've seen a ghost!"

"Nah, nothing's wrong, Shand. In fact, things couldn't be better."

"Oh yeah?" she smiled at him. "Come over here."

Chuck walked over to her, and she stood and wrapped her arms around him, kissing him on his lips. He had forgotten the taste, the feeling of her mouth.

Suddenly, he heard the television come on from the bar behind him, and voices. How could that be? There was no one home but them, and the television had been off when he walked past it. Chuck was confused.

"Do you hear that?"

"Hear what?" she asked.

"Hold on," he said and gently pulled away from her.

"Chuck, wait!" Shandi called.

Chuck walked back through the doorway to the bar and saw Mike and Mitch sitting on the stools, talking to each other and watching a movie.

"Hey guys! What are you doing here?" Chuck raised his voice to get their attention. How could they be in Chuck's basement at this moment in time? They had never Met Shandi because she was murdered before Chuck met them.

Mike swiveled his chair halfway to face Chuck. "Hey there, Rockstar! We're waiting for you. Look, I got our movie on."

Chuck was in disbelief. "What movie?"

"A Bridge Too Far!"

Chuck looked at the screen and sure enough, there was a scene playing with the actor Sean Connery as a soldier, running through the streets and taking gunfire from German soldiers.

"Did you guys meet Shandi? Let me go get her," Chuck said.

Mike and Mitch looked at each other, confused as to what their good friend was talking about.

Chuck turned back and walked into the studio, which was empty. No Shandi. He felt lightheaded, like that fateful day he had returned home from his parent's house and found Rupert by himself crying on the front steps with her blood on his collar.

"Shandi! Shandi! Shandi!" Chuck called out in a panic.

He blinked and Paul was looking down at him where he was lying on the chiropractic table.

"Hey Chuck, how do you feel?" asked Paul.

"Feel? How long was I out?" asked Chuck.

"Maybe a second or two. You yelled out someone's name, I think."

Chuck was embarrassed. "I'm sorry about that."

"No, don't worry about it. Nothing to be sorry about."

The doctor then had him turn to his opposite side for a few more adjustments, then sat him up and made two more slight adjustments to his neck.

"Man, you were very tight and tense. How do you feel now?"

Chuck got up off the table feeling a little loose and rubbery, but good. "I can't feel the pain in my back or leg. What did you do?"

"I think, for precaution's sake, you should come in twice more so I can make sure you stay on the right track. You needed some major adjustments."

Chuck felt like a new man, or rather, like his old self. "OK, absolutely. I will."

"Remember, you're living your best day today. And tell your brother, Gary, I said hello," said Paul.

Chuck quickly caught on to what that catchphrase meant, and he liked it. "OK, Doc, I will. See you in a few days."

CHAPTER 9

TEXAS

FEBRUARY 2003

KELLY RACED DOWN a long road in Dougherty, Texas, her beautifully manicured toes laying heavily on the pedal. She wore a coral, off-the-shoulder sundress with peplum sleeves that blew in the wind of the topless red BMW she had rented at the Lubbock Preston Smith Airport. Her long red hair was pinned tightly in a bun, and she was humming along to the Bob Seger song playing on the radio.

"It seems like yesterday/ But it was long ago/ Janie was lovely, she was the queen of my nights/ There in the darkness with the radio playing low, and/ And the secrets that we shared/ The mountains that we moved/ Caught like a wildfire out of control."

In the center console, her flip-phone rang. Kelly turned down the volume and flipped it open, smiling.

"Jeff!" It was her lawyer friend and confidant.

"Where are you, Kell? It sounds loud, wherever you are."

"I'm driving to my daddy's ranch. I rented a convertible from the airport."

"Oh, very nice. How's the single life treating you? Fancy-free again?" asked Jeff. He heard an uncomfortable pause. "Sorry, Kelly, that was insensitive. So, what are you doing out there?"

"Oh, just a visit, Jeff. A quick getaway and then I'll be back home. I stopped to see Chip. He's going to help us with those zoning issues for the Birch Group."

"Excellent. How is our newly elected senator? We can get a lot done with Chip on our side."

"He's adjusting well, as I'm sure you can imagine. That's the plan, Jeffrey. After the loss, I took on my failed marriage, Gussy's Pitts, and MoonRiver, it would be nice to get something else going."

"You know, Kell, you never needed that bum. Without you, he never would have gotten his ranch running in the first place. Or his book sales. And let's not forget his new Hollywood status." Jeff avoided bringing up the fact that she put her sister on Chuck's ranch to distract him while Kelly fast-tracked deals behind Chuck's back to build on his father's property.

Kelly felt her phone vibrate in her hand. She had another incoming call. Her heart fluttered.

"Jeff, I'll have to pick this up with you later. I have an incoming call I have to take."

"OK, enjoy your visit."

Kelly clicked over to the other line. "Hello there, stranger. Miss me already?"

Chuck was pulled over in his vehicle at the entrance to the ranch, still relishing his restored back and clammed up at Kelly's remark.

"Ah, hi Kelly," Chuck cleared his throat. "I just wanted to call to thank you for your help in California. Have you heard anything from Jed about needing your help in court? That information you gave us on that Devine Group really paid off."

"No, nothing yet," she replied. Yeah well, ya know, when I was tied up in the living room of that mansion I kept hearing Silus on the phone with a broker from LA, discussing that particular property they wanted for a new group they were going to be forming out there called Devine. So, you guys got your culprit?"

"We did. It went off without a hitch."

"I'm glad. Really, Chuck, and I know you didn't care much for Nick, but he didn't have that coming". Chuck kept silent about that one. "Well, we're square now, right ex-hubby?"

Chuck almost choked, not knowing if she was joking or not. "Sure."

"How's your mother getting along with my dear little sister?" Chuck heard the jealousy in her voice, and Kelly noticed Chuck's uncomfortable silence. "Well, that's all right then. So your television show was a tremendous success this week. At least no one's upset with me over that one."

"Kelly, things got complicated and confusing real quick between you and me and–"

"Yeah, and the answer for you," she cut him off accusingly, "was to have our marriage annulled and hook up with Shalon. I'm sorry, I mean Samantha!"

Chuck's face was beat red. He was always left speechless in dealing with her brash personality. "Kelly, what can I say? I'm sorry."

"Yeah, me too, Chuck. Anyhow, I'm pulling into my father's ranch right now. I'll talk to you when I do, I guess." She hung up the phone.

Chuck sat in his Jeep a while longer, feeling like shit and not knowing how things got so screwed up so quickly after he met Kelly. Could she have a point about him, or was she just grandstanding? Maybe she wasn't completely at fault; his affair with Samantha wasn't innocent

Boy, what did Vic think about all of this? He probably wants to kill me, that's what. Chuck had liked him a lot when he first met the man. At the time, he didn't know he was Samantha's stepfather also. Thanks to both of them, keeping that a secret from Chuck. Boy, oh boy, he thought, then shook it off.

He pulled forward down the drive with the vision of Shandi still on his mind, wondering why she had been singing that song they never ended up recording.

Kelly smiled as she saw the big archway to the home she grew up in. Over the wide opening, it said "TEIXEIRA RANCH" in weathered steel letters. The gates were wide open for all to come and go, Texas style. She slowed down a bit and took a sharp right onto a long dirt road surrounded by a wide open prairie. White wooden fencing surrounded the property to keep the livestock contained as far as the eye could see.

Kelly spotted a man to the left of her, riding a gorgeous black and white horse and tending to a small herd of cattle. He saw her slowing and turned his horse towards the fence. She knew the tall, slender drink-of-handsome right away. Stitch Lunger was one of her father's many ranch hands. She steered the car over to the left, put the car in park, and lifted herself up to sit on the headrest, her dress blowing in the warm breeze.

"Stitch!" she waved and called excitedly.

He galloped the rest of the way to the fence and jumped off the animal with ease, tied the stirrup to the fence, and took his hat off. "Miss Kelly! Shucks, Vic didn't tell me you were coming down here."

"Just for a few days, then it's back to the salt mines in Massachusetts."

"It's real nice to see you back home, and as usual, you're a sight to see on this dusty, old ranch."

"Why, thank ya kindly, Stitch. Whatcha doing out this way alone?"

"These here cattle broke loose from the north end. I'm just bringing them back."

They exchanged pleasantries for a minute longer and then Kelly continued driving to the house. There was a certain allure to living on a big ranch, but she was more interested in working on the business end of things. She knew that Texas businessmen would never give her the same respect that a man would get in big oil, so she had set out to the east to build her own real estate legacy. The memory of her mother was certainly a factor in her decision to move out of Texas as well. Shortly after, Shalon had followed her upon her invitation. Maybe that was her first mistake.

Back in Woodrow Massachusetts, Chuck pulled into his driveway where an unfamiliar vehicle was parked. It was a dented and rusty 1993 Pontiac Duster. Saying it was in really awful shape would have been a nice way to put it. Chuck thought that maybe it was a new horse client, but that was doubtful considering the state of the car. He got out of his Jeep with ease, still in amazement at his pain being gone, and walked up the stairs to the house, shouting hello to anyone who might hear him.

Uncle Armond was in the kitchen having coffee with someone Chuck hadn't seen in a long time.

"My God! Jemel, is that you?" Chuck yelled. It was his Army buddy from Panama, Jemel Landau.

"You always did get my name wrong," Jemel laughed.

"Sorry, bro," Chucked said, also laughing.

Jemel walked over to him and gave him a bear hug.

"I'll let you guys catch up," said Uncle Armond.

"OK, Unc. Hey, where's Rupert?"

"He's at the barn with Samantha."

Chuck nodded and turned to his friend. "Buddy, how the hell have you been? Whatcha been up to?"

Jemel sat down and Chuck refilled his coffee, as well as poured one for himself. Then Jemel told him a sad tale.

After the military, he met a woman, got married, and got her pregnant. He had to get a job working at a chemical factory to make ends meet. He injured his right knee and got hooked on painkillers, and after a few years of not being able to kick the habit, his wife and young daughter left him and moved to South Carolina. He explained to Chuck that he was desperately in need of a job, and he was trying to save money to move out to the Carolinas to be closer to his daughter. Mike had reached out to Jemel and told him about a possible opening at the ranch.

"I have no experience with horses and can't do much with my leg, but would appreciate any kind of work. If there is nothing, believe me, I fully understand," Jemel concluded.

Chuck noticed Jemel was sweating buckets in the middle of the winter and that he seemed a little twitchy. This was not the man he remembered. He had the look of someone in dire straits. Chuck felt bad. He saw this kind of thing before when he worked at the prison with inmates that were jacked up on drugs.

"Can you sit on a lawn mower and a four wheeler with a plow alright enough?"

"Yeah, I can do that," Jemel replied anxiously.

"I need a landscaper. My last one was terminated prematurely," Chuck smirked.

Kevin Chapman, the captain of the Pocomtuc Prison, sat at his desk in the early afternoon. He was a very young captain, only 26 years of age, and had his wit, cockiness, and swagger to carry him. The number one lieutenant under him, Mick Loya, sat across from him working on reports and feverishly eating a big bowl of peanuts.

"Hey Mick, have you called Sergeant Venkman to the office yet?"

Mick looked up quickly while almost biting his fingers off. "Yeah, I sure did. He's on his way, Kevin."

Suddenly the big metal door buzzed behind them and the sergeant opened the door.

"Hey Cap, hey Lieutenant. What's up? What's going on?" he asked as he walked over to the captain's desk and sat down opposite of Chapman.

"Dennis, I have to talk to you about an inmate coming into one of your blocks tomorrow." Sargeant Venkman was in charge of blocks, LJ, XL, and a special protective block for inmates that were in high risk of being harmed by others.

"Yeah, Cap, who's coming in?"

The chipper young captain stroked the long mustache hanging over his upper lip, his bright white chiclets showing and a DOC baseball cap turned backwards on his head.

"The inmate's name is Silus Kobol. Have you heard about him?"

"No, never. Who is he?"

"He was allegedly involved in murdering the Attorney General last year in Wolford City and trying to kill a former officer, Barreto."

"Oh, bloody hell! Yeah, I remember. Speaking of those guys, how's Ferrari doing?"

"Looks like he's the AG for now. He was sworn in until the next election cycle," said Chapman. "See, Dennis, here's the thing. I'm putting this guy in block XL for now. I want you to talk to your officers that work that unit to make sure they're on point. We don't need another incident like the one we had with CO Guardian and Father Schaffner getting beheaded."

Dennis straightened his posture. "That won't happen, Cap, but I'll reiterate with them to have eyes on him at all times."

"You know that idiot, Rick Guardian, is on his fourth damn suspension now! They put him in your unit on the overnight shift, and the captain on that shift says they already caught him on camera in the middle of the night rounds not looking inside the cell windows."

Dennis shook his head disgustedly. "Some guys, Cap. Just can't learn 'em."

"Dennis, I want you to see if you can find a way to get him on the right track, okay?"

"Yes, I will try, Captain," he said with zero confidence.

"One more screw up and I'll be forced to have a more progressive hearing on him."

Kelly's car pulled into a large, round driveway. The outer facade of the house was of pressure treated barnwood, and to say the home was expansive would be an understatement. There were two large, man-made ponds on the front lawn, surrounded by rolling countryside. Vic and her stepmother, Cheryl, sat outside on an Amish-made wooden swing having drinks. Chance, her father's right-hand man and confidant, was standing against the wooden porch rail. Both men wore the usual leisure suits with cowboy boots and hats.

Kelly pulled her car close to the house and shut the vehicle off. Cheryl and Chance started waving.

Vic got up and shouted with glee, "My baby girl, get up here! Don't worry about your luggage. We got it."

Chance met her at the car, grabbed her luggage with one arm, and hugged her warmly with the other. "Welcome home, little girl." He looked her in the eye to see if she was okay, and he knew she wasn't, not exactly.

Kelly ran up the steps to the porch and as Vic embraced her, she felt a bit emotional. "Daddy, it's so good to see you!"

He picked her up off her feet, relieved to have her home after having worried so much about the kidnapping and separation from Chuck. Vic put her back down and gave her a kiss on the cheek. She quickly wiped her teary eyes.

"Come on over here and sit with me and Cheryl," Vic said. Cheryl hugged Kelly and they all sat down. Kelly decided not to be icy to her stepmother for once, having been slightly humbled by her experiences.

There was iced lemonade on hand, and Cheryl poured her some as Chance brought Kelly's luggage into the house. As a warm breeze swarmed across the great big porch, she looked around her childhood home, memories good and bad washing over her. They sat on the porch enjoying the breeze, talking about the goings on with the ranch, and purposely staying off certain topics for the time being.

"I think I'll go inside and get dinner ready," Cheryl said eventually.

Then, Kelly knew it was coming.

"So honey, what's going on there with Chuck and Shalon?"

Kelly put her head down and pulled an envelope from her purse, extending it to him. "Daddy, here's the money back from the wedding."

Vic touched her hand gently. "No Kelly, I don't want that. You keep it. But what happened out there?" He saw sorrow in her eyes and wanted to help, but didn't know how.

"Things got screwed up between him and I, Daddy. I only meant well. Let's just leave it there for now."

"Who are these people that tried killing him and kidnapped you?"

"Bad judgment on my part, Daddy. I made a mistake and now I've paid the price."

"I don't understand, things can't be all that bad that Chuck couldn't forgive you. Why is Shalon living on the ranch and not you?"

Kelly's complexion turned red. He could see that his questioning, which was out of concern and love, was getting her upset. He softened his tone. "Okay, okay. Not to worry about any of this stuff right now. Good enough?" He patted her on the back. "On a lighter note, what would you think about coming to work for me and taking charge of my oil company?"

She shot him a look.

"OK, but you know when you're ready, it will be waiting for you," he said.

Kelly half smiled, "Thanks, Daddy."

Cheryl came out onto the porch to tell them dinner was ready, followed by Chance.

"Go on in now, you two," Vic said to Cheryl and Kelly. "I've just got to talk to Chance about something and then we'll be right in." He waited until the women were safely out of earshot before continuing. "Chance, we need to go to Massachusetts and pay a visit to Shalon and

Chuck to find out what in tarnation is going on between her, him, and Kelly. I have to do this face-to-face. When can we get up there?"

"Well, we still have that fire to put out on well number 23. It's still going like a bat out of hell, but I believe the hell fighters are getting on top of it."

"I certainly don't want to lose that well. It's brought us a fortune so far. I'll look at my calendar, and you and I will pay them a visit and square this shit away."

CHAPTER 10

THINGS A-COMING

MARCH 2003

ALLAN MILLER AND his men set up a classic sting in an abandoned parking garage to see if he could nail down the primary culprit involved in moving some major drugs in and out of Wolford City. Two of Allan's men, Doug and Sean, waited in an old Impala for a possible drug buy from a man who was known on the streets as "The Cowboy". His reputation was so that it was almost mythical; many were unsure if he really existed. Five more unmarked police cars were hidden nearby, the officers armed and ready for a bust.

As they awaited the arrival of The Cowboy, Allan was talking to Jed on his cell phone. Jed was asking Allan about another new player in the city, The Birch Group.

"Jed, the guy who started the company, his name is Elliot. He began with some help from his father, but he's basically an entrepreneur. The more I look into his past, the more he seems to be legitimate. Everyone I talk to, or everything I dig up on this guy, tells me he's very ambitious, but an honest business executive. Don't worry, though, I'll keep looking until no stone is left unturned. Believe me," said Allan.

"I know you will, Al. This guy Thorn is like a ghost, but somebody has to know something."

"It's only a matter of time before the answer presents itself."

"Any sign of the dealer yet? Isn't he overdue?"

"Way overdue. Hopefully he's just being cautious."

The two men hung up and Allan put his phone down on the dashboard, looking out the windshield for any signs of movement in the dark garage.

* * *

Chuck was in his kitchen waiting for his mother, who had just arrived to take Aunt Joanne to look at houses for sale. Rupert was lying underneath the table at his feet as he sipped a warm cup of coffee.

Rita walked in the front door. "Hello," she greeted her son.

"Hey, Mom. Want a cup?" he said, pointing to his mug.

"Sure. Whew, it's cold out there!" she said as she took her heavy coat and gloves off.

"Massachusetts, Mom! Call this the coldest month of the year," he said as he poured her coffee.

"Boy, you're not kidding. Where is everyone?"

"Ah, Aunt Joanne is still upstairs getting ready. Armond and Richard took off into town to get something to eat. Everyone else is down at the barn, where I'm headed soon too."

Rita gave her son a look, one he knew well: there was an incoming criticism.

"What, Mom? Let's have it."

"Well… you know, that big helicopter you and Junior have sitting out front really takes away from the beauty of this place, that's all."

"Ma, lots of people have their own helicopters."

"Very funny, Chucky, but not in their front yard this close to the house! And you're not exactly on the front of Forbes yet," she joked.

He brought over her coffee and sat down. "So Ma, why didn't you ever tell me about who Dad really went to meet in New York? I just found out about the phone call from his lost brother, Charlie."

Rita looked at her son directly. "I just thought you, Gary, and Stacey had enough to deal with. Why make it any worse than things already were at the time? And I thought it may have been more than Vovo's heart could handle. It was bad enough to lose one son once, but to lose both of your sons, and one for the second time…"

Chuck digested her comment for a moment. "Yeah, you may be right, Ma. What do you think happened to Charlie?"

"My guess would be that he was engulfed in the crumbling buildings with everyone else that day. Otherwise, I think he would have reached out to one of us at some point in time."

Deep down, Chuck felt a level of denial that his father actually ever died that day. There was a part of him that continued to hope that maybe he had survived it somehow. Maybe he had been injured, forgotten who he was, and had a whole new life somewhere.

Why did he keep randomly having visions of his father when he was sleeping? Was Chuck losing his mind? He kept the thoughts to himself. Rita didn't need to hear it.

"Have you reached out to your friend, Bob, yet?" Rita asked.

"Oh shoot, yeah. I've been meaning to do that."

Aunt Joanne walked into the kitchen. "Hey, everyone. Good morning." They both smiled and greeted her. Chuck got up to get his favorite aunt a cup of coffee.

* * *

Chip Karrington was reviewing the week's schedule in his office in the Capitol with one of his aides when there was a knock at the door.

"Yes, come in," Chip called. His aide, Lisa, opened the door and his campaign manager entered the room with an urgent look. "Alicia, what's wrong?"

"Maybe a word alone would be more prudent," she replied.

"Sure. Lisa, would you mind? This shouldn't be too long."

"Sure, Senator," Lisa said and she exited the office, closing the door behind her. No matter how many times he heard his new title, he never got tired of hearing it.

"Well, Alicia, don't leave me in suspense."

"The Democrats have chosen their candidate for the next election."

"We knew that was coming. Who is it?" he said, bracing himself.

"Erick Blackwell, and he's very popular in Massachusetts, as I'm sure you are aware."

"Are we going to run solely on issues or is there anything we can use against him?" asked Chip.

"I've got my people on it already, but it's not good. This guy is like a choirboy."

"You mean an altar boy?"

Alicia grinned. "Sure, if you like!"

"Should I set aside my schedule today so we can work on a strategy for this? You know we're going to get slammed with questions for the next two weeks, at least from the fake media."

"Oh, no doubt, but no. Don't worry for now, Chip. Carry on. In the meantime, I have three fantastic speech writers making you look like Abraham Lincoln."

Chip laughed. "Honest Abe. I like the sound of that."

"Don't worry, Chip, we'll get through this. I'll find something on Blackwell."

Chuck, Mitch, and Dave were inside the barn working on a horse named Lucky Star. Dave had taken charge and was very efficient. It was definitely not Mitch and Chuck's forte, and they were doing more of cracking jokes than they actually were helping. While Dave worked feverishly, guiding his buddies, he pressed his right hip against the horse's hind leg that they were working on.

"Good girl," Dave made sure to reward the stallion with praise for cooperating with him as he lifted her hoof. Occasionally he would chime in to the conversation. "Dude, what's going on with your car? Did you fix the lock on the door yet?"

"No, I thought maybe water could have frozen inside, but after heating it using a blow-dryer, that turned out not to be the case. The lock mechanism itself is broken, so I ordered a new one."

"How long before you get the part, Rockstar?" asked Mitch.

"Well, I had to special order it. It's too damn cold to rummage through a junkyard this time of year. I'm not sure. Maybe a few weeks. In the meantime, I used a thick bungee cord and hooked it from the inside handle to another mounted to the dashboard in case I want to take her for a drive."

"The dashboard lights, dude," Dave said, in all seriousness.

Chuck understood his dry humor and love for classic tunes so he replied back, "Gotcha, Meatloaf Dave."

"Rockstar, speaking of, did you ever…you know?"

Chuck smiled. "I don't know, Mitch, did I ever do what?"

"Fool around in the backseat?"

Chuck mimed being surprised. "Mitchell! A gentleman never tells."

"Ah, dude. You, a gentleman?"

"Oh, wow, you're funny today, David," replied Chuck.

As they continued working on the horse, Chuck's cell phone rang. He looked at the small screen. "Fellas, I gotta take this." He walked over to the staircase leading up to the hayloft to hear better.

"Ken, what can I do for you?" Chuck answered.

"Well, Mr. Television Executive, you could move out here to California and write for me full time."

"Ah, Mr. Carlson, I'd love to, but I got too much going on right here at the ranch."

"Chuck, I'd pay you enough to have four ranches. Think about it. Anyway, what a fantastic script to follow up the show. The ratings went through the roof!"

"Thank you, Mr. Carlson," Chuck replied humbly.

"No, thank you, son. We'll begin filming the next one in about three weeks. I wanted to ask if you'd be able to get started on a third script right away. I'll send you out another contract, compensating you appropriately."

"Wow, another one that fast?"

"Television is quick and lucrative. I could also set you up with a team of assistant writers if that helps."

"Hmmm… that's alright. I think I can finagle it, Ken. When do you need it?"

"May or June sound good?"

"Yeah, okay. I think that's doable."

"OK, let me know if you change your mind about wanting any help."

They hung up and Chuck thought, Damn, I love the money, but we're about to expand at Gussy's Pitts. Gary's wedding is coming up. He shrugged to himself as he walked back over to the guys and Lucky Star. I'll get it done somehow.

Allan pulled into his apartment complex after a long, unsuccessful day. He didn't want to disappoint Jed, but he knew it would only be a matter of time until he got his man. When it came to work, he was restless and hated to lose.

His apartment was in the town of Chicopee, right outside of the city. Allan needed very little because he was always on the job. Oftentimes it seemed like all he did at home was sleep, which was fine by him because he liked to stay busy.

Allan parked his red and white Impala up front, fairly close to the office manager's building. As he was getting ready to get out of his vehicle, his phone buzzed. It was a text message from Jed.

Chin up, good buddy, We'll get this schlub next time.

Allan smiled at the message. He admired Jed's tireless pursuit for justice. He closed his phone shut . He'd text him back after he'd settled in and had something to eat.

Allan walked up the flight of stairs to the second-floor landing. He looked at his watch. Damn, 8:40 PM already, he thought. Holding his leather briefcase, he took out his keys with the other hand, opened the door, and walked inside, closing the door behind him. He went to turn the living room light on when a man's voice coming from a dark corner of the room startled him.

"Leave the lights off and don't make any sudden moves," he said.

Allan always knew his job was dangerous and had feared that someday one of his enemies would catch up with him.

Allan shakily cleared his throat. "Can I put my briefcase down?"

"Slowly, then you turn around with your hands up."

Allan followed the intruder's instructions, and as he turned toward the dark figure sitting at the end of the room in a chair, he retorted, "How did you get in here? And who is it I am talking to?"

He could make out that the man had a gun pointed at him with a silencer attached to it.

"I'm the guy asking the questions right now!" he shouted. With his free hand he pulled the chain on the lamp next to him, lighting the area well enough for Allan to see the face of a striking younger man wearing a large cowboy hat on a mound of curly hair. "I believe you were looking for me today. I thought I'd introduce myself formally, Mr. Miller."

Allan was taken aback. "You're the Cowboy?"

The man smiled, exposing a gold tooth. "Call me Mr. Logan."

While Allan was trying to process the situation, he noticed a small black duffel bag on the floor next to the island that separated the kitchen and living room.

"OK, Logan. What's the black bag over there?"

"Slowly put your left hand in your pants pocket, and with your right hand, slide that kitchen chair over here in front of me so we can talk. And when I say slow, I mean fucking slow. Oh, and Allan, I know you have a piece holstered underneath that jacket of yours. Do not try to go for it, 'cause I promise you, you will not make it."

As Allan proceeded with the man's instructions, he wondered why Logan would let him keep his weapon on him.

"Now slowly sit down and put your hands in your front pants pockets so we can talk."

Allan sat down knowing his situation was not looking too good.

"What's to talk about? You're going to kill me, and let me take a wild guess, that bag is filled with either drugs or money to make me look like I was dealing and had this coming. How am I doing so far, Mr. Logan?"

"So far so good, Allan. Smart guy for an ex-pig. How did you get kicked off the force?"

"I was chasing a scumbag like you and an innocent woman was killed in the pursuit."

Logan smirked. "So maybe you do have this coming. But I'll tell you what, I will make it fair. I'm going to put my gun on the night-stand right here. I will count to three, and on three, you can go for your gun and I'll go for mine. How's that?"

"I can't ask for more than that, Mr. Logan, because you're the one in control here. Just one thing because, no matter the outcome here, it won't matter, right?"

"True that, Allan. True that."

"You work for Thorn and Silus?"

Logan snickered and snorted. "You got it partially right. I work for Thorn. Silus is under me. OK, enough Allan. One, two–"

Allan pushed himself up, grabbed the chair he was sitting on, and threw it at Logan to buy himself a second to unholster his weapon. Logan grabbed his gun first and dodged the chair, which hit the wall and made a loud thud, throwing him off balance. He fired a shot, wounding Allan in the left thigh, as Allan also fired and grazed Logan's left shoulder. Blood spattered on the wall behind him. Logan got off three additional shots, hitting Allan directly in the chest. He fell sideways onto the ground, blood pouring out onto the shag carpet.

"You go to hell, scumbug!" Allan sputtered.

Logan hobbled over to the dying detective and pointed the barrel of the gun at Allan's head.

"You first."

CHAPTER 11

NEW PLAYERS

MID-MARCH 2003

POWDERY SNOW BLEW around Woodrow Cemetery. Two men dressed in long winter coats, hats, and gloves stood at the freshly piled earth over the body of Allan Tiberius Miller, who had been laid to rest. It was another defeat for Jed and Chuck. Chuck looked as if he could rip the head of a hippopotamus right off its shoulders.

"So this is how it ends for a good man, alone and six feet below. No family and few friends," said Chuck, his breath visible in the cold air.

"I guess his line of work didn't make too many. His parents are both deceased. There were no siblings or kids, just three ex-wives. He kept himself busy doing a job he loved. It was kind of your mother to give him this plot."

"Yeah, actually, it was one of mine in case I ever got married." Jed kept quiet on that one. Chuck pointed to another group of tombstones close to Allan's. "My dad's is right there next to my grandfather and my grandmother."

"Your father's father?"

"Oh no, that's my mother's father, Armond Senior, a great man."

"Where is your father's dad? Is he still alive?"

"Another story for another time," said Chuck and he changed the subject. "What the hell happened to Allan? Who did this to him?"

"I don't really know for sure," said Jed hesitantly, "but I have my suspicions. I can't say more than that. It's an open investigation. I could get fired."

"That's total bullshit, Jed. You're the boss. It's me. After all we've been through this last year?"

Jed looked his old partner in the eye. "No matter what, this goes no further than here, and I mean no matter what."

"Yeah, yeah, of course."

"There was some kind of scuffle in his apartment, but what really got me was that we found a black duffel bag in his kitchen filled with narcotics."

"Didn't you find a bag of drugs in your colleague's apartment after he went missing?"

"We did, and it was the same exact kind of bag."

"There's no way in hell Allan would be mixed up with drugs. No way," said Chuck, shaking his head.

"Of course not, Chuck, he's being set up by someone. Likely the same person or people that had set up Alfred."

"It can't be Silus. He's in jail."

"That kind of thing is probably below his pay grade anyway, but it's got to be someone affiliated with him or this Thorn guy, if he exists."

"He's out there somewhere. I know it in my heart," said Chuck. "So what happens to Allan now? He goes down in the papers as a drug dealer?"

"No, not quite."

"What do you mean by that?"

"Chuck, I did something terrible."

"Come on, buddy, what? Don't leave me in suspense."

"I put a couple of heavy rocks inside the duffel bag, zipped it back up, and threw it over the Wolford City bridge, into the river. Our boy Allan died clean."

Chuck kiddingly punched Jed in his shoulder. "Goddamn, I'm proud of you buddy."

"I'm not sure that's something to be proud of. I broke the law, big time."

"Let me ask you something. Is all this really worth it, Jed? Your pursuit for justice?"

"Do you like all your capitalist gains and freedoms? Your ranch? Your novel? The show? Your land at Gussy's Pitts? Then it's people like me that protect those freedoms, pal, from people like Silus. The creeps, you know? The bad guys?"

Chuck was excited by Jed's pep talk. "What next, then?"

Jed squinted his eyes. "Next? Now I go see that little Jumpin' Jehoshaphat in Pocomtuc!"

"Silus?"

"Yes, Silus."

"I'm coming with you."

"Fine. You can come along for the ride when I go, but I don't know if I can actually get you inside."

"I got faith. You'll find a way, bro, said Chuck. "You know, I never heard you swear before."

"That's not really swearing, Chuck. Compared to your vocabulary, I still sound like a choirboy."

Inside Block XL, Silus Sin Kobol sat at the far end of the tier at a small table wearing a fresh pair of oversized, orange scrubs. He was making the best of his time, with the assurance from his attorney that he would be a free man come May at the pre-trial.

The first day Silus came onto the block, an inmate by the name of Derek Guardian approached him. A guy like him was called a "heavy". He was the guy in charge of the inmates on the block, and at times would even keep the peace between inmates and block officers. Guardian said that outside forces had paid him to protect Silus from harm by funneling money into his canteen.

Guardian nonchalantly looked around the unit to see if the officers at the desk station were going to make a round before approaching Silus who was sitting at a small table cemented to the floor, playing cards with another inmate. The coast was clear.

"Hey Jeremy, take a hike. I have to discuss some personal matters with Silus," said Guardian.

Jeremy was a short, nervous man who may have been dropped on his head one too many times. "Sh-sure, no problem, Derek." He quickly got up and shuffled off to his cell.

Derek sat down opposite of Silus. "Derek. Everything OK? Anything I can do for you? Do I owe you any money?"

Derek gave him a stern look. "Shhh! Lower your voice! To answer your question, no, I don't need anything right now. I am being taken care of by one of your people. I believe they call him The Cowboy."

"Oh that's great, Derek. I'm glad." Silus had never done so much groveling in his entire life. It was downright humiliating. In fact, it was usually people under his command that were groveling to him. Every second behind the prison walls was torture. No wonder he heard about convicts hanging it up.

"If you see one of the officers leave the desk to make a round, we stop talking about what we're about to discuss."

"I understand."

"In a few days, maybe less, we have to get you out of this block and transferred to the protective custody block."

Silus was confused. "Why? Am I in danger here?"

"Not exactly. You will find out more once you're there. My brother is an officer in the block you will be going to. He works nights there. His first name is Rick."

"They let him work in the same prison where you reside?"

"As long as I don't live on the block where he's working. Listen, I don't have time for all this silly talk, Silus. Here's what needs to happen. My boys and I are going to stage a fight in your cell. You're going to take a good enough beating to send you to the hospital, and when they send you back, I'm betting dollars to donuts you will automatically be sent to protective custody. From there, you'll be under his protection and you'll receive your next set of instructions once you are housed in the block."

"Is the beating really necessary?"

"Trust me, there won't be any permanent damage. Just enough to have you sent out and then PC'd to the special block."

"What does 'PC'd' mean?"

Derek exhaled impatiently. "Protective custody. Silus, this is what your boss wants. I don't have time for explanation. You're in good hands. It'll all make sense later on. My men and I are more at risk than you, so stop worrying."

"OK Derek, sorry, this kind of thing is all new to me. I am used to a different world of crime."

"Silus, I know that just from looking at you, but no worries. We will show you the ropes. Then you will be an old pro wherever you are." He smiled at Silus.

Kelly Texeria was in a meeting at The Silver Bell when there was a knock on the door.

"Excuse me, Elliott," she said to the man sitting across from her. "Yes, come in."

The door opened and Paige's face popped in. "The assistant attorney general is here to see you."

"If you'll excuse me, this shouldn't be too long," Kelly said to Elliot.

"No, no, that's quite all right. I've got to be going, anyway. I'll talk to you soon enough."

He stood up as Abby Taylor walked into the room. She couldn't help but notice how well-tailored the suit was to his five-foot-nine frame. Abby took notice of his shoulder-length hair and well-groomed beard and mustache. As they made eye contact, his radiant blue eyes and gleaming white teeth struck her.

"I'll talk to you later, Mr. Birch," said Kelly.

As the man was putting on his black leather gloves, a lightbulb went off in Abby's head. "Excuse me, sir." He turned to smile at her again. "Are you Elliott Birch?"

His smile grew. "Why yes, and who do I have the pleasure to address?"

Abby thought, Oh boy, not only is this guy cute, but he's a charming devil. "I work for the Attorney General's office. My name is Abby Taylor. We've been trying to reach you with some questions about the property on the south end of Wolford City."

He reached over and gently grabbed her right hand, raising it to his lips to kiss it. "I'm so glad to meet you, Miss Taylor." She quickly took her hand away from him. "Maybe we could discuss this over dinner tonight?" he asked.

Her face felt flushed. She sharply rejected the suggestion. "How about in my office, Mr. Birch, instead?"

Elliot's face adjusted slightly though his smile never faltered. "Oh well, I tried. I'll tell you what, Miss Taylor. I'll be in my office, on the top floor of the SkyTower if you'd like to discuss anything. Anything at all. Good day, ladies." He walked out of the office with a debonair swagger.

Abby looked at Kelly, her heart still fluttering. "Well, he's a rude man!"

"Oh, I don't know. He seems rather charming." Kelly smiled.

"You certainly have a type," said Abby.

"A type?"

"Sure, he looks like Chuck, but older and more distinguished."

"You seemed taken aback by him from what I saw," Kelly retorted.

Abby shook her head and made a face. "Ha, no. Definitely not my type."

"Anyhoo," said Kelly. "What is it I can do for you, Miss Taylor?"

"I just wanted to stop by personally to talk with you about the court hearing on testifying against Silus Kobol."

Kelly's expression changed. "A phone call would have sufficed."

"I also thought I could go over some things that could pop up in the courtroom, so as to better prepare you."

"Again, I already know, Miss Taylor. I'll be there. Is there anything else? I really have a lot of work today."

"Ah, no, that's all I guess. What was Mr. Birch doing here in your office?"

Kelly's face turned red. "Miss Taylor, I've had enough. Is Mr. Birch now a corrupt businessman that is under your scrutiny?"

Abby lowered her voice. "No, no, of course not. I was just curious. Occupational hazard. Sorry to bother you. I'll go now."

Abby walked out of her office and Kelly shook her head. "What is it with these people?"

Chuck pulled into a small plaza in the town of Wilbraham, which bordered Woodrow. He had just come from another visit to the chiropractor and was feeling fantastic. He had been keeping up with the therapy and it had really been helping.

He looked up at the sign of the office he had pulled up in front of. It read "Palluzzi Construction", and it was a family friend's business. Chuck was meeting with Chad Palluzzi, Rita, and Stacey to go over their plans for Gussy's Pitts.

Chuck had a quick thought. He grabbed the yellow legal pad sitting on his passenger seat and wrote down a few lines quickly. He brought paper with him everywhere, trying to get the manuscript done for the third production in a timely fashion. His phone rang from the middle console. He looked at the small screen and was pleasantly surprised to see it was his book publisher, Linda Mansfield. Wonder what she wants.

"Hello, Linda, how are you?" Chuck answered.

"Chuck! Or should I call you Mr. Hollywood? I am doing well and I see that so are you. They're already filming your second manuscript, I heard."

"Yes, ma'am. Ken said it should be airing in the summer."

"I'm actually calling you about that manuscript. My company would like to have it made into a book, and we would release it after the show airs. What do you say, Chuck? Please say yes."

Chuck couldn't believe his good fortune. He never thought of himself as a writer, despite the book's success. It had always been Shandi that could write, especially when it came to music. What would she think if she were here now?

"OK, Linda, let's do it."

"Fantastic, Chuck! You won't regret this."

"Oh, I know, Linda. You haven't steered me wrong yet."

Chuck hung up his phone and got out of the Jeep. He went into the small lobby and Chad's mother, Jenny, greeted him from behind reception. "Chuck, how are you, sonny boy? Come on around the desk. Everyone is in the back office." She was always cheerful, a real people person like Chuck's mother.

"Hey, Mrs. Paluzzi. Nice to see you too."

He denied the offer of coffee and they walked into the back office that he had been to many times before. When he entered the room, everyone greeted him with hello's and condolences.

"Hey, son. Sorry about Allan. He was such a nice man. Did Jed learn anything more about what happened?" Rita asked.

Chuck kept his promise. "No, nothing, Ma. No one's heard anything yet."

"Well, I'm sure Jed will catch whoever broke into his apartment. Maybe he should call Jack Bufford."

Chuck just wanted to change the subject. "Yeah, we'll see, Ma." He shook Chad's hand and hugged Stacey and then they began their meeting. Diagrams and blueprints for their new project were spread across the long wooden table. There were specs of different sections of

Gussy's Pits, which would be utilized without actually destroying the beauty of the landscape.

Chuck and Stacey were floored that the plans lived up to what they had envisioned. There would be corrals, barns, private cottages for guests, beautiful horse trails, a small restaurant, and a convenience store mapped out. All of it was designed to be built into the landscape, so it wouldn't interfere with nature or the environment. All guests would be parking in an area out at the entrance of Gussy's Pitts and shuttled in. Rita was equally as excited as her children.

"What a brilliant idea to build these units right into the hillside of Indians Leap. Chad, how long before it will be completed?"

"I'll get started next month. The ground will be thawed enough by then. I should have most of it ready for next summer."

"Wow, that's amazing!" She was so proud of Stacey and Chuck for not selling the land and deciding to do something more profound with it to carry on her husband's legacy.

"How is Gary with all this?" Chad asked, looking at Chuck and Stacey.

"Oh, he's going along with it, I think because he can't get as much for his parcel of land without ours. Plus, he stands to make out once we start bringing in business," said Stacey.

"Oh Stacey, that's not altogether true. Your brother is happy to be part of this venture, I'm sure," Rita scolded.

Chad was sorry he even asked the question.

Chuck pivoted the conversation by bringing up the good news about his second manuscript being turned into another novel by his publisher.

"What are they going to call it?" asked Chad.

"Ah, I don't know. Maybe they should name it How Booze, Women, and Corrections Saved My Life," he said jokingly.

Everyone laughed except for Rita. "Chucky, that's not a good title. I really didn't care for the tone of the first one."

"That title was Kelly's idea, Ma."

"Exactly," said Rita, crossing her arms.

Jenny entered and asked if they would like to grab lunch at the restaurant next door.

"I'd love to guys, but I'm picking Joanne up at Chuck's and then we're off to look at more houses. I think she's coming close to a decision on one. We'll see."

Stacey and Rita went their separate ways, and Chuck and Chad remained to talk more about the finer details of the plans.

CHAPTER 12

POCOMTUC

LATE MARCH 2003

CHUCK WAS LOOKING out his kitchen window having coffee and waiting for Jed to pick him up at the house. The snow was melting and you could finally see patches of the earth showing through. It was around 9:00 AM when Samantha came inside with Rupert from being out at the barn.

Chuck smiled. "Hey there. The little fella had enough?"

"Yeah, his rear quarter is bothering him in this cold weather. His age is catching up with him, I think," Samantha replied.

Chuck didn't want to believe his buddy was getting old.

Rupert walked over to his master, wagging his curled up tail. Chuck petted his head. "Good boy! How's my little man today?" Chuck looked at Samantha. "You want some coffee, Sam?"

"Why not? Everyone's doing alright outside without me for now. Well…almost everyone."

Chuck had a feeling he knew who she was referring to. "Jemel?"

"I didn't want to say anything, but he seems to be struggling with his duties. I've been pulling Andy to give Jemel a helping hand. He's not quite getting it yet."

"He's having a rough go of it. I'll see if Mike can help him."

"I'm sure Mikey will be good for him, the big teddy bear. He was your Sergeant back in the day?"

"He was."

"What's this package on the counter?" Sam pointed to a small box on the island, changing the subject.

"The parts store delivered it this morning. It's the new lock for the Charger. Right now I got it rigged closed with a bungee cord. I'll put it in the garage on my way out when I leave with Jed."

"How's Jed taking Allan's death?"

Chuck had told a little white lie to her, that he and Jed were going to Allan's apartment to clean it out. Samantha was no dummy. She was pretty sure his place was still a crime scene, but she didn't want to let on that she knew he was being untruthful.

"Ah, you know, he hides his feelings well, but I'm sure he's most bothered because Allan had been working on a case for him when it happened."

Samantha felt annoyed and hurt a little by being left out of the loop. She cleared her throat after sipping some coffee and put the cup in the sink.

"I'd better get back to the barn. I'll see you later on." She gave him a quick peck and walked outside. Once outside, she put her hand over her mouth to muffle a scream as she walked over to the four wheeler.

What do I need to do to gain his trust? she thought to herself. I think he loves me, even though we haven't said it yet. It all felt helpless at times. Maybe Kelly had been right all along, and he couldn't let go of the past. She looked like a dead woman he was still in love with. Tears trickled down her cold, red cheeks.

Inside the house, Chuck was wondering if he should come clean. Maybe he would tell her everything that night.

He tidied up the kitchen and was putting out some food for Rupert when he heard a car pulling in the driveway. He looked up at the clock on the wall. Jed was early, but that wasn't exactly surprising. He walked over to the window and saw his sister's car pulling in instead. What was she doing there?

Stacey slammed the car door shut. She stormed up the porch into the breezeway and into the house, taking her gloves off as she plopped into a chair.

"Hey, sis. What's going on? Are you here to go to target practicing with Sam?" Chuck joked.

Stacey took her hat off. "You got some coffee, Chuck?"

"Always," he said. He walked over to the pot and poured her a cup with cream and sugar. "What's up? What's wrong?"

"You might wanna sit down for this one, big brother. The governor is going to try and write an executive order to make an access road through Indians Leap to connect Woodrow and the surrounding towns."

"What! Why? How is that even possible?"

"They had an inspection done on the city bridge and it needs some repairs, so they're going to shut one side of the bridge down at a time until the project is completed."

"So that means the bridge will still be operational."

"Partially, yes, and it will cause major traffic issues for people trying to get in and out of the city."

"They can still go around at the far end of Chicopee to get in."

"That will not alleviate the problem enough to meet their standards."

"Well, damn them. Damn them all to hell! They're not coming through our land. What can be done?"

"I'm way ahead of you. Your attorney, Jessica Farnsworth, is filing an emergency hearing in court as we speak. It should take place tomorrow."

"Damn, you're on it, Stace. Nicely done. How did you find out about all this? And can Jessica stop them in their tracks?"

"She has already assured me they will not dig one inch of dirt on our land and not to worry. I found out from a friend of mine that works in the governor's office and she gave me a heads up. Can you make it into court with us tomorrow?"

"Yeah, I'll be there," he said, looking up at the clock again. "Hey, Chip Karrington have anything to do with this?"

"My guess would be yes."

"Do you think you could call Chip and talk to him about this craziness?"

"I already did. I left a message with one of his aides. How about you? Ask Jed to get a hold of him about this too."

"Oh I plan on it, Stace! Chip came to me last year asking me to develop our land before LoneStar made their attempt to kill me, and now here we are once again," Chuck said as he heard Jed's vehicle pulling up to the house.

Abby exited the elevator on the top floor of the SkyTower. She had decided to take Mr. Birch up on his previous invitation, though she came unannounced to catch him off guard. She was ready for battle, undeterred in her pursuit for answers. Abby would cut through his smugness like a knife through butter.

Elliot was pacing around his carpeted office and gazing through the large rectangular windows overlooking the city. He felt a kinship when he was talking to his one and only hired security man, Eddie Chellis.

Eddie was in his early fifties and taller than his employer at six foot three. He was well-dressed in his Armani suit and fully armed underneath his coat, a hint of potbelly sticking out. He had been with Elliot for over 10 years now and they had become very close friends. Security wasn't his only speciality; he would also take care of other problems for Mr. Birch from time to time. They made a good team and Mr Birch was quite happy with his abilities, but Eddie often warned him about not having enough security for his status.

Elliot would laugh cavalierly and say something like, "We got this, Eddie. Plus, you know I'm pretty handy with my piece." Elliot carried a gun strapped to his backside. He was too proud and assured of himself to put anyone else on the payroll, so Eddie worked extra hard to keep his boss safe from any dangers.

Elliot went back to looking out into the big city, sipping on a robust black coffee while Eddie was reviewing an assortment of duties.

"Ya know, Edward, it's absolutely amazing to me how one man can make such an immense difference in this city," Elliot said.

"Ah, for sure, Elliot, and that man is...?" said Eddie in his gravelly voice.

Elliot smirked at Eddie and the intercom on his desk buzzed. He walked over and pressed a button. "Yes, Miss Ryder?"

"Mr. Birch," a soft voice replied, "there is a Miss Taylor out here in the lobby to see you. She says you told her she could come by anytime."

He smiled at Eddie deviantly. "Yes, I did tell her that, Miss Ryder. You can send her in, please."

"Yes sir, and don't forget you have an appointment today with Delta Investments at 1:00PM."

"Thank you, Miss Ryder."

Abby walked into the room, her short blond hair frizzed about her head and wearing a pinstripe suit under an overcoat. Her tan heels clicked across the floor.

Eddie could see his employer wanted to be alone with the stunning young lady, so he excused himself, greeting Abby before closing the door behind him.

Elliot's intense blue eyes lit up as he engaged her. "Well, Miss Taylor, I'm so happy to see you. You are looking rather ravishingly gorgeous today, if I may say." His unrelenting charm once again took her aback, but her game face never wavered.

"Mr. Birch—"

"Please, Miss Taylor, call me Elliot. What do you say if we go out for a bite to eat? There are some pretty fantastic restaurants around here."

"No, thank you, Mr. Birch. I just stopped by to ask you some questions about your affiliation with the LoneStar Group and a man named Thorn."

Elliot made a dramatic pouty face. "Okay, okay, Miss Taylor. We will play it your way, for now." He smiled at her. "Well, at least sit down and relax."

"I'll stand, Mr. Birch."

"OK, Miss Taylor. Can you repeat your question?"

Abby pursed her lips. She didn't like the games this man played. "The LoneStar Group. And a man associated with them, Thorn." She was watching him for any tells, but there were none she could see. He was calm and relaxed with her line of questioning.

"I only know that this LoneStar Group was bought out by smaller groups looking to invest. Shareholders put out bids to finish the project that had only just barely broken ground on the south end of the city, as you know. My company won the bid to complete the hotel in the casino, Miss Taylor. I also own shares, which makes me part owner. If I knew anything otherwise, I'd tell you. I am just an earnest businessman."

"Are you looking to expand your project into Gussy's Pitts, beyond the city?"

"That would be a little tough. There's a big ridge in the way owned by a wealthy rancher, as I understand it."

"Yes, it's called Indian Leap, and that rancher is Mr. Barreto, who was almost murdered by some unsavory characters that worked for LoneStar. What my office is trying to understand is if you're affiliated with them in any way, shape, or form."

"Miss Taylor, building is my business. Those are some outrageous suggestions. I would only be interested in developing that valley if that was something Mr. Barreto wanted. If not, that's his prerogative. I have developed in almost every major city in this country so far, and now I'm here to do the same in Wolford."

"And what's next after you're finished here?"

"I go where the money is, Miss Taylor."

"And you don't care about the destruction you leave behind?"

"Excuse me? If anything, I'm making lives better. My work brings new homes, businesses, and jobs to the areas I develop."

"What about the small businesses destroyed or people forced out of their homes that you put out on the street, Mr. Birch?"

"I don't see it that way. I upgrade the area. Progress for all."

"Some might say that's progress only for the wealthy."

"Well, we could argue about this at length, Miss Taylor. Over dinner, perhaps?"

"We could, but people of your nature are very shortsighted about these kinds of matters and I must get going. Thank you for your time."

"The pleasure was all mine."

She walked towards the door, then turned back to him. "Do you know who these shareholders are who hired you, Mr. Birch?"

"I know some of them. Why?"

"Is it possible you could provide me with a list of them?"

"This is your city, Miss Taylor. Wouldn't your boss have a list of all business dealings? Well, never mind. I'll tell you what– even though I believe it's considered unethical– I'll bring the list to dinner tonight."

Abby stared at him icily. She walked a few brief steps back to his desk, pulled a business card from her purse, and gently placed it on the corner of it. "Call my office when you have it. Good day, Mr. Birch."

She walked out of his office, leaving the land mogul impressed. "Well, it's not going to be easy getting her to see things my way, is it?"

He pressed the small gray button on his intercom. A voice came from the speaker, "Yes, Mr. Birch?"

"Miss Ryder, can you get me the list of shareholders from the casino hotel project?"

"Yes, Mr. Birch, is that all?"

"That'll be all for now. Thank you, Miss Ryder."

Elliot stroked his well-groomed beard as he walked over to the wall of windows. He took out a flip phone and hit a button, placing the speaker to his ear.

"Eddie, I need you to look into something for me."

"Of course. What do you need, Elliot?"

"I'd like you to look into the shareholders for the project we're working on. See if you turn up anything inconspicuous in nature. See if there is a person named Thorn involved with any of them, or the LoneStar Group."

"That's the group you took over for."

"Yes, exactly."

Jed and Chuck drove towards the Pocomtuc Prison. Jed was trying to calm his friend down over the recent development with the governor. He was assuring Chuck that he obviously had known nothing about it and would call Chip to see what was going on. Jed himself couldn't believe his own boss would try to do this, putting him in a tough spot, especially after the events of the last year.

Jed pivoted to a new subject. "So when are you taking me for a ride in the Charger, Chuck?"

"Ah, not for a bit. I have to fix the passenger door first."

"What's happening with that?"

"The lock mechanism is busted. She won't stay closed. So anyway, you never told me how you got it approved for me to see this mutt today," said Chuck, his mood lightened some.

"I'm going to keep that to myself for now, buddy. I'm still not so sure any of this is a great idea, but thankfully Kobol won't actually see you because you will be looking through the one-way glass."

Chuck had had little choice but to agree with this procedure.

"So given that, that's four you owe me now," Jed joked.

"Four? How do you figure?"

"The barn, when the assassin tried killing you. Outside the hotel, when the bomb went off."

"Okay! So what's the third?"

"Oh, the time you almost got muckled by that inmate, Kevlin, in his cell."

Chuck laughed out loud. "Ho, ho, ho. I'm pissing myself, bro. I had that asshole all day long 'til you punched him and he staggered backwards into me."

Jed smirked. "OK, maybe. Maybe it's just three." His vehicle took a sharp right ascending an access road that was way overdue for repairs.

Jed hummed along with an Ozzy Osbourne song that was playing low on his radio. Chuck never figured his friend for a classic rock guy before. It struck him as funny.

"Hey, I didn't know you like Ozzy, Jethro."

"I love this guy and Black Sabbath."

On each side of the road were thick woods and up ahead the structure of the prison facility was visible.

"Boy, I don't miss this place. It's starting to look like an old castle," said Chuck. Jed's car pulled up to a big metal gate. An officer came out to greet them and immediately recognized Jed. He approached the car window and said excitedly, "Why, is that Jed Ferrari? Nice to see you, brother."

"You too, G-man."

The officer then noticed Chuck sitting next to Jed. "Holy cow, and Mr. Hollywood himself."

They reminisced for a few minutes and then the officer let them in through the gate. Jed drove to the front parking lot and shut the vehicle off. They unholstered their guns by reflex. Jed carefully placed his inside the glove compartment and Chuck stashed his weapon underneath his seat. Jed grabbed his brown, leather briefcase from the backseat.

115

"You think this guy is ready to sing, Jed?" asked Chuck.

"I doubt it, but you never know. We'll soon find out."

They walked through the double doors of the prison that led to a large lobby area. Inside there were ten male and female officers waiting at the podium to greet Jed and Chuck. Whereas normally there would be only one officer posted in the lobby for incoming visitors, they were excited to see their former coworkers.

They immediately started shouting at Chuck and Jed with glee, especially at Chuck because of his book and show. They were calling him Hollywood or Steve Burnett, after his character. Jed got a kick out of his buddy's newfound fame.

Officers Murray, Marlo, and Daniels were telling Chuck about how much they loved the television show and that they were all glad that he was actually not dead. Chuck was blushing and not quite comfortable with the attention.

After they were done catching up, Captain Chapman announced that he needed to talk with Jed and Chuck alone before they entered the trap to see Silus Sin Kobol.

"Gosh, Chap, when are you going to shave the caterpillar off?" Jed razzed on his mustache.

Chuck chimed in as well. "I've only seen one man in my lifetime with a stash prettier than this one, Jed."

"Who?"

"Magnum PI." Chuck and Jed shared a laugh and Chapman smirked.

"Okay, okay, wise asses," he shook their hands. "Welcome back from the dead, Chucky!"

"Roger that, Cap. It's good to be back."

Chapman turned to more serious matters. "OK, guys, I have to tell you about this piece of shit before you go in to see him. Kobol recently came back from a hospital trip. He got beat up pretty badly in your old block by a couple of inmates. We sent him out to the hospital for a few days and now he is in the protective custody block, J-7, for his safety."

"Couldn't have happened to a nicer guy," said Chuck under his breath. Jed shot his buddy a look to knock it off.

"Sergeant Dennis Venkman, the officers that work that block, and myself caught a lot of crap for that happening to him." Jed and Chuck looked at one another with dread, still remembering the day they both got investigated about the injuries of an inmate. Chapman knew what they were thinking. "No guys, it's not Ned or Warren. I have officer Fuentes going inside with you."

They both let out a sigh of relief, knowing that this specific officer was a solid person and would avoid getting others in trouble at all costs. He wasn't a rat.

"Are you boys ready?" asked Chapman. They nodded and the captain walked them to the big metal door that would let them into the world of convicted felons.

Chapman looked at the officers in the glass control room off to the left and raised his right thumb to give them the OK to open up the door. A large, blue metal door slowly slid across its tracks until it made a loud clanking noise. They walked inside and were greeted by Officer Forest Elmore, who also knew Jed and Chuck very well.

"Well, how are you guys? I thought I'd never see the likes of you two again. Mr. fancy-pants Attorney General and Mr. Big Hollywood." He shook their hands before using a metal detector wand on them, which was a protocol that couldn't be avoided. Then he jokingly told them, "I'll see you two troublemakers on the way out."

Captain Chapman walked them down a long hallway to their final destination. Jed and Chuck, once out of earshot from Officer

Elmore, said to Chapman, "So, he is still working in the trap after all this time, Captain?"

Forest was notorious for getting himself into mischief, a real glutton for punishment, they would say.

"Yeah, well, you think Forest being confined to this one area would do the trick to keep him out of trouble, but this guy always finds a way."

"Why? What did the big dummy do now, Chap?"

"You wouldn't believe it if I told you."

Chuck looked at his partner and rolled his eyes. "Oh yes, we would, Chap."

"Forest went to fill his water canteen in the maintenance area on his break." Jed and Chuck shook their heads, waiting for the plot to thicken. "The maintenance staff were using one of the water bubblers to put their chemicals in. There were homemade signs everywhere on the damn thing that said, 'Do not drink! Chemicals!' What does sleepy Forest do?"

Jed and Chuck laughed before the punchline was given.

"He fills his jug up and drinks a big old gulp of it, then spits it out, realizing what he'd done." They all laughed, knowing it was a typical Forest move. "Hey Chuck, you should put that in your next book!"

Chuck appreciated the glossy, waxed tiled floor they were walking on. It reminded him of the days he worked his old block with Jed, and they had inmate runners shine the floors to gain them the accolade of the cleanest unit. They reached another locked inner door and Jed kindly reminded Chuck that he was not to interact, no matter what. The captain looked through the thick, secured glass doors and knocked at the window to get the officer's attention. She hit a button on her desk to open the door for them.

Chuck and Jed were not familiar with the officer. She must have come in after they had departed. Chapman opened the door and said, "OK fellas, this is where I leave you. Good luck with that piece of shit, and I'll see you both soon."

They thanked him and walked into the visiting area to talk with the female officer, Sue Bardot. She was courteous to them and had been previously instructed to help them with everything they needed, within the rules. Then the Inner Perimeter Security Officer, Fuentes, came out from another secured area where he had already been with Kobol.

"OK Jed, this guy is all ready for you. I don't have to tell you what to do, you're an old pro. He's sitting in room number four waiting for you. Chuck and I will be sitting behind you in the private room, watching and listening. Good luck. I hope you can get something out of him," Fuentes said in a low voice so that Silus would not hear.

"How has he been? What do you think?" asked Jed.

"It's hard to tell. He keeps pretty much to himself and looks scared most of the time, but you never know. Before he was moved to this new block, he was chumming with Derek Guardian back in Block XL."

They looked at one another and rolled their eyes knowing that Derek Guardian was officer Rick Guardian's brother and a total screw up.

"OK, boys, let's do this," said Fuentes.

Jed walked down a narrow hallway until he reached door number four, while Chuck and Officer Fuentes went through a different door and walked down another narrow hall shaped like a tunnel that had a futuristic look and feel with lowlights embedded in the walls.

"Fuckin' A, Miguel. I heard the rumors about this little place you IPer's had hidden back here, but always took for granted its actual existence. It reminds me of an old Planet of the Apes film set or something," said Chuck, astonished.

"Yeah, it's pretty cool, huh, Chucky?"

Further down the hall there were built-in alcoves for each visiting cell that were used to spy on the inmates and their visitors. Officer Fuentes stopped Chuck and said, "This is us right here, my man."

They pivoted to their right and inside the alcove were two old, leather chairs bolted to the carpeted floor facing a one-way mirrored glass looking into the visitation room. There was a middle console between the chairs with several colored buttons embedded into it.

"Go ahead, Chuck. Take a seat."

They sat down and Chuck's eyes widened. Through the glass in front of them was Silus Kobol. His hands were cuffed in front of him and he wore a bright orange pair of scrubs. Chuck immediately noticed his two black shiners. They were awfully striking in conjunction with his odd-looking eyes. Silus looked as if someone had sucked the life out of him, and it gave Chuck great satisfaction to see him trapped like a rat and looking pathetic. Maybe, just maybe, Jed could get to him somehow.

"Don't worry, he can't see or hear us," said Fuentes, and he pushed a button on the console to turn on the speaker.

"Boy, they really worked him over. And he looks as if he's lost weight," said Chuck.

"Yeah, he took a pretty good beating. The inmates kicked the shit out of him in his cell, and as far as his weight goes, this pansy ass is probably not used to eating small portions of state food," he chuckled.

Chuck laughed too. "They should reward them and make those inmates, wherever they end up, as head unit runners."

"Yeah, that would be nice, but no. They were transferred out of our county to Walpole and they're all doing time in the hole out there."

"Oh, that's too bad."

They stopped talking so they could hear Jed's conversation with Kobol. The sound was piped into the area that Chuck and Fuentes were in.

"Hello, Mr. Kobol," began Jed. "Sorry to hear about the attack on you."

Silus gave the Attorney General a stony stare. "Please, spare me the nonsense, Ferrari. What is it you want from me today? I know the game. Before your pals abducted me, I was an attorney and will be again soon."

Jed quickly responded. "Sure, right, an attorney who is in for kidnapping and murder."

"I am innocent, Ferrari. In this country, we have laws. I will have my day in court with a jury of my peers, but I doubt it will go that far."

"Then why did you agree to see me today with no legal r epresentation?"

"Mmmm, mostly boredom and insatiable curiosity."

"Curiosity?"

"What is your proposal? You didn't come here without one, I'm sure."

"Boy Chuck, this guy is one self-assured little prick. I thought he was scared out of his mind and in over his head, but that's not the case at all," Fuentes said.

"Nope. This dirt bag is insidious."

In the visitation room, Jed continued. "The governor has a deal, and it's the only deal on the table. After today, it will automatically be dissolved."

Silus paused for half a minute, and Chuck and Fuentes were wide-eyed waiting for his response.

"OK, Ferrari, what is this deal?"

Chuck and Fuentes exhaled.

"A reduced sentence in a federal prison. Ten years. This doesn't include time off for good behavior, and when you get out, witness protection is an option if you choose to enter it. All of this is in exchange for the whereabouts of the persons involved in the LoneStar Group. We know you were taking orders from a person who goes by the name of Thorn."

Silus paused again.

"He's going to bite, Chuck!" said Fuentes.

"No, I don't think so Miguel," replied Chuck, shaking his head.

Silus leaned into the glass window between him and Jed as far as the metal restraints allowed. "Are you out of your mind? You want me to turn an alleged powerful conglomerate over to the likes of you so that I can do ten years in prison? No federal prison or witness protection program could protect me for two minutes. After my hearing in May, Mr. Ferrari, I will be a free man. Free! And you will be looking for a new job."

Officer Fuentes and Chuck exchanged a glance.

Jed maintained his game face. "Kobol, when I leave this room, this offer is immediately off the table, forever. Why did you agree to even see me today without a lawyer present? You had the Attorney General murdered, and this is the best it will ever get for you. After today, the state will be asking for a life sentence. And we will get it. I would think it over if I were you. Take a minute."

Chuck and Fuentes waited on the edge of their seats, and then Silus looked straight at Jed with those evil eyes, gritting his teeth. "You were already suspended once before they stupidly gave you this job. When I am released in May, you sir, will be looking for a new job. But at least you can have your old job back, here at the prison as a guard again."

Jed's face turned beet red with anger and humiliation. "We will see about that, Kobol!"

"Oh yes sir, Mr. Attorney General, we will. And let me just say one more thing."

"What's that, Kobol?"

Silus looked over Jed's head at the glass and smiled evilly. "Peek-a-boo, Barreto, I see you!"

Chuck's eyes bulged out of his head and he leaned back and kicked the small metal counter in front of him in disgust. "Motherfucker! He can see us. He knows we are in here."

Fuentes attempted to calm him down. "Chuck, no way. It's not possible. He's just fucking with Jed right now."

"No! You've been compromised somehow. You got a damn snitch somewhere inside this facility!"

Fuentes was half in agreement with him, but didn't want to admit it to Chuck openly.

Chuck jumped up off his chair. "Miguel, buzz me out of here. I've heard enough! I'll meet Jed in the lobby."

Fuentes wasn't going to argue. He knew this attempt to get Kobol to sing was a bust. Chuck walked down the hall alone in complete disgust, shaking his head.

CHAPTER 13

CAPTAIN GILL SELLER

APRIL 2003

A MAN SAT in a large, rustic-European kitchen that had gold-streaked granite counters with a white marble backsplash that glistened in the morning sunlight. The man was drinking a glass of fine H.M. Borges Terrantez vintage wine. The bottle of Portuguese red sat on the island next to the television, in which the man was engrossed.

The man was the ever-elusive Mr. Thorn.

What he already knew was being reiterated to him on the television screen; bad news for him. The newly nominated candidate, Erick Blackwell, would be running against Chip Karrington next year for Senate, and he was making a scorching statement against Chip and the governor.

"Governor Graham was just beaten in court by a local rancher and author. His lawyer blocked Graham from closing down the Wolford City bridge, which is long overdue for repairs according to the inspectors. The poor taxpayers of the surrounding towns that work in the city will have to suffer by waiting in traffic to get home every night, thanks to Senator Karrington and Governor Graham's incompetence."

Thorn cringed at Blackwell's rant and lowered the volume on the TV. He reached over and grabbed his red flip phone from the counter.

"The hairs on my arm will stand up, at the terror in each sip and each sup," he said to himself aloud, an unusual reference he often made to an old song. He opened the device, selected a contact, and patiently waited for an answer.

Mr. Logan answered as he drove his black Hummer. "Good morning, Mr. Thorn. What can I do for you, sir?"

"I am calling to inform you that I have returned home to personally see through Operation Kawaii."

"Very good, sir," Logan replied enthusiastically. "Nice to have you back."

"It's good to be back, Mr. Logan. Polishing seats in Washington gets redundant after a while. You did a fantastic job keeping up with the maintenance of the house. Thank you."

"I had help, Mr. Thorn, from a few trusted members of my crew."

Thorn walked over to the glass French doors, opened them, and walked outside onto a wrap-around deck, which featured an incredible view of the river that curved around Wolford City. Two of Thorn's security guards stood at the perimeter for the safety of their boss. He looked at them both to let them know he needed some privacy and they walked out of earshot.

"What's the status with this operation? Because things just went south with my other plans."

"I am actually on my way to talk with our expert, Mr. Sellek, right now."

"Excellent. Keep me up-to-date."

"Yes, I will do that, Mr. Thorn. Is there anything else you need, sir?"

"Actually, Logan, I'm calling about two other assignments as well. One I need done right away. The other can wait until I assess the situation a little further."

"Sure, it will be my pleasure."

"Chuck Barreto, the rancher in Woodrow. Have you found out anything pertinent?"

"I have. I infiltrated his ranch with a trusted operative, sir. My man has reported back to me that the rancher has a girlfriend that works on his ranch."

"I'm going to need her removed from the equation."

"Yes, sir. How soon?"

"Immediately, Mr. Logan. Is that going to be a problem?"

"Consider it done, Mr. Thorn."

"Maybe that will slow him down some. This young man needs to be taken down a notch before our grand finale."

"I concur with that, sir. And what was the second job, Mr. Thorn?"

"I may have a problem with a certain senator in Washington. He just announced his nomination to run against my guy, who already has the seat. His poll numbers are really good. Actually, too good for his own good. Is there anyone you could get close enough to him to cancel his candidacy if need be?"

"Who is the candidate, Mr. Thorn?"

"Erick Blackwell."

"Let me get to work on it right away, sir. We may be able to use the operative that is meeting with the rancher's brother in Richmond, Virginia. He owes us big time."

"Yes, of course. What was his name?"

"Matt Helfer."

"Oh yes, now I remember. A genuine character. He has a very special skill set when needed. Very good, Mr. Logan."

"OK, Mr. Thorn, I'll let you know when the rancher's girlfriend has been taken care of. I'm pulling into Gill's driveway right now, sir."

"Thank you, Mr. Logan. I will let you get to it."

Thorn walked over to the titanium deck railing and sipped some more wine as he looked out into the distance at the structure that was the bridge going into the city.

Logan was driving down the south end of Lime Street, a rough section of the city. They considered most of the homes in the area to be slums, and criminal activities of all sorts went on in the streets. Many simply referred to the area as "The Projects".

Logan felt right at home, as he had been recruited from streets like these at a young age by some of Thorn's men. It had saved him from becoming a gangbanger, going nowhere in life. Thorn excelled at finding talented thugs and turning them into first-class criminals. It had actually been Karl Eiden who discovered him. Of course, Allan Miller had killed Karl after his attempt on Chuck's life.

Logan pulled into the driveway of Gill Sellek's home, which he had been to on previous occasions. It was a small two-bedroom ranch with a chimney between the one-car garage and house. There was a rusty chain-link fence surrounding the property.

Mr. Sellek was working in his garage with the door open. He had an old '57 Chevy Belair engine propped up on a block. He was turning wrenches on the beauty, keeping his mind off of his subpar existence.

Logan had used Sellek for jobs before. Some of Logan's recruiting scouts from the neighborhood knew Gill and had introduced them. He had always paid him just enough to grease his palms for a while, but never enough to set him up in style. He wanted to keep him hungry in case he needed his expertise for future projects.

Gill Sellek was an ex-Navy Seal and Green Beret. After the 9-11 attack, he had volunteered with a special team that defused bombs in Afghanistan. Before Staff Sergeant William James became famous, there was Captain Sellek. He would have been the original Hurt Locker, except for one fateful day he had been defusing a bomb in Kandahar. It was detected underneath a vehicle, but he did not see the secondary device until it was too late.

The explosion took off half his face, which had to be reconstructed. They replaced his right leg with a mechanical one and gave him a functional mechanic arm from the elbow down. Unfortunately, Gill's gorgeous young wife could not handle his new abnormalities and left him high and dry. He turned into a very bitter man, especially towards the government that he once believed in. His dedication had turned him into a half man, half machine.

Logan shut his vehicle off and stepped onto the cracked asphalt. Gill looked up from what he was doing, and seeing who it was, kept turning his large wrench as he listened to the music that was playing from an old radio on a worn-out wooden shelf in the garage.

"Jesse is a friend, yeah/ I know, he's been a good friend of mine/ But lately something's changed that ain't hard to define/ Jessie's got himself a girl and I want to make her mine."

Gill put his wrench down on top of the engine and walked over to lower the radio as Logan grabbed a black duffel bag from the back of his vehicle. It was similar-looking to the one that had been found in Allan and Alfred's apartments. He slowly walked towards Gill to greet him with an offer, he hoped, the man could not refuse.

"Hello, Captain Gill."

"Just Gill will do, Mr. Logan. I'll never be a captain again," Gill said somberly.

"I respect that. How you doin'?"

"As well as I can be, I guess. But I'm sure you're not here for pleasantries. What did I do to deserve a visit from you today?"

Logan looked over at a pile of wooden boxes stacked to the left of him on the ground. "What're the boxes for?"

"Oh, those are traps."

"What are you trapping, if you don't mind me asking?"

"Stray cats. They're everywhere in this dump of a neighborhood."

"I see. What do you do with them after you catch them?"

He smiled and some of his facial scars pierced through where his grizzly beard did not grow anymore. "I have a burn pit in the backyard I throw them into."

Logan knew it was a serious answer. "Well, OK then, Gill. I was just wondering if you would reconsider working for me full-time."

"Sorry, Logan, but I am a freelancer. I'll always only be a gun for hire, you know what I mean?"

"I hear you, but the last couple jobs you did for us– burning down that old couple's place and the car bomb you did at the Holiday Inn– were very much appreciated. I have another job for you."

"I heard you boys had quite the shootout down there in the parking lot with the authorities," Gill responded sharply.

"And we missed our target. But we got away safely after a kick-ass car chase. Win some, lose some. We'll get 'em back. We always do."

Logan threw the duffel bag next to Gill's intact foot. He reached down and carefully unzipped the bag, revealing what was inside: crisp stacks of $100 bills. It was more money than he had ever seen in his life. He zipped the bag back up and stood.

"I'm listening. What do you need done for this kind of money, Mr. Logan?"

Logan buttoned his jacket against the stiff wind. "Something big, Gill, something really big. And that's only half the money. After we complete the job, you get the other half. What do you say, Gill? Are you in or out?"

The ex-captain took a third of a second to think. "That's enough money to get me out of this hell. Oh yeah, Logan. I'm in!"

"This operation may need you to do some scuba diving. Can you do that?"

"My new limbs work good enough underwater, Mr. Logan. It's not even a factor."

"Good. Let's discuss the plan in more detail. It will be the biggest thing we've ever done, by far."

CHAPTER 14

FLYING HIGH

MID-APRIL 2003

CHUCK WAS OUTSIDE on the helipad at the Silver Lake Air Force Base with Junior. He had been there many times since the summer of 2002, when he began working towards getting his private pilot's license by taking lessons with Junior. Today was the last day he would be flying under the supervision of his instructor. He'd already done more hours in the air than needed and passed all the written tests that the FAA required with flying colors.

Junior had always told Chuck from day one that he was a natural and born to fly. Chuck just loved being in control of any type of fast-moving machinery.

For this special occasion, he was wearing his old, white leather NASA jacket from his rock band days and his hair was neatly tied up in a ponytail. He had driven to the base in the '72 Charger even though he still had not fixed the passenger door yet. He had been so busy dealing with his recent victory in court against Karrington and the governor, writing his new manuscript, and ranching that there was no time for such things as fixing a car door.

Chuck and Junior stood by the car and shared a little history about how he and his father restored it, Junior admiring its beauty. Junior couldn't get over the roll cage inside, like an old stock race car.

"Hey Rock-o, shall we kick the tires and light the fires on this little puppy?" Junior said, referring to the two-seat Robinson 127 helicopter that he was borrowing from the base for his last test flight.

"Hell yeah, let's do this!"

The weather was mild for April, around 60 degrees, and most of the snow had melted. Only some of the heavier patches remained. Chuck sat in the pilot seat as Junior climbed into the copilot's. He had a clipboard on his lap with paperwork detailing what Chuck had to exhibit. He already knew without a doubt that Chuck would pass.

They put their headsets on and Chuck tested them. He turned the key, and the blades began turning on the helicopter. Junior gave Chuck a few technical commands and Chuck implemented them as if it were second nature. They lifted off and the bird levitated ever so gently off the pad. Chuck took it up until they could see the whole Army base below them and Junior gave him directions.

"Like the pro I know you are, smooth sailing. A true helmsman. Let's head out to Wolford City for now."

"OK, JuJu. How's about a little music while we fly?"

"Now you're talking my language, Rock-o!" Junior turned on the radio and a song Chuck knew well played through their headsets.

"Make the world go away/ Get it off, get it off my shoulders/ Say the things you used to say/ And make the world, make it go away."

Junior laughed loudly as Chuck captured Eddy Arnold's sound. "Sing it, Chuck, sing it!"

"Do you remember when you loved me/ Before the world took me astray," Chuck crooned.

"So Rock-o, what's going on with your land? I saw your name mentioned on television. You won in court against the governor. He was trying to use some of it as a highway?"

"Yeah, my attorney held them up for now. We'll see what happens. These people are relentless in their pursuit for their endeavors."

"Bro, when did you become a politician?"

"I'm not, JuJu, by any means. I'm just trying to hang on to my family's land as long as possible."

"What does your lady think of all of this? Did you end up telling her about what we did in California?"

"I was thinking about that the other day when I went to see Kobol at the Pocomtuc Prison with Jed."

"You saw that bastard? What happened?"

"Nothing good, Junior. I'm going to hold off for a while before I come clean. Just looking for the right moment."

"Alright, I hear ya, Rock-o. Wise move."

Gary was on his way to meet with a gentleman representing a company called The Devine Group to discuss the possibility of selling his portion of Gussy's Pitts. He wasn't telling anyone what he was up to, especially not his family. Construction would begin any day now on Chuck and Stacey's horse ranch. He was envious of his brother's success and wanted his own fame and fortune.

Gary walked down a cobblestone sidewalk in Richmond, Virginia towards a restaurant called The Boathouse at Rockett's Landing. He was conflicted and confused about the meeting he was about to attend. He had been closer to his family when he was younger and living in Massachusetts, but lately he had been missing his family and felt even more disconnected from them since the death of their father. To complicate it all, his fiancé was adamant he make a deal and had been reassuring him that his family didn't treat him right, that he should strike now while the iron was hot.

Gary approached the restaurant and noticed several people sitting at tables outside. One was a bigger man built like a bulldog with a blonde buzz cut and a tan complexion. He was dressed in a tailored suit and sat by himself. The man looked at Gary, who was seriously thinking of reneging and going back to his car. He stood up and called out, "Gary?"

"Yeah, that's me," Gary said nervously and walked up to him. "Nice to meet you."

"Nice to meet you, Gary. I'm Matt Helfer. I do a lot of the legal work for The Devine Group," said Helfer energetically.

They sat and the server came over and took their coffee order.

"Well, Gary, it was certainly nice talking to your wife on the phone. She couldn't make it?"

Gary had purposely told Lilly not to come along because he knew she'd make him seal a deal on the spot and he wasn't ready to do that just yet. "Oh, uh," he cleared his throat, "we are getting married in May. She's working today." He was lying his ass off.

"Congratulations. If we can come to an agreement today, you will be in pretty good shape to take an extravagant honeymoon."

"Actually, we have everything already booked," said Gary, pulling at his collar. He felt like he was sweating even though it was a comfortable seventy-degrees outside.

"That's great. Where y'all going?"

Gary's face lit up. "Hawaii."

"Wow, nice choice."

Matt pulled files out of his briefcase and explained what was detailed on the paperwork. Gary's eyes virtually rolled with green dollar signs as he made his sales pitch.

He thought of his family, only briefly. Should I tell them what I am considering before I sell?

"So, Gary, what do you say? This offer may not be as generous in, say, a month from now."

Gary gave Matt Helfer a look of dilemma. Do I act now or get paid less?

Half a dozen police cars and ambulances surrounded the far end of the construction site of Elliot Birch's casino, which was still in its infancy. When one of the steel workers was high on a girder fastening beams together, he spotted something suspicious-looking in the ravine at the bottom of Indians Leap. He called it in over his radio to the foreman in charge. The site supervisor walked over to the ravine with two of his subordinates. They found two mutilated bodies, and then about thirty yards from that scene, two more.

The city police were called immediately. The foreman then also placed a call to Mr. Birch to inform his boss of the situation. The Lieutenant quickly had his officers block off the area to protect the integrity of the crime scene. Jed had also heard the call come over the scanner and jumped in his car to see what was going on.

When Jed arrived, officers moved one of the wooden horses for him to drive closer to the scene. Jed let out a deep breath as he looked out at the chaotic scene. He opened the car door and a nearby officer pointed towards a crowd of police officers where a Wolford City detective was taking notes.

Prior to becoming a detective, Vincent Giovanni was in the Air Force Reserves. He had fulfilled his service requirement of four years and got out right before 9-11. While he had been seriously considering signing for another tour of duty, the city offered him a place on the force as a detective. About the same age as Jed, he was in very good physical shape and single, but he sometimes juggled several girlfriends.

Detective Giovanni walked away from his men to greet Jed.

"Hello, Mr. Ferrari!"

They had become acquainted fairly recently as Vincent had been working on the case of Allan Miller's murder, which was still unsolved.

Jed shook his head at the detective. "Vince, what have you got so far?"

"Something's amiss here. There are two white males over there in the ravine." He pointed in the opposite direction. "About 200 yards over there... two more white males."

Jed interrupted. "Cause of death being a fall from the top of Indians Leap?" They both looked up at its facade.

"That's not what killed them. There was gunfire up there. They were all killed by an AR-15, looks like maybe a .223 caliber. I would say only one shooter killed all four men, then sent them over the side. All forms of identification were removed."

"What makes you think there was only one shooter?"

"I've been around the block, Mr. Ferrari. I believe there was a gunfight up there on that mountain, only it wasn't much of a fight. I'm only guessing, but I think our shooter got the jump on these guys. They probably knew who he was and trusted him," said Detective Giovanni as Jed's brow furrowed. "I can't be sure right now, but I think there may be a connection to the murder of Alan Miller."

"What? You think it's the same guy?"

"That's my instinct. Hard to tell right now because these bodies have been decomposing for some time, at least since February. We will need to go up there to see if we can find any other evidence, so I will notify the Woodrow Police and the owner of the land about our investigation."

"That shouldn't be a problem, Vince. I happen to know the owner of Gussy's Pitts. And actually, I personally know the Chief in Woodrow."

"That's great. I'll get up there right away then."

As they continued talking, another police officer walked over to them.

"Mr. Ferrari, the owner of the casino has arrived and is asking to be let inside."

"Elliot Birch?"

"Yes, sir."

Jed looked across the way at a black limousine behind the barriers. He had yet to meet the man who had been getting a lot of attention for his rapid takeover of the LoneStar Group. He had let Abby deal with him and she hadn't gotten very far. "Let him in."

The officer grabbed his walkie-talkie and spoke into the receiver. "Let Mr. Birch through."

While Jed continued talking to Detective Giovanni, he kept an eye on Birch approaching. From afar, he had a commanding appearance, his long hair and jacket flowing in the breeze. He walked with a confident swagger. Giovanni noticed Jed observing him intently and turned to watch Birch's approach as well.

"So that's Elliot Birch? Do you think these murders have anything to do with him?"

"That's what you're going to find out for me, Vince," said Jed. He walked up to Birch and extended his arm for a handshake. The powerful men looked at one another with curiosity and respect. "Mr. Birch, it is good to finally meet you."

"Likewise, Mr. Ferrari. I have already had the pleasure of meeting your lovely assistant, Miss Taylor," he smirked at the mention of her name.

Jed was not sure what the expression was for. He was pretty sure no one knew of the personal side of their relationship. He couldn't help but feel protective over Abby even though he knew full well she was more than capable of handling herself.

"Unfortunately, Mr. Birch, we're meeting under some pretty gruesome circumstances here today. And by the way, I have not been over here in this part of the city in some time. I'm impressed with how quickly the project is progressing," he said, referring to the skeleton of metal girders that had been erected, stories high.

"Thank you, Mr. Ferrari. Regarding that, how long before my men can get back to work? I have many schedules to keep. You know the saying. Time is money."

Jed could see he had a silver tongue. "I am sure we will finish up in a timely fashion. What do you think, Vince?"

"Mr. Birch, do you know what's happening here?"

"I know my workers found four half-decayed bodies in the ravine over there, and that's all so far."

"Would you have any idea who they could be?"

"No idea, Mr. Ferrari. In all my years of business, I can say this is my first murder. I can also say all of my men are thoroughly vetted and accounted for. However, would I be able to see the bodies to make sure?"

"You could, but I will tell you that the faces are unrecognizable, and it's probably going to ruin your lunch," Detective Giovanni responded.

"I'll tell you what, Mr. Birch. If it's all right with Mr. Ferrari, I'm going to barricade this entire area as a crime scene. That way, it will not interfere with you getting back to work. The next part of our work will be up there." He pointed to Indians Leap.

Elliot looked up. "That's a long way down."

"Exactly," said Jed. "Vince, that will be fine. Mr. Birch's men can get back to work as soon as you barricade that area." He pointed over to the ravine where a group of police officers were combing for evidence.

"This is going to cause some scandal for the landowner," said Birch.

"He's used to that by now," replied Jed.

Junior and Chuck were flying over the city having the time of their lives, like two high school kids joking around. While Chuck completed his instructional maneuvers, Junior played his favorite game with Chuck, quoting famous movie lines that Chuck would then have to guess.

"So Rock-o, here's one for you. 'Hey Landon! Join the expedition!' Come on Rock-o, you know that one," he laughed.

"Oh, come on, buddy. You gotta give me one tougher than that. It's Planet of the Apes. The original one too, not that crappy Wahlberg remake!" he said jokingly.

Junior belly-laughed. "Rock-o, you're a funny dude!" Junior became suddenly serious as something on the ground caught his eye. Police cars and ambulances were clustered. "Hey Rock-o, look down below. Looks like some sort of accident. Doesn't this land belong to you?"

Chuck looked down at the flashing lights. "Yeah, that's Indians Leap, but that side of the mountain belongs to the new developer that took over for Lonestar Group."

"Wow, I wonder what that could all be about."

Chuck paused in thought for a moment. "Hey JuJu… would we get in trouble if we landed down there somewhere to check it out?"

"Eh, I don't know. Circle around the area for a second." Chuck deftly moved the throttle and the chopper rotated over the scene below as Junior looked around."The heck with the scarecrows, Rock-o!" It was another reference from Planet of the Apes. Chuck smirked.

Junior pointed. "You see that big, empty lot off to the right of the casino that is going up? That's past the barricades. We should be OK to land there. Can you do it?"

"You bet I can, Juju." Chuck had never made a landing like the one that he was about to attempt, with buildings surrounding the lot, but the prospect excited him.

"OK then, Rock-o, make it happen."

Chuck turned the throttle and lever slightly and simultaneously pressed some switches, preparing to land. The sleek-looking helicopter began to descend. Below them, everyone involved in the murder investigation looked up, including Jed, Elliot, and Vince.

Jed looked at Vince. "That's not a police chopper, is it?"

"Ah, no, definitely not. And it doesn't look like a news chopper either. It looks to be a private one. Is that yours, Mr. Birch?"

"Oh no," Birch smiled, "that's too small for one of mine."

The men watched the chopper make a perfect landing.

Vince got on his walkie-talkie. "Mac, come in!" he said to the officer by the barricades.

"Mac, here," he responded.

"Mac, can you take a walk over to the helicopter that just landed and find out who the hell that is?"

"Yes, sir." The officer walked to the helicopter as the three men observed.

"It must have something to do with these murders, right?" said Birch.

Vince retorted sarcastically, "Never know in this city."

Jed nodded his head, concurring.

"Giovanni, it's a guy named Chuck Barreto and his copilot. He says he owns the mountain next to the ravine where we found the bodies," Mac said over the walkie.

"Speak of the Devil, and he appears!" said Jed.

Jed gestured to Vince to let them through. "Mac, you can let them in around the barricades. Have them walk straight to us."

"They're en route to you now."

Chuck had left his jacket inside the cockpit, so as not to attract any more attention than they already had by landing a helicopter right in the middle of a construction site next to a crime scene.

Chuck and Junior were about a football field away from them when Vince said to Jed, "Which one's your friend, Mr. Ferrari?"

"The smaller guy with the black T-shirt on. The bigger one is his instructor and buddy."

Elliot chimed in. "Wow, this guy gets around. I like it."

"You have no idea," replied Jed. Birch and Giovanni looked at Jed questioningly.

Chuck and Junior walked up to them, grinning.

"Great Caesar's ghost, Chuck! You never cease to surprise me," said Jed.

Chuck laughed. "I wouldn't want to disappoint you, bro."

Jed introduced everyone to Chuck and Junior. "What are you boys up to, flying around the big city today?"

"Oh, just taking my final lesson to get my license."

"Impressive, Mr. Barreto," said Birch. He shook Chuck's hand. "I've heard a lot about you. All good, of course. And congratulations on your recent victory in court preventing the governor from encroaching on your land."

"Thanks," said Chuck warily. "Did you have anything to do with that nonsense?"

Jed rolled his eyes at the fact that Chuck would go right after Birch upon meeting him, but that was Chuck. If anything threatened Chuck's orbit, he'd go for the jugular. It was a side of him he often admired.

Elliot quickly replied with a chuckle, "Mr. Barreto, I am just hired to build buildings. I have no interest in your land, unless, of course, you wanted me to build something for you on it."

As they had a friendly-enough verbal joust, Jed couldn't help but notice how much Elliot looked like an older version of Chuck, just more distinguished.

"Right where you parked your helicopter, we will be starting a project on a retirement community that I partnered with the Silver Bell to build." He said it as if that would give him some sort of credit for helping old people. It didn't work.

"Silver Bell, huh?" said Chuck with a snort.

"Yes, why?"

"You're doing business with Kelly Texeira?"

"Yes…"

Jed and Chuck looked at one another.

"That is Chuck's ex-wife," said Jed.

"You really do get around," said Birch.

Chuck was amused by the familiar dry sense of humor. He wasn't getting any bad vibes from Birch like he had with Nick Colombo, even though Elliot more or less stood for everything Chuck did not.

You could tell Junior was getting a kick out of the friendly banter going on back-and-forth from the shit-eating grin the size of the Grand Canyon he wore on his face.

Detective Giovanni interrupted them. "Mr. Barreto, I am actually glad you're here. I need permission to go onto your land, specifically up on Indians Leap."

"Why what's up there? What's going on?"

Jed touched his friend's shoulder. "Chuck, there have been four murders. Four men with no identification were shot up. We think it happened on Indians Leap and then they were thrown from the top. The bodies are in pretty terrible shape. We figure that this happened in January or February. We will know more after the coroner's report."

When will this craziness ever end? Chuck thought to himself. He looked at Jed, but kept his thoughts on the seemingly never-ending trail of bodies that seemed to follow him to himself in front of the mixed company.

"Mr. Barreto, it's possible there may still be useful evidence up there."

"Sure, no problem. Whatever you guys need from me."

"Chuck, would you mind taking a look at the bodies, see if you recognize anyone?"

"Of course," said Chuck.

"Mr. Birch, you can come as well. But like I said earlier, there's not much to see. The bodies are really decomposed."

"I'm sure I wouldn't know any of them, but yes I will come along."

Jed told Junior to stay behind while they adjourned to one of the ambulances. He wasn't going to argue with that. Even though had seen combat during the Gulf War, he mostly just flew helicopters and didn't have the stomach for something as grotesque as that.

Two bodies were outside of an ambulance, while the other two had been loaded. Detective Giovanni asked one of the EMTs to unzip the body bags halfway. When the bodies came into view, all you could see was dirt and decay. Vincent was right on all counts- the deceased men were unrecognizable.

Elliot tried to disguise his reaction. He grew nauseous and put his hand over his mouth, coughing repeatedly. "Sorry about that. Just allergies."

Chuck was unaffected. His instinct was that he had somehow come across these poor sons-of-bitches before, but couldn't put a finger on it. It reminded him of the time Leroy Stick had confronted him in the barn, and Chuck didn't realize who he was until after half his head was blown off.

They viewed the other two bodies.

"Well gentlemen, anything?" Giovanni asked.

"No, nothing. Sorry," said Birch, his face a bit green.

"No, me neither," said Chuck. "Jed, did you contact Buford?"

"I've been in touch. He's away on another assignment right now."

"Who is that, Mr. Ferrari?" asked Detective Giovanni.

"He is an FBI agent that was involved in the case with Silus Kobol, LoneStar, and Nick Colombo."

"Do you think there is some connection to all of this?"

"It's possible. Maybe we'll find something up on Indians Leap that will tell us. Or maybe once we process these dental records, we'll have the identities and be able to draw some lines between them."

"We might find casings from the bullets fired, but tire tracks from whatever vehicle drove them up there are likely gone. It was a heavy winter. Well, let's just hope we find something."

"What do you think, Vince? A professional hit?"

"It's what my assessment indicates so far, but I need more evidence."

"Excuse me," Birch interjected, "but why would a professional kill them up there and then throw them down here. One would think they would be found sooner down here."

"That is a question, Mr. Birch, that I hope to resolve."

Detective Giovanni was keeping some theories to himself while Elliot and Chuck were in his presence. He looked at Chuck and said, '' Mr. Barreto, do you know of anyone that was on your land this past winter?"

"Just some surveyors that worked for Paluzzi Construction. We're getting ready to begin a project in about a week or so. Is that a problem?"

"Mmm, no, but I will need to get my men in there first to investigate the area. Should only be a few days at most. Also, I'll need to talk to those surveyors about whether they saw anything suspicious," said Giovanni. He looked at Jed. "I would also like to speak with this Kobol character."

Jed and Chuck looked at one another, knowing how that would most likely turn out.

"That will not be an issue seeing as how he's locked up tight in the Pocomtuc Prison. He's not the most cooperative individual. You can take my word on that one," said Jed.

"I'd like to try with him anyhow, Mr. Ferrari."

Chuck rolled his eyes, knowing that conversation would go nowhere.

"Excuse me, gentlemen, I have to take this," said Elliot as his cell phone buzzed.

"That's OK, Mr. Birch. You are all set here. Thank you for coming down."

Birch walked out of earshot and flipped open his phone to answer.

"Eddie, I hope you have something for me. You will not believe the mess I am dealing with down here at the construction site!"

"What's wrong?" asked Eddie. "Elliot, you want me to come down there?"

"No, no, that's quite alright, Eddie. I'm just leaving now and it is mainly under control. I will fill you in later. Tell me what you found."

"Hold on to your seat," said Eddie. "The shareholders involved in the casino project, as you are already aware, are not your usual investors."

"Yes, despite my inclination toward routine, I took them on as a favor from an affiliate in D.C. I owed him a favor."

"Well, I was surprised, as I know you will be too, that most of these new shareholders reside right here in Wolford City."

"You don't say. OK, what is so unusual about that, my friend?"

"What's so unusual is that literally almost all of the shareholders live in the same dwelling."

Elliot paused for a moment. "You mean an apartment building?"

"Not exactly, Elliot. Try an old age home."

"You've got to be joking. What home is it, Eddie?"

"It's on the west side of the city, The Cavalier Old Age Home."

"That's the name of it?"

"Yes, Elliot. You want me to look more in depth?"

"I am beyond curious about what is going on here."

"There's a slight hiccup in gaining intel. This place is for the extremely rich. They will allow no one in without an appointment, and the only way to get an appointment is if you have a family member currently living there. Or if you are looking into it as a residence for a family member."

"How do you get a family member admitted?"

"It appears difficult. They told me it was by application only, and there is a long waiting list."

"Who did you speak with?"

"Just an intake staff member. Maybe a receptionist. The establishment is run by a woman named Laurie Turner."

"OK, my friend. I think I may know someone with connections in this fair city that may be able to help us." He was thinking of his new business associate, Kelly Ann Texeira, who he still could not believe was once married to Mr. Barreto. "OK, Eddie, marvelous work. I will see you back at the office later on today and fill you in on the other shenanigans going on out here."

Gary arrived home from his meeting with Matt Helfer. He was sitting in his driveway with the engine shut off, puffing away on a cigarette and scratching his head. Hair fell out onto the steering wheel. He took a few more puffs before smashing his butt into an already overflowing tray of ashes. He dreaded going inside to Lilly. She was already home and was no doubt waiting eagerly to see what transpired during his meeting.

After procrastinating for as long as he felt he could get away with, he got out of the vehicle and headed inside the house as quietly as he could, making a beeline for the bar in the dining room. A large, gold bottle of Grey Goose vodka had his name on it. He took hold of the bottle and uncorked her, his hands shaking as he poured some of the smooth liquid into the crystal glass in his other hand.

"Hey sweetheart!" said Lilly, startling him. Gary jumped and spilled half his glass on the floor.

"Hey Lilly."

She laughed at his clumsiness. "Sorry, Gary, I didn't mean to scare you."

"Oh, no, you didn't." He reached for a nearby towel and cleaned up the spill. Then she started in on him.

"Are we rich, my handsome hubby?" she asked, her eyes bright. She could tell by his posture that something was wrong. "Gary, what happened?"

One thing he dreaded more than anything in the world was going up against his mother or his soon-to-be wife. Both women were strong-willed, hard-headed, and persistent. He felt his anxiety rise as the words came from his mouth. "Lilly, I need to talk to my brother first. I'm thinking he could buy me out and that wouldn't mess up what he's trying to do with my sister."

Her body arched sharply to the right and her hands sat on her hips. "You're worried about him? Are you fucking kidding me right now?" she spat, frowning.

Gary grew more anxious. He twitched and lowered his tone to see if that would calm her down. "Lilly, he's my brother."

"And I am going to be your wife!"

"I'll talk to him when we go to Massachusetts next month for the wedding. If he can't or won't take me up on my offer, then Mr. Helfer said he's ready to make a deal. Lilly, please, I'm just trying to do right by everyone involved."

"Do right by Chuck? He doesn't give a rat's ass about you!"

Gary felt like crying. "That's not true, Lilly."

"We'll see! I am the one who is here for you, not your family. Let's just hope we're not sucking on a tail pipe by the time you and your family figure it out," she blurted.

"Lilly, take it easy. We'll stay afloat. May is right around the corner. One way or another, I'll get us enough to push back to the top again."

Lilly looked at him with disgust.

CHAPTER 15

THE CAVALIER RETIREMENT HOME

LATE-APRIL 2003

ABBY SAT IN HER office working on some depositions for Jed when her phone rang. She listened while her secretary spoke.

"Oh yes, of course, Leslie, put him through right away," Abby responded. She waited for a second for the transfer. "Hello, Mr. Karrington. Nice to hear from you, how is everything going out there in Washington?"

"Very well, Abby, but as you can imagine, extremely busy. I see you and Jed have been busy as well, with the recent murders."

"Yes sir, that was a heinous one. Four bodies."

"Any news on that investigation?"

"Detective Giovanni is doing a fine job so far, sir. He has learned that the men were out of Chicago. All of them had priors. What they were all doing here in Wolford City is still a mystery so far. Maybe a drug deal gone bad. There are a lot of mules that go back and forth from city to city."

"Well, certainly keep me posted. You're all doing a great job, Abby, but what I'm calling for is an actual favor."

"Anything, Mr. Karrington. What can I do for you?"

" I hate to ask– and you know I wouldn't if I didn't need to– but there's an issue with that darn bridge in Wolford City. It is going under repairs and Jed's pal, Barreto, won't bend an inch with Indians Leap to ease the pain of our taxpayers," Chip schmoozed. "And also, as you know, I have an election against a tough opponent next year, and this problem is causing my poll numbers to drop some."

Abby was instantly uncomfortable with what seemed like an extremely unethical conversation. "Senator…what could I possibly do about that? We're an independent crime commission, coming straight from your office. I would love to help, but…"

"Of course, I know that, Abby. And again, I'm sorry to ask, but these are times of desperation. I am doing everything I can out here for our state. It would be shameful to let the corrupt other party get back into power over a silly bridge. All I am asking for is Jed to talk to Barreto."

She knew that any attempt Jed made would be a waste of time, but she wasn't going to bother trying to explain that to Chip. "OK, Mr. Karrington."

Abby hung up the phone. Something about the conversation made her wonder if the senator had secrets.

Kelly was in the SkyTower office reviewing a lucrative sale that one of her agents made in the town of Woodrow. Paige sat at the other end of the desk, confident in her recent work, but also craving the acknowledgement from Kelly.

"Paige, I am so proud of you!" said Kelly as she pointed out her employee's earnings on a colorful chart. Paige blushed and smiled. "You are the top earner of this company now. I will be giving you a promotion and a raise. I would like you to take charge of my office in Woodrow, full-time, starting next week."

Paige leapt up out of her chair to hug her boss. She wasn't one to normally cry, but she was overjoyed and a few tears rolled down her cheeks. "Oh thank you so much, Kelly. Thank you so much! I won't let you down."

"I know you won't, and you deserve it, Paige. You will do well. I'm sure of it."

The intercom buzzed. "Miss Texiera, you have a visitor. Mr. Birch," said the secretary.

"OK, thank you, Liz, you can send him in."

Elliot Birch walked in, saying hello to Paige as she passed by him on her way out of the office. Elliot smiled and made himself comfortable by sitting in a chair and putting his feet up. "Well, hello there neighbor. I mean, partner."

She smiled coyly. "So good of you to come in and visit with me. Looks like I'll be around here more often so we can focus on our new project. Where have you been?"

"Oh, you know, just dealing with the nonsense from a few weeks ago. The police finally released the area that had been taped off. We are fully operational again."

"I can see that. The casino and hotel are going up fast. It looks great so far. What happened with the police investigation?"

"Nothing so far, unless they are not keeping me informed," he said. "I forgot to tell you who I ran into when they called me down there that day."

Kelly then sat down across from him. "Who?"

"Your husband."

"Oh? You mean my ex. Where did you run into him?"

"He flew a helicopter right down by the construction site the day they discovered those bodies. I didn't know you were married to the famous rancher and novelist from Woodrow."

"It's not that important, Elliot."

"Well I will say, he makes quite the impression. What happened between you two?"

"Ask my sister," she scowled.

Elliot got the feeling he may have crossed a line. "Enough said then." He took his heels off the desk. "I just wanted to thank you for helping me get my man Chellis inside the Cavalier Retirement Home. And our other little project should be breaking ground any day now."

"I'm super excited. You never told me...why did you need to get inside that old age home anyway?"

Eddie Chellis pulled up to the wide, gated opening of The Cavalier Retirement Home in his Toyota Corolla. Just outside his vehicle was a barrier with a small, brick guard shack only big enough for one or two people to fit inside. A short, heavy-set African American man in his early sixties dressed in a dark brown security uniform came walking up to Eddie's window, which he had already rolled down.

"Good morning, sir. Who are you here to see?"

"Ah yes, I'm here to see my mother's sister, Mrs. Diaz."

Using bifocals, the guard looked at a roster attached to a clipboard underneath his arm and scrolled down the sheet. "Yes, I have you right here. Mr. Lombardo?"

It was only Eddie's last name for the purpose of the visit. He was taking a risk in that Mrs. Diaz – who really was not expecting him – may blow his cover.

"Yes sir, that's me."

Luckily the man did not ask for an ID. He walked over to the shack, reached inside quickly, and walked back to hand him a visitor's pass attached to a thin, red lanyard.

"You're all set, Mr. Lombardo. Just drive up the road until you reach the main building. Park anywhere and go through the main doors. I'll call ahead and somebody will be waiting for you inside. Enjoy your visit."

Eddie thanked the gentleman and the guard raised the barrier for him to proceed onto the grounds. He stepped on the gas pedal lightly and the vehicle rolled slowly up the winding, inclined drive lined with topiary. He came to a large rectangular sign that read "Hospital and Long-Term Care Unit" and pointed towards the assisted living building. He noticed the parking lot was mostly empty, with the exception of the staff spaces. Eddie pulled his faded, red Corolla into a spot and turned it off.

Kelly had informed him that Mrs. Diaz was 98 years old and senile. She would be courteous to him and go along with the charade unknowingly, just happy to have company.

Eddie looked in the rearview mirror. "OK, here we go Edward!"

As he exited the car, he grabbed the large paper bag on the passenger seat which contained something he had brought for Mrs. Diaz. He walked to the main entrance with a slight limp. Eddie opened his flip phone and looked at the photo Elliot had sent him of Mrs. Diaz.

Upon his approach, the large glass doors slid open. He walked through the breezeway and another set of glass doors into a carpeted, dim lobby. Various plants surrounded a desk off to his left where a thin, older woman sat in white scrubs and a cap. She smiled as she greeted Eddie.

"Mr. Lombardo?" she said. The first thing that came to his mind was that the security seemed awfully tight. The second thing he thought was that there was something eerie-looking about the woman. She reminded him a bit of Nurse Ratched.

"Yes ma'am, I am here to see Jane Diaz."

"Oh yes, we just love Janey! I've never seen you visit before," she said pointedly.

"Oh yeah, I travel a lot for work."

"I see. What do you do?"

Eddie's inner monologue suggested that she was suspicious. He had to think of a plausible lie quickly.

"I install laundry units for the military. Keeps me pretty busy." He had an acquaintance years ago that did that for a living, though he wasn't sure why it came to him just then.

"Sounds very interesting. Where do they send you?"

Eddie's mind was working overtime. Damn, why is this lady asking a million questions?

"You name it. Germany, Mexico, France, Afghanistan, and on and on. Wherever they need me."

"I never thought about how all those Army men need their clothes done just like the rest of us. What's it like in Paris? I've always wanted to go there."

Eddie was getting a little perturbed. "Ah, Paris is great, but there's nothing like the good old US of A! Actually, Miss, I'm due to fly back out tomorrow morning so…"

"Of course. Mrs. Diaz is up on the fourth floor, room 437. If she's not in her room, she will either be in the rec room or the cafeteria." She pointed towards the elevators to him. "Do you need a staff member to help you find her?"

"No, thank you, I think I can manage. If not, I will most certainly give you a holler."

"Very good. Enjoy your visit, Mr. Lombardo, and have a safe trip tomorrow if I don't see you again."

Eddie nodded and started walking toward the elevators.

There was a dark, ten-by-ten room lined with built-in counters upon which stood monitors that displayed the views of security cameras hidden throughout The Cavalier Retirement Home. Four black, leather office chairs filled the confined space. One security officer, wearing the same uniform as the man at the guard shack, and an older woman with slicked-back silver hair were engrossed in watching one specific monitor.

"How long before we get the guy's information, Laurie?" said the man in the uniform. The security guard at the shack had recorded Eddie's license plate number and called it in to Laurie Arnold, who was in charge of running the home. Once she received the plate number, she called in a favor with an acquaintance to find out what they could learn about the man.

The phone rang and Laurie anxiously picked up the shiny, red phone handle. It was indeed her contact calling her back. Her mouth turned down into a frown and she began writing on the pad of paper next to her.

"Eddie Chellis. And he works for The Birch Group? OK, thank you, Claudette, thank you so much," said Laurie into the receiver. She hung up and turned to Spencer. "I goddamn knew it. Gotcha! Spencer, do not lose him on camera. Follow his every stinking move!"

"You got it. What would an employer of The Birch Group be doing, snooping around here?"

"I don't know." She picked up the phone again. "I'm going to call you-know-who. Let him handle this."

Eddie approached Mrs. Diaz's door, confirming he was at the correct one by reading the number 437 on the plaque above the door. He took a breath, unsure how it would play out. He knocked gently on the door three times and waited for a response, but there was no answer. He could hear through the thin wooden door that The Price is Right was on the television. Eddie waited a few more seconds, then knocked again a bit more loudly.

"Yes, come in, please," responded a delicate voice. He slowly turned the knob and opened the door.

"Hello, Mrs. Diaz," said Eddie.

Mrs. Diaz was sitting on a couch reading a book, wearing very thick eyeglasses while the television remained on in the background. She had curly, white hair and appeared to be of short stature; the picture-perfect embodiment of someone's adorable grandma. She wore a pink housecoat and brown moccasins.

"Hello there. Do I know you? You must be new to the staff."

"Ah no, Mrs Diaz, I am a distant cousin to your sister, Janice Lombardo."

She stared at him through her thick lenses for a minute. "I'm sorry. That does not ring a bell."

"I just came to visit you and bring you some books. I heard you like to read a lot."

"Yes, I certainly do, young man. But I can only read large print these days."

Eddie raised up the large brown bag in his right hand. "Well, that's exactly what I brought for you. I hope you'll like them. They're mostly thrillers and dramas."

"Oh yes, thank you so much!" she said enthusiastically. "Come in and sit down for a spell. I'm just sorry I can't remember you right now."

"That's quite alright, Mrs. Diaz. I don't see my family much because of my job." He closed the door behind him and proceeded to empty the bag of hardcover books onto the small wooden coffee table in front of her. He sat down on an old chair next to the sofa.

"Is it alright if I sit here, Mrs. Diaz?"

"Oh yes, of course. Now tell me everything about what you've been up to. And my cousin, how's she doing?"

Inside the control room, Laurie grew more anxious while waiting for further instructions from her superiors. She paced back and forth and ranted obscenities under her breath.

"Is that fake still in her room?" she asked the guard.

"Yes, ma'am," said Spencer nervously.

"If he doesn't call me back in two minutes, I say we have to pull the plug on her visit."

"Yes ma'am."

Laurie began chewing on her fingernails and then the phone finally rang.

"Yes, Mr. –"

Before she could finish her thought, the caller told her to hold off: the cavalry was en-route to their destination.

Laurie put the phone back on the receiver. "Stay on him. They're on their way."

Eddie and Mrs. Diaz were getting along famously, discussing everything from the weather to city life to the family that she loved so much. Though Jane Diaz was like a superstar amongst her companions in the home, it was always refreshing to see someone from the outside world.

Eddie got to the point that he felt comfortable enough to ask questions that could help him discover why so many shareholders were said to be living right there at The Cavalier Retirement Home. He pulled out a crumpled piece of paper from the inside pocket of his blazer. On it was a list of twenty names of shareholders for the new casino that lived at the home.

Eddie didn't want to overwhelm her, so he decided to only ask her about the first five.

"My friend's grandfather lived right here in the city for a long time. Before I came here today, he asked me to ask you if you knew any of them."

"Oh, really! What is his name? I probably know him too. Your friend's grandfather, I mean."

"Ray Withers," Eddie produced a false name.

"Hmm, can't say I knew him. What neighborhood did he live in?"

Now Eddie was stumped. That was a question he was not prepared for.

"Oh, I believe his family grew up on Baker Street," he said after a moment of thought. Now he was just hoping she wouldn't know the area.

"Really? I know that neighborhood, but that was on the other end of the city. I did have friends over there, oh yes. Have you ever heard of the Giovannis?"

Eddie was surprised. "No, I don't recall them."

"Well, young man, who are the people your friend's grandfather knows that live here?"

Eddie looked down at his cheat sheet. "I had to write them down. My memory is bad." He squinted at the paper. "Let's see... I have Terrance Shane, Ronald Quintana, Joseph Connors, Patricia Simpson, and Kara Kolowski. And I apologize in advance, Mrs. Diaz. I know that's a lot."

She looked at him intensely before her face lit up. "Of course I know those people! Ron Ron, my little bear, smiling Joey, Patti-Cakes, and Scary-Kari," she listed her nicknames for them all.

"You know all of them?" he said with a surprised look.

"I sure do. Let me tell you about Ron. He's the devil in disguise, always hitting on me! But I put him in his place."

Eddie chuckled. "I bet you d0, Mrs. Diaz."

"Most of them are probably in the television room right now, or in the cafeteria. Would you like to go downstairs to see if they are there and get a bite to eat, too?"

"That sounds really nice, Mrs. Diaz."

"Very good, young man, because I'm starving. And let me tell you, they have the best apple crumb cake I've ever tasted."

Eddie was really taken with her, particularly her entertainingly sharp wit. "Let me help you, Mrs. Diaz."

"No, no, I got it." She reached over to her left and pulled her walker closer. She gently rose off the couch and started trucking it across the carpeted room like a little speed demon. Five feet tall, if that, and she had more life and spunk in her than most average young adults.

"Come on, try to keep up, will ya!" she said as she moved steadily along. Eddie caught up and opened the door for her, which she told him not to bother locking.

On their trek to the elevator, Eddie examined every detail of the place. Like a loyal man of security, he had the eyes and ears for observation ingrained in him.

Mrs. Diaz pressed the button for the elevator and continued to lead the way.

"Even for an elevator, this is pretty small, huh?"

"Absolutely, Mrs. Diaz."

Eddie observed a generic oil painting of a wintry mountain landscape of birch trees. He could see that engraved right into the frame were the words "Printed by the Lonestar Group". Now that caught his attention.

A chime sounded and the double metal doors opened up.

"Come on, Eddie, keep up!" said Mrs. Diaz. She took a sharp left down a long hallway. Peers who passed by greeted her.

"Janey! Janey! Look out everyone, she's got her guns!" one of her friends joked.

Even the staff members brightened at seeing her in the hallway. She clearly had an iconic presence and seemed to revel in her popularity.

An elderly lady who was exiting the hairdresser sporting a head of curly locks called out to her. "Janey, look at my new -do!"

"Oh my, Nancy, your hair looks just fabulous! Really fabulous!"

Mrs. Diaz introduced Eddie to her and invited Nancy along for lunch. The three of them continued on down the hallway until they reached the generously-sized cafeteria. Mrs. Diaz greeted more friends and led the way to her usual table.

The sun beamed through a wall of windows on the far end, adjacent to a kitchen that reminded Eddie of high school. Old folks were either going up and helping themselves or waiting for a caretaker to come and take their food orders.

Two men were already sitting at Jane's table. Nancy and Jane sat and gestured for Eddie to do the same. Mrs. Diaz introduced Eddie.

"Eddie, this is The Bear and Patti, otherwise known as Terrance Shane and Patti Simpson. The other two fellas and lady you asked about do not appear to be down here right now."

They all looked at Eddie curiously. He could tell he was going to have to do some work to get what he wanted.

"Very nice to meet you all. A friend of mine, his grandfather said he knows a lot of you fine folks and wanted me to say hello to everyone. You know, just to see how everyone is doing and if anybody needs anything."

Before they could respond to him, a female caretaker approached with a small clipboard and menu. They all chose the chicken, mashed potatoes with gravy, and a slice of apple pie, except for Terrance who chose the hamburger and fries.

"Just a coffee for me, if it's not too much trouble," said Eddie.

"No trouble at all!" she said cheerfully and made her way to the next table.

Eddie noticed a symbol on the wall over the kitchen.

"What's that stand for?" he asked, pointing.

"The home is where the heart is, or something along those lines, if memory serves," said Nancy.

He smiled at her response.

"Oh no it's not, silly goose!" Mrs. Diaz cut in. "That was the logo for the company that built this place. It's some ancient symbol, stands for loyalty I think!"

"You mean Cookie's old company?"

Eddie's ears perked up.

"That's right, The Lonestar Group."

Before anyone could interrupt them further, Eddie asked, "Do you all know that you're part owners of a new casino and hotel being built in Wolford City?"

"Who is?" asked Nancy, shocked.

Terrance looked at Eddie like he was crazy and Jane laughed.

"If my friends were all part owners of a casino and hotel, I think I'd be the first one to know about that one. We sure as hell wouldn't be living here," she chuckled.

"The only reason I'm here is because of my son, Herbert Graham," said Patti.

Eddie was startled at the name. "Your son is the governor?"

"Oh yeah, Mr. Fancy-Pants himself!"

"And Mr. Shane, who are your children?" he asked Terrance.

"My daughter is Kimmy Shimmerlik, married to Chester. If you didn't know, he is a congressman in Washington."

Eddie was beginning to get a clearer picture of what was going on. These rich politicians had their parents living here, confined from the public, and they were putting their shares of the project in their names. But why?

Eddie lowered his voice. "So who is this 'Cookie'? You mentioned he owns the Cavalier Retirement Home, or built it?"

They looked at one another and started chuckling.

"Why, young man, he's right behind you!" said Mrs. Diaz.

Eddie felt something hard tap on his shoulder from behind. He turned his head and saw an olive-skinned older man in a wheelchair holding a cane with a silver wolf head. He was grinning at Eddie.

Cookie had a thick head of curly gray hair. He was definitely on the thinner side but appeared to be healthy. For an older man living in a retirement home, he sure looked like he spent a lot of time on vacation.

"Hello, sir, nice to meet you."

"Eddie, his voice is almost gone. He had a brain aneurysm ages ago."

The man called Cookie lifted his right arm in the air and extended his index finger at Eddie, curling it towards him to come closer.

"It's OK, he doesn't bite too much," joked Mrs. Diaz. "Cookie just speaks quietly so you have to move in closer to hear him."

Eddie cautiously got up from his chair and bent over closer to the man. Cookie smiled at him and continued to beckon him closer with his finger until Eddie's right ear was a whisker away from the old man's lips.

Cookie spoke with a rasp of a whisper that no one else at the table could hear. Whatever he said lit up Eddie's eyes, but before he could respond, a female voice shouted his name.

"Mr. Lombardo!"

He straightened, looked over towards the voice, and saw a furious woman looking at him. Laurie Turner stood next to a large Asian gentleman wearing a brown security uniform. A young female orderly walked out from behind them and took the handles of Cookie's wheelchair.

"Time for your bath," she said to Cookie.

"And it's time for you to leave the premises, Mr. Lombardo. And I mean right now!" Laurie shouted at Eddie.

Someone must have blown his cover, and he knew why after what Cookie just whispered to him. He decided to get out of there while the going was good. He desperately wanted to relay the fresh revelations to Elliot anyway.

"OK, miss, I have to leave anyway. I am running late for an appointment," said Eddie.

As the orderly wheeled Cookie out of the dining hall, he looked directly at Eddie and winked.

Eddie quickly said goodbye to Mrs. Diaz and her friends, then exited the uncomfortable situation, walking past the manager and security guard. He could feel the palpable tension in the room, and he couldn't help the feeling that something wasn't right. Without turning around, Eddie could hear them following him out.

He finally arrived at the lobby and smiled at the receptionist.

"Have a wonderful day now," she said awkwardly.

"I'll try, you too," Eddie replied.

He took a deep breath of relief as he walked out of the home. Once he got a distance down the walk, he turned his head to see Laurie and the guard watching him from the breezeway. He continued to his vehicle and thought, I can't wait to get in my car and call Elliot with the information I just received.

A few rows behind his vehicle, a big black Hummer with tinted windows was parked. He noticed both because the vehicle would stand out anywhere, and it certainly hadn't been in the lot upon his arrival.

Eddie reached his door, unlocked it, and took one last look at the entrance of the home as Laurie and the guard were going back inside the building. As he got in the vehicle, he observed dark clouds were rolling in and there were sounds of thunder in the distance. He looked in the rearview mirror and turned the ignition, feeling accomplished. He turned the knob up on his radio as he reversed.

Thunder rumbled louder and raindrops hit the windshield audibly. Eddie turned the wipers on, and pressed the gas pedal as he pulled forward. Music played through the speakers.

"I was once your diamond, you said you were mine/ And you burned inside me, when you looked in my eyes/ I should've seen clear through you..."

The rain poured down now, but Eddie didn't care. He wanted out of that place. His vehicle reached the main gate and the security officer did not come outside. The barrier lifted for him to exit the premises. Eddie pressed down on the gas pedal, not looking into the guard shack as he passed by, and took a hard right onto the main road. He floored it as the song continued.

"...the crystal was clear/ When I reached to touch you, the magic disappeared/ It was fadin', fadin'/ Like ice out in the rain/ So cold inside when you feel the pain."

Eddie was cruising down a road that was beginning to flood and pulled out his flip phone to call his boss. The wipers scraped on the windshield as they flickered back and forth rapidly. He dialed Elliot's phone number and felt a rumbling coming from the rear of the vehicle. It was bouncing up and down as if he had a flat tire or something was caught in one of the wheels.

Elliot answered the phone while Eddie was contemplating the issue.

Elliot shouted through the receiver, "Eddie, are you there? Can you hear me? What's happening?"

Eddie pulled the vehicle over to a grassy area on the side of the road. "Elliot, hold on a moment, will ya? I got some really big news!"

"Everything OK?"

"Yeah, but I might have a rock in my rear tire, so just bear with me, boss."

"A rock?" Elliot said, confused. "OK, Eddie." He was antsy to hear what Eddie had learned.

Eddie put the vehicle in park and turned on the hazard lights. He tilted the steering wheel up so that he could move more freely without the obstruction of his large stomach. He turned around, holding the phone and looking for an umbrella somewhere in his messy backseat. He rummaged around on the floor with his right hand until he found one.

"Hang on, Elliot. I got it!" He struggled to open the umbrella as he clumsily got out of the car. He quickly scanned the back tire on the driver side and saw nothing wrong with it. He tried turning the lug nuts on the tire counter-clockwise. They were all perfectly tight.

Elliot waited impatiently on the other end of the phone as he watched the rain fall through his office window.

Eddie walked over to the rear passenger tire and examined it carefully. At first he saw nothing, but upon looking again he spotted two lug nuts missing on the rim. He reached down to feel the remaining nuts and they were all barely on the threaded studs.

"Shit! Son of a bitch!"

"Eddie, what's going on?" said Elliot.

"Hang on a sec, Elliot." Eddie placed the cell phone on the roof of the car, holding the umbrella over the device to keep it dry while he reached down to try to tighten the remaining lug nuts. When he went to pick up his cell phone again to let Elliot know he would probably have to call him back, the phone shattered right before his eyes.

Elliot heard what sounded like a shot before the line went dead.

Eddie, startled, looked behind him as bullets sprayed. As he squinted through the rain, he saw the black Hummer, doors wide open. Two men with automatic weapons fired at Eddie as he instinctively ran to the passenger-side door. He opened it to use it for cover as he drew his .38 Special, which was comfortably strapped on his left side. He had never been so thankful that he was too big to button his jacket.

Eddie got into a defensive stance and steadily returned fire. He quickly realized his extra rounds were in the glove compartment inside the vehicle. He could vaguely make out that the person behind the driver's door of the Hummer was wearing what looked like a cowboy hat. And then one of the many bullets shattered the window and appeared to pass into Eddie's stomach.

Elliot redialed his associate's phone number, but the line was completely dead.

CHAPTER 16

THE HAYLOFT

MAY 2003

IT WAS MID-morning and Chuck was sitting in his Jeep at the entrance of the ranch. The sign hanging above looked grander to him than ever these days. The sun was beaming down and it was a fabulous spring day. Chuck was engrossed in writing his new manuscript, which he would soon be turning over to Ken Carlson.

Chuck laughed out loud to himself at what he was putting down on paper. "Oh yeah, this is good, Chuck. This is good!"

He heard a noise outside his vehicle and looked up. Jed was driving down the turnoff road leading to the ranch. He put down his pad to greet his friend.

Jed pulled up alongside Chuck and rolled down the window.

"Hey pal, thanks for meeting me," said Jed.

"Yeah, no problem. I just came from the chiropractor.. Do you want to come up to the house for some coffee?"

"Nah, that's all right. I only have a few minutes. I have to get back to the city. I just wanted to touch base with you in person real quick to go over the investigation and the court date coming up with Silus."

As they talked, the mail truck rolled down the hill to Chuck's mailbox on the right of the entranceway. Jed moved his car behind Chuck's to get out of the way and Chuck got out.

"Nice day, isn't it, Mr. Barreto?" said the mailman. Chuck concurred and the mailman handed him a few envelopes before continuing on down the road. Chuck shuffled through the envelopes and one of them put a smile on his face.

"What do you got there, bud?" asked Jed, who was now standing next to him.

Chuck quickly opened the envelope and pulled out some stamped paperwork and a plastic card. "My pilot's license, bro!"

Jed smiled back. "Look out now! Congratulations, Chuck, really. How did it come so fast? You just took your final flight test."

"Good old Junior put a rush on it for me. So what's happening with the investigation?"

"The workers are all cleared to return to work in Gussy's Pits. Detective Giovanni has not turned up anything except that three of the guys were ex-convicts from Chicago. We're still trying to figure out where the other guy came from."

"Chicago? Just like that a-hole that tried executing me last year."

"That is correct, Karl Eiden. We think there's more than likely a connection with Kobol. Maybe, Chuck – and I'm just saying this for you and your family's safety – we should hire some protection around here."

Chuck shot him a look of disapproval. "Not a chance. Never again. Between me, Mike, Mitch, and Dave, we got it."

Chuck thought to himself, My buddy never changes. Just like the old days, always planning and strategizing. Chuck liked to face the unknown head on and unfettered, take the bull by the horns if need be.

"OK, just looking out for you, bud. If you haven't heard already, Elliot Birch is having a few issues of his own."

Chuck's ears perked up. "Really? What's going on?"

"He filed a missing person's report on his head of security."

"That's weird, I guess. Did he elaborate on why?"

"I don't know. He was somewhat evasive about our questions. He just said the guy didn't show up for work and that it was unlike him. He reported that his man had been visiting a relative at the Cavalier Retirement Home, and that's the last he heard of him."

"Hmm, I think I know the place. Driven by there a few times on Fauci Street. The only reason I remember is the name 'Cavalier' is my grandmother Mary's maiden name, coincidentally. Who knows, maybe the guy tied on a few good ones and is sleeping it off somewhere."

"Could be. So Gary will be here in Woodrow soon, huh?"

"Yep, he'll be here this coming weekend for his wedding."

"Are they all staying with you?"

"No, they'll be at my mother's house."

"You practice your best man's speech? It must be great after all the writing you've been doing."

"I think it's okay. Hopefully, anyway."

"I have no doubt. Well, I really have to get back to the office. Friendly reminder, the court date is still set for the day after your brother's wedding. It would really be best if we do not see you inside the actual courtroom. I am going to have a really tough defense on my hands with this one. Jack is flying into town to help out, especially with Allan's absence."

"Don't worry, I'll wait outside. I just need to be there, okay Jethro?"

"OK, buddy. I will see you this weekend. It was surprising that Gary invited me after last year, with what we did in faking your death."

"He's a kind-hearted guy, my brother. Holds no ill will about stuff like that. My family understands, Jed, and they're thankful it all worked out in my favor. Oh, by the way, before you go…you bringing a date, bruh?"

Jed blushed a little. "Well, not exactly a date. Abby's coming."

Chuck smirked. "Ahhh, shit! Get out of town! You two?"

Jed's face got redder. "No, no, we are just friends."

"OK, sure, sure! I gotcha," said Chucking, winking.

"I'll let you know if anything comes up between now and then," said Jed, eager to get out of the conversation. He congratulated Chuck on his license once more and took off.

Chuck drove up the driveway whistling an Elvis tune, and thought, Hot damn, my buddy is finally getting laid.

As he pulled up to the house, he looked proudly over to Junior's helicopter sitting on the helipad. "Oh yeah, I'll be taking you up real soon baby."

He parked the Jeep and got out, still whistling, and walked into the house to be greeted by Uncle Armond, Uncle Richard, and Aunt Joanne. They sat at the table by the window as a shocked Mitch poured everyone coffee. Everyone laughed at Mitch who was just caught wearing Chuck's NASA jacket. Chuck had left it hanging on one of the bar stools after his last day flying with Junior.

"Hey Rockstar, would you like some coffee?" he said guiltily. Everyone could see that Mitch was unsure about the stern look on Chuck's face.

"Hey there, Meathead. Mitchell looks cooler than you with that jacket on."

Everyone in the room laughed harder, except for Mitch, who hurriedly took the jacket off and hung it back where he had found it.

"Sorry about that, Rockstar. Just wanted to try it on for size."

"No worries, Mitch," said Chuck who broke out in laughter with everyone else. "It looks much better on you, really."

"I just stopped inside to get a sip of coffee. It's a warm one today, but I gotta get back out there. Dave and I are working on some fencing down by acre 11. I'll see everyone later."

"OK, Mitch, I'm heading there soon myself."

Chuck put his legal pads on the breakfast bar and poured himself a cup of coffee, the police scanner audible in the background.

"Hey, nephew, how's the manuscript coming along?" asked Uncle Richard.

"I'm getting there. Working on the last couple of chapters now."

"Proud of you," said Aunt Joanne. "Well, Chuck, looks like I will be leaving you soon. Your mom found me a really nice house not too far from here."

"That's great. Congratulations. But it is kind of a shame because I love having you here."

"At least I'll be close. It's a really nice Cape on Gaudreau Street."

"Oh wow, that's a great area. Truly awesome, Aunt Joanne."

"Thank you, Chuck, for everything you have done for me."

"No thanks needed. It's been a pleasure having you stay here." Chuck felt his cell phone ringing in his pocket. He took it out and checked who was calling. "Excuse me, everyone, I have to take this."

He walked out of the kitchen and onto the porch. Chuck had been avoiding calling Bob since his mother told him that she had hired his old band to play at Gary's wedding, but it looked like time was up on that.

"Bobby!" said Chuck excitedly. "How are you doing?"

"Hey, I'm doing pretty good, Capricorn Man, '' he joked. "Not as good as you, I see, but not too bad. I was just calling to ask you a favor before the wedding."

"Sure. Everything okay?"

"Oh yeah, everything is peachy. As you probably already know, we put the old band back together. All the boys are back! Well, except for you and–"

"Yeah, I hear ya, Bob," said Chuck, interrupting him before he had a chance to mention Shandi.

"Well, anyhow, we have a new singer," Bob paused. "Her name is Madeline Star. Of course, she's not Shandi, but she has her own unique sound. You know, we'd love you to come back too, but I felt weird asking you."

Chuck put his friend at ease. "No, no, it's alright, Bob. I'm done with that part of my life."

"Yeah, I figured that, Chuck. I was happy to hear, though, that finally justice was served and they got those bastards, Leroy and John Stick." Bob still felt awkward discussing the events of that period of their lives.

"Yep, they got what was coming to them."

Bob cleared his throat. "Sooo… you still play guitar?"

"I kept all my equipment, but no, not since that day, Bob."

"Well, you never forget. I'm sure you'd pick it up in a heartbeat, knowing you. So I also called because I wanted to tell you that our old producer, Kenny Saxon, now runs the old studio. Bill Arkin has since retired, and me and the boys are back recording some new material."

"Oh, wow, congrats man. All of you? Dan and Harry too?"

"Yeah, and some of the stuff sounds really, really good. But I was wondering about an old song that we never used that Shandi had written. I think it was called–"

Chuck interrupted. "An Angel in Hell."

"Yeah, yeah, that's the one. If you don't want us to use it, I completely understand, really. But I was wondering if you had the original tapes that we recorded and if we could use it on our new album?"

Chuck paused for a few seconds before responding. " I'll tell you what, Bob. If I can find the tapes, absolutely, they're all yours. When do you need them?"

"If you find them you can just bring them to the wedding rehearsal, if that works. Thanks a million, Chuck."

Close to the ranch, two men crept quietly through the woods, close to the tree line. Across from where they were positioned, they could see an open field upon which stood a large, red barn surrounded by corrals. The first man, who was obviously in charge, motioned for the other man behind him, who had an enormous bald head, to get down and make a temporary camp in a gully while they observed.

They had trudged through the woods for miles to get to this spot. Mr. Logan, the leader of this two-man expedition, had an oversized cowboy hat strapped around the middle of his back, exposing a head of curly black hair. He seemed to know his way around the area pretty well. Butch Gro wore an old green jumpsuit and brown construction boots in a failed attempt to blend in. He was a peculiar looking man. If you saw him at a quick glance, you'd do a double take. He was seven feet tall and had a thick build. The only hair on him was a full goatee, in sharp contrast to his glistening head.

They got down on their stomachs and carefully crawled up to the edge of the grass line. Logan held a pair of binoculars, while Butch positioned a rifle with a scope on top of it. They looked through their lenses towards the barn. Logan took out a small glass vial, put a bump of cocaine on the upper part of his right thumb, and snorted with a proficiency that suggested it had long been a habit.

"Is that her?" asked Butch as they saw a woman walking a horse in circles in the corral.

"Butch!" Logan snapped. "Keep your voice down. This rancher is ex-military and retired corrections officers are working everywhere on these grounds. They're on point all the time, trust me. They put a man of mine, Karl Eiden, six feet under.

"So Mr Logan, that was one hell of a shoot-out we had the other day at the retirement home," whispered Butch.

Logan shot him a look of annoyance. "Yeah, our target is one lucky son of a bitch. For now, but not for much longer."

Butch nodded his colossal head. "Certainly. How 'bout that Matt Helfer I dropped off at the airport last week? He's an interesting dude. What happened with him and the rancher's brother? He went to cancel him out too, right?"

Logan was struggling to remain calm. "We had a change of plans. The boss has other ideas for him."

"What happens if your inside man on the ranch boffs it up today?"

"He won't. That's why today we're here, to supervise it all and confirm the kill to the boss. If somehow my man gets into trouble getting off the ranch, you know what to do. We will give our boy plenty of cover to get out. If something goes awry, we might have to blaze fire and fury from this position. I have a good line of sight on her right now."

Butch could clearly see the woman through his gun scope, the thin, red crosshairs right on her pretty, platinum-blonde hair.

"How much longer before he makes his move, Mr. Logan?"

"I'm about to send him a message to proceed. She's the only one at the barn. I don't see anyone else there right now. This is it."

He reached into his right pants pocket for his flip phone.

Sam was walking side-by-side with a client's horse, training the gorgeous beast. She was teaching the horse, She's a Lady, to gait. Rupert was sitting close to the fence of the corral, watching them both patiently. He knew not to interfere with Sam taming the horse, content to watch his favorite person work.

Another horse, named Bullseye, was in the next corral. He was walking around freely, and every time Samantha and She's A Lady walked by, he would snort at them and pound his right front hoof into the dirt.

"Easy boy, easy," Samantha said to Bullseye. "I'll get to you soon enough. You can wait your turn."

Above them, up in the hayloft of the barn, music played on the radio that Dave and Mitch had left on earlier when they were baling hay. They had taken off to fetch some supplies just outside of town, and Mike and Candie were at the far end of the ranch fixing fences.

Jemel loomed against the wall in the loft's shadow. He was supposed to be out mowing, but instead he was peering nervously down at Samantha. It wasn't just the warm day that was causing him to sweat buckets.

He felt his cell phone buzz in his back pocket. He quickly took it out and saw the number that just sent him a dreaded text message.

Jemel started rubbing his forehead, immensely conflicted about what he was about to do. He flipped the phone shut, put it back into his pocket, and edged his way forward along the wall until he could see Samantha clearly.

His inner voice kept repeating, We live together, we all die alone, over and over, to the point that he thought his brain was going to explode.

Jemel extended his torso to the window and slowly reached around the backside of his shirt, lifted it, and pulled out a 9 millimeter from his waistline. He couldn't help but think at that moment of everyone in their unit in Panama. They used to call themselves "The Magnificent Seven". They had all trained together. They were brothers.

They wouldn't be after this.

Jemel, with great reluctance, raised the gun straight across his mid frame. He closed one eye and used the other to focus Chuck's lady in his line of fire. The gun in his hand shook so badly that he could not aim. Back in the field, Mike would tell the boys that you could be a world-class expert at shooting targets, but when it came to hitting a living, breathing target, the game changed.

Jemel was in torment. Thoughts of what he was about to do plagued his mind.

My God! How did I come to this place in life? I am going to murder an innocent woman and betray a man that saved my pathetic life a decade ago. I screwed up my life so bad, this is all I have left. You have no choice, Jemel. It's you or him. Here we go!

Jemel managed to steady his hands and put on his game face. He realigned the target's golden head for the kill. His right index finger still twitched slightly, but he was committed to the task, so he started to squeeze the trigger.

Suddenly, down below, Rupert jumped up onto all fours and swung around toward the barn opening of the hayloft. The short hairs on his back stood straight up, and he barked so loudly that the sound echoed against the barn.

Jemel's finger eased off of the trigger and he stepped backwards clumsily, almost tripping and falling down. He couldn't believe the dog's instincts. He thought to himself, This has to be some kind of sign.

"Hey Rupey, it's okay. There's nothing there," Samantha said as she looked around, seeing nothing out of the ordinary.

The music continued to play from the barn loft. Rupert scoped the area and sat straight up in an alert position.

Samantha kept walking with She's A Lady, and Jemel tucked his gun back into his waistband and quietly scurried down the spiral staircase to the barn floor. Sweat poured down his body as he looked around to see if he was still alone. He pulled out a pack of Newport Lights and a Bic lighter from his pants. He sparked up the cigarette and took a long drag.

Fucking A, I can't do it, he thought to himself.

Before he could contemplate any further how to get himself out of the major dilemma he was in, a loud familiar voice interjected.

"Hey! Jemel, what the fuck do you think you're doing?"

Jemel almost dropped the cigarette, he was so startled. He turned to see Mike standing in the wide doorway of the barn.

"Oh, Mikey! I was just taking a cigarette break," said Jemel.

"That's great, Jemel. I don't care if you take a break, but there's no smoking in the barn. You know, hay and fire don't do well together."

Jemel took the cigarette and smashed the burning tip of it into his left palm, then took out his crumpled pack and put it back inside.

"Sorry, Mikey, I forgot."

"That's alright. Just be more mindful, brother. We don't want to foolishly make that kind of mistake."

"Of course. Won't happen again."

Mike could see that Jemel seemed out of sorts. He was even more disheveled than usual.

"Hey Jemel, is everything good with you?"

"Yeah, I just don't feel too good today. Could be allergies. I don't do too well this time of year, and there's a lot of pollen floating around."

"Sure, sure, I understand."

"Mike, do you think Chuck would mind if I take off early today?"

When Chuck wasn't around, Mike, Samantha, or Candie were in charge of the day-to-day operations on the ranch.

"You know what? Get the hell outta here, brother. Go home, get some rest, and we'll see ya tomorrow, okay? Oh, what sections of the ranch still need to be mowed?"

"I still need to do areas 7, 8, and 11. Thank you, Mike. I'll see you tomorrow."

Mike was concerned for his friend and unconvinced that allergies were the problem, but he didn't push. "Hey, don't worry, I'll get it Jem. Feel better, brother. If you need anything, call me. And don't forget."

"Forget?" asked Jemel, confused.

Mike smiled. "We all live together, we die alone!"

"Right," said Jemel, giving him a small smile back.

As he shuffled past, Mike clapped him on the back. "Just take the four-wheeler back to the house. I'll get it later on."

Jemel nodded his thanks. He was relieved to get off the ranch, but now he would have to deal with disappointing Mr. Logan.

* * *

Logan and Butch watched from their position at the wood line.

"What now, Mr. Logan? Your man is leaving. He chickened out, looks like."

"Yeah, it looks like that. On to Plan B then."

"We're going to take her out ourselves?"

Logan was looking through the scope on his binoculars as Jemel got onto the four-wheeler. Mike was on the riding lawn mower and Samantha was still walking the horse.

"No. The text message I received a minute ago was for me to hold off on this operation if Jemel failed."

"Why don't we come here with a crew and wipe them all out for good?"

"Yo! Do me a favor, Butch?" said Logan, annoyed. "Stop with the stupid questions. If he wanted that, we'd have done it already! C'mon, we gotta get outta here without getting noticed and regroup with Jemel to see what went wrong."

The two men slowly crawled backwards into the thick of the woods.

Chuck and Uncle Armond were on the golf cart, joking around as they rode towards the barn.

"So Meathead, when are we getting fitted for our tuxes?" asked Uncle Armond.

"I have it written down on a post note stuck to the fridge," said Chuck. He could tell that Uncle Armond was excited to be a part of Gary's wedding party. He often asked about the details as it grew closer to the date.

They saw Jemel heading towards them on the four-wheeler. Chuck slowed down to a stop alongside Jemel.

"Hey. What's up, buddy?" said Chuck.

"Ah, I gotta go home Chuck. Not feeling so hot today. Plus, I forgot I had an appointment with the VA. I promise I'll be back tomorrow. Mike's finishing the sections I had to do as we speak. I'm really sorry, dude," said Jemel, avoiding eye contact.

"Don't worry about it, Jems. Go home and take it easy today. If you're not feeling better, take tomorrow off too. We'll cover you. And if you need anything, let me or Mike know."

Jemel felt terribly ashamed. "Thanks, dude. I appreciate ya."

Chuck proceeded to the barn feeling sympathetic about Jemel's ongoing struggles, but he did not know how to help him. He knew it was going to be a long and possibly rough road of recovery for him. Chuck recalled his own days of self-destruction after Shandi's death before he joined the Army and met his buddies. After returning home, he felt like a new man. Ever since, he had tried to share whatever good fortune that came his way with those he loved.

The golf cart pulled up to the entrance of the barn and they walked over to the corrals where Samantha was still walking She's A Lady. She and the horse saw them coming as they rounded a corner.

"Whoa, Lady," Samantha said to the horse. Lady stamped her front hooves on the ground to communicate to Sam that the horse wanted to keep going. She chuckled at the stallion's insistence and tugged her close enough to tie up the stirrup to the fence. Then she patted her on the head before walking towards Chuck and Uncle Armond.

Rupert barked with enthusiasm, jumped up, and ran to greet them.

"Hey, Unc!" Sam said and then turned to Chuck. "You just missed Mike. He headed out to mow the far end."

"Yeah, we just ran into Jemel. He told us."

The way they looked at each other, Armond felt like he was intruding on a lovers' conversation, so he quickly got Rupert onto the golf cart with him and took off back to the house.

Chuck looked at his girlfriend like he hadn't seen her in years.

Sam was wearing a faded pair of tight, worn jeans with beat-up, brown Duluth cowboy boots and one of her classic Def Leppard t-shirts, torn in all the right places. Her long, blonde hair was pulled back out of her face. She could not help but smile back at Chuck as she saw the longing for her in his deep green eyes.

"Miss me, boy?" she said coyly.

"And then some, girl!"

"Well, we got too much work to do this afternoon," she smirked at him.

"Yeah, work, work, work!"

"I'm working with She's a Lady and Bullseye right now. You wanna give me a hand with them, boss man?"

"Why, sure thing, ma'am, but they both look a little riled up today."

"They are, for sure. They're in heat."

"I know the feeling," Chuck said under his breath.

"What's that?"

Chuck raised his eyebrows. "Oh, nothing. I just said the poor devils."

She giggled. "OK, get serious, will ya, Chucky? I have an idea."

"Oh yeah? What's that?"

"You take Bullseye and I'll take Lady, and we'll ride it out of them."

Chuck grabbed two saddles that were hanging over the fence and fastened them to the horses securely while Samantha adjusted them. He opened up the gates and they walked the horses outside the perimeter of the corral. She's A Lady and Bullseye were excited to ride, their heads bobbing up and down and hooves stomping.

"You ready?" Chuck asked once they were situated.

"No, mister. The question is, are you?"

"Lead the way, ma'am."

"You making fun of me?" Sam laughed.

"Definitely not," he retorted and he jumped up on Bullseye like he was in a Clint Eastwood western.

It never got old when he did that. Samantha admired how fast he had learned how to ride and to run a ranch. Having grown up on one, she knew it wasn't for everyone.

Chuck, on the other hand, loved watching her get up onto a horse as well. The female form was something he always appreciated, but this was something more than that. She was perfect.

As Samantha swung her right leg over the saddle and sat in a ready position, she felt Chuck's eyes on her. She winked at him. "Boy, oh boy. You're something else today!"

"What? I'm just making sure you got up there alright."

"OK, let's ride it out of all three of ya's." Sam tapped the sides of Lady with her boots and the stallion leapt forward like a bolt of lightning.

Chuck followed in pursuit, yelling, "Yah, Bullseye!"

A song continued to play from the radio up inside the barn loft as the two lovers blazed across the land.

"I wonder why it took so long for us to meet/ And if I ever passed you on some street/ And I die just a little every time/ I count the days you should have already been mine."

Lady and Bullseye's lust caused them to run so fast that they were leaving divots in the ground. Chuck thought, Oh well. I'll have to have Jemel fix the lawn later.

Samantha had her head down and her legs pointed up like she was on a rocket. Chuck came up alongside, and she turned her head, yelling, "Come on! Try to keep up!"

Chuck laughed and yelled back, "Oh, I am. Don't you worry, girl."

They blazed past Mike who was riding the lawnmower.

"Hey, Mikey!" Sam yelled.

He smiled and shouted back, "Hey, all work and no play makes Chucky a dull boy!"

They were moving so fast, Chuck couldn't hear what was said. He just waved back and gave chase to his lady.

The music still played, though no one was close enough to hear it.

"I have waited all my life for you/ No one no one else would ever do/ Baby, we were meant to be together/ Yeah, you and me/ We're gonna be/ The love affair that lasts forever."

Logan and Butch were still trudging through the woods when they heard the thunder of horse hooves and the sounds of voices behind them.

"Do you hear that, Mr. Logan?" asked Butch.

"Shhh! I thought I told you, dumbass, to keep your voice low," snapped Logan. "It's probably Barreto's ranch hands or something. Let's just get back to the car."

"How much further do you think? Is this the way we came?" Butch whispered.

Logan couldn't help but think, My God, I should've come alone on this one. This guy is more trouble than he's worth.

"Yeah, this is the way we came. It's not much further now."

"What about Jemel, Mr. Logan?"

The frustrated cowboy took another breath. "I already told you. I'll deal with him when we get back to the Hummer. Please do me this favor: no more unnecessary chitter-chatter or stupid questions until we get there."

Before Butch could respond, the branch Logan had moved out of his way snapped back and smashed Butch square in his protruding forehead.

"Ouch!" he yelped.

Logan looked back at him and shook his head. "You can't teach stupid."

*   *   *

Chuck and Samantha were reapproaching the barn, She's A Lady still in the lead. They slowed their horses, trotting them to the corrals. Once close enough, Samantha leapt off her horse and held onto the stirrup.

"Hey, Chuck, put Bullseye over on the other side," Sam said.

Chuck jumped down and followed her direction. The horses immediately started drinking the fresh cold water from the trough, thirsty after a hearty run. Samantha patted both of them on their heads. Bullseye snorted his returned affection.

Unbeknownst to Chuck, Sam had another mission in mind.

"Well, I think we certainly ran it out of them. They both look pretty content for now."

"They do. I believe they are," said Chuck.

She smiled at him like she had a dirty secret. "Now, my other stud, let's take care of you."

Chuck looked at her innocently and feigned ignorance. "Me?"

"Yeah, you, cowboy. Now that I see your back is feeling better, get your little ass in here!" she said. She disappeared into the barn.

Samantha was right about Chuck's back. Ever since his chiropractor got all the kinks out, he had been feeling great. And he had none of the strange flashbacks of Shandi since the first visit.

Chuck wasn't going to waste any time. He chased after her into the barn. She was already halfway up the staircase to the loft, removing her clothing as she went.

The radio played a fitting soundtrack for their love.

"You bring to life every single fantasy/ You and I, love how you make a mess of me/ What I feel has never been felt before/ We have it all, and all I want is more."

He reached the top and quickly pulled off his cowboy boots. She lie in her birthday suit on a couple fresh bales of hay.

Chuck's eyes bulged out of his head.

"You want me to get our secret blankets?" he asked. They had some stashed away in a wooden chest at the far end of the loft for occasions such as this one.

"Hell no, silly, come on. I need you right now before anyone comes back."

Logan and Butch finally emerged from the woods onto a crumbling, paved side road in Woodrow, but the black Hummer was nowhere in sight.

"Mr. Logan, where is your vehicle?" asked Butch.

Logan looked over to the left, and approximately a quarter mile up, he could see the black Hummer parked off to the side. Logan pointed. "Right up there, Sherlock. Keep your weapon low and on your left side in case anyone drives by, and let's pick up the pace."

Logan whipped a cell phone out of his right pocket as they moved towards the Hummer. He looked through the contacts, scrolled down to Jemel, and hit the dial button. It went to voicemail.

"Hi, this is Jemel Landau. I can't get to my phone. Leave a message and I'll surely get right back to ya."

Logan hung up without leaving a message. "Goddamnit!"

"No Jemel?" Butch asked stupidly.

"No flies on you, Butch," said Logan sarcastically. "After we get to my vehicle, we're going to find his dumb ass. And then I'll be having a talk with my man, Pete."

Butch tried to keep up with Logan. When they finally reached the vehicle, he said through labored breaths, "Why do you want to talk to Pete, Mr. Logan? Isn't he the guy who recruited me?"

Logan looked at him sidelong. "Precisely."

Samantha was lying on top of Chuck. She cleared her throat to ask him a long awaited question that she had been building the courage to ask.

"Can I ask you a question, Chuck? And I mean, it's just out of curiosity. Believe me, the answer will not upset me no matter what. Really."

Chuck felt sure she was going to ask him if he was in love with her. He cleared his throat, too. "Sure, you can ask me anything. You know that, Sam."

"I know I look like Shandi. But you're not with me cause of that, are you?" she blurted.

He didn't want to lie to her.

"Ah, well…" Chuck began, but he was saved by a voice from down at the bottom of the stairs to the hayloft.

"Hey, anyone in here?" Mike called.

Samantha jumped up. "Shit, shit, shit!" She grabbed her clothes and hastily put them back on.

"Yeah, we're just straightening up some of the bales for the horses, Mikey!" Chuck yelled back.

Mike shook his head at the response. He was grabbing a saddle off the wall when they both came shambling down the stairs with pieces of hay still in their hair.

Mike smiled. "You two need to get a room."

"No, Mike, we were just fixing up the loft a bit," said Chuck.

"Sure you were."

Samantha giggled and stood on her tip-toes to reach Mike for a big hug.

CHAPTER 17

THOUGH LOVERS BE LOST, LOVE SHALL NOT

MID-MAY 2003

IT WAS 10:00 A.M. and flight 457 United Airways was arriving in Hartford, Connecticut at Bradley Airport in approximately one hour. Sitting in two first-class seats, drinking whiskey and scotch and dressed in their usual leisure suits and cowboy hats, was Vic Texeria and Chance. After finally extinguishing the fire in Texas from the main oil rig, they were on their way to Woodrow to surprise Chuck and Shalon. Vic needed to understand how Chuck and Kelly got so far off-track and how Shalon was entangled with it all.

A young, attractive flight attendant approached the two older Texans. "Would you two gentlemen like another?"

Vic smiled. "Absolutely, young lady. Keep 'em coming."

She laughed and refilled their glasses, then walked off to help another passenger.

The two boisterous men had the luxury of exercising their usual volume because they were the only two in the front of the plane on this particular flight.

Chance, who was snacking on Planters peanuts, had a dry wit that Vic admired and it often sent him into a fit of laughter.

"So Vic," said Chance, about to utilize such wit. "There's a guy, and he's tired of having sexual relations with his wife." He went on for a few minutes just telling a very crass joke until he finally reached his intentional punchline. Vic busted out laughing heartily. Luckily no one was around to hear it, lest anyone should think it was inappropriate.

"Did you ever end up telling Kelly or Shalon that we were coming down to see them?"

"Only Kelly knows. I told her I had some business in Wolford City and that we'd be stopping in to see her this weekend at her apartment. I told her we could all go out for dinner, and she said she can't wait to see us."

"What's the plan for the other two, Vic?" asked Chance.

"Well, I decided to give Rita a call to let her know my intentions and promised her I wasn't coming down to make any trouble. She's a classy lady and deserved a heads up. She said she has tried to talk with them, but they aren't very forthcoming about their relationship. Rita did tell me that she and Shalon get along well. Given all that, our timing is somewhat impeccable because her younger son, Gary, is getting married this weekend. She invited us and didn't tell Chuck or Shalon."

"Is that what we're going to do? We're going to the wedding?"

"I told her we'd sleep on it. She told me where the church is and where the reception is taking place. I thought we'd skip the ceremony and head over to the reception. If I decide to go there instead of just confronting them both at the ranch, you and I can sit down with Chuck and Shalon to speak with them in private somewhere."

"That's ballsy."

"Sure is, and it's perfect," said Vic. "Where are we staying for the weekend?"

"I wasn't aware of the wedding, and I figured you wanted to be close to the ranch, so the only hotel in Woodrow is the Holiday Inn."

"Holy Toledo, Chance. Isn't that the same hotel Chuck was holed up in when we were all at his funeral?"

"I believe that's the one."

"The same hotel where a vehicle exploded and there was a shootout with the sons-of-bitches that kidnapped my daughter?"

"I'm sorry, Vic, do you want to stay somewhere else? Perhaps somewhere in the city closer to Kelly?"

"No, my friend, I'd rather be closer to Chuck's ranch. The H-Inn will be just fine and dandy," he said sarcastically.

The bell dinged throughout the hull of the plane, making the announcement for everyone to buckle up for landing.

Samantha was pacing around on foot inside a glossy-floored laundromat located in the same plaza as The Silver Bell. She was impatient as she waited inside, and the Pepto-Bismol feel of the place was not improving her mood. Other than an elderly woman towards the back, she was the only soul there. The machines were coin-operated so there was no need for staff. Unlike the other woman, Sam had no clothes with her to launder. She had told Chuck she had to leave early to run some errands, and then she would be off to meet up with Stacey and Lilly to try on their dresses, as she was asked at the last moment to be a bridesmaid. Sam was excited to be given the honor as though she was part of the family.

Kelly's little red car finally pulled into a parking space right in front of the window. The driver's door opened up, and a sharply-dressed Kelly Ann stepped out wearing a loose-fitting black pinstripe suit that still somehow accentuated her curves. Her mane of red, silky hair was pulled back tightly into a ponytail in a similar fashion to Sam.

Once Kelly got closer to the entrance, she moved her oversized sunglasses onto the top of her head. The laundromat door opened and a bell rang to announce her arrival.

"You always did know how to make an entrance," said Sam dryly.

Kelly smirked. "What, this old outfit? Only wear it when I'm coming to the laundromat!"

"Why meet here at the laundromat, anyway? What's wrong with your office upstairs?"

"Paige is running that office for me right now. We're doing some remodeling there, too, and I always thought this was a cute, quiet little place when I passed by."

Samantha wanted to roll her eyes, but she decided to take the high road. Even with all she, Chuck, and Kelly had gone through, ultimately she missed her only big sister.

"It's nice to see you, Kell," said Sam stiffly.

"Hmmm, I bet that must've hurt to say," replied Kelly. "Even though I didn't deserve what you and Chuck did to me, believe it or not, I've missed my little sister too. That will never change, Shal. Anyhoo, how's the ranch doing? And how's Chuck?"

Samantha knew eventually they would have to talk about what actually happened between the three of them. She'd been avoiding it, having fallen so hard for Chuck. Feeling like an outcast in her adopted family hurt like hell.

"He's doing well," Sam blushed. "He's actually out with Gary. He's in town for the long weekend because him and Lilly are getting married."

"Oh, how nice. Hopefully he'll stay married and won't get it annulled right afterwards," said Kelly spitefully.

Sam paused and chose her next words carefully. "Kell, when I heard that you and Chuck were going through with that I tried to talk him out of it. I even texted you that I didn't want you all to do that, and I would've stepped aside and left the ranch for a spell, but you never answered me. I didn't mean for any of this to happen. You asked me to come here to Woodrow to deceive and distract Chuck. Remember?"

"The choices I made were for his own good. Look at how he's prospered from it all. Shalon, I never told you to sleep with him, and I tried telling you once before that he is not all that innocent either."

Samantha knew she didn't want to hear what Kelly was going to say about Chuck, but she had to know anyway. "What do you mean, Kell?"

"Do you know how the police captured the man that kidnapped me?"

Sam had a confused look on her face; she didn't know what her sister was talking about.

"Let me take a guess. He never told ya?" said Kelly.

"Told me what?"

"Through my real estate connections, I learned that Chuck and his buds captured the guy. They got him locked up right now at Pocomtuc Prison and his pretrial is next week. I'm going to be testifying as a witness to help Jed Ferarri put him away for good. Chuck told me he was going to tell you about all of this. I guess he never got around to it, huh?"

"When did all this happen?" asked Sam, trying to keep her emotions in check.

"Listen, little sis, it wasn't my intention here to cause issues between you all. The main reason I'm helping is to keep the peace with Chuck's family."

"What do you mean by that?"

"You just moved out here last year. I've been living here for a while now, trying to build my own little legacy, and if I do know one thing to be true in life, it's power is money. Rita is an influential person in this area. Just her word of mouth alone could ruin me and run me out of here, if she was so inclined. I'd have to pack it in and head back to Texas, work for Daddy instead. I really had no choice but to try to make good with Chuck and his mother in some way."

"Rita doesn't exactly strike me as a vindictive type. She's a sweet woman."

"It may seem that way, dear sis, but I've seen the woman in action and she is a force to be reckoned with. Even I know I have limitations."

"Then why would you even try to develop Gussy's Pitts right under her nose?"

"It's complicated. But Chuck and his friends were somehow able to extract the man responsible for my abduction back in January and lock him up."

Samantha thought to herself, That's when Chuck went to California on the trip with Mitch, Mike, Junior, and Uncle Rich.

"Where did they find this man, exactly?"

"It had to be in California because I had some connections there. They lured him to an expensive piece of real estate. I thought he would have told you by now, but Chuck does have some bad habits."

"Why wouldn't he tell me, Kelly?"

"You tell me, sis. He definitely has many things he keeps secret."

"Like…?"

"I am still hurt, but I just want to make sure you know that's not at all why I'm telling you this. When you sleep next to him at night, does he seem at peace?"

Samantha's face reddened. She was disturbed, but kept silent. Kelly could read her just by her expression.

"Shal, the three of us have some deep issues that may be parallel to one another."

"I'm not following you. What?"

"OK, I'll spell it out better, Shal. The loss of your biological parents, my mom, and his father and lost love."

"Right, Shandi, the girl I look like. And you knew that when you had me go work on his ranch."

"I know, Shal. I made a mistake in that, and I paid the ultimate price over it. But my point being is that our losses are different from his."

"How so?"

"You and I mourned and then accepted and moved on from our losses."

"And so what are you saying, Chuck hasn't?"

"On the surface, Chuck is handsome and strong and confident. But when he's sleeping, you can see he's tormented. You do see that, don't you?"

If Shalon admitted to that, she would also be admitting to her sleeping with Chuck, which she still could not do aloud. She just blankly stared back at Kelly.

The old woman in the laundromat couldn't help but eavesdrop on the two of them as she folded. She thought to herself, Mmm, what it is to be young!

"He'd probably never admit this to anyone," said Kelly, "but I get this strange feeling – intuition, call it– Chuck believes somewhere in that thick head of his that Shandi and his dad are not actually dead, but still alive."

"That's insane, Kelly. He doesn't think that! Why would you say something so awful?" Sam scowled, upset.

"You remember Chuck's fake funeral, that hoax you were in on?"

"You don't understand," said Sam defensively. "Chuck had no choice but to keep everyone safe from those thugs you invited into our lives."

"That's fine, Shal, but did you see the gravestone near his?"

"No, I didn't. I was a little too busy worrying about other things. Why?"

"Go see it for yourself. After that, think about all his peculiar mannerisms and you can form your own conclusions from there." Kelly turned to leave the laundromat. "Oh, by the way, I also wanted to let you know that our father will be here this weekend. He wants to see you. It's time, Shalon. He doesn't deserve this from you."

"OK, fine. We can get together sometime after the wedding."

"Sure. Daddy, Chance, and I are going out to dinner at the Villa on Sunday. Call me before then."

Kelly walked out to her vehicle and Samantha hunched over one of the tables and began to cry. The old woman stopped folding her clothes and kindly walked over and enveloped her in a hug.

"You sweet, dear thing! It's alright. It gets easier, I promise you."

Samantha cried as the woman patted her back.

In a rundown section of town on the border of Chicopee and Wolford City was a seedy apartment complex that looked like it should've been condemned a decade prior. The Blisswood Apartments was a series of buildings painted in a dark green that was now peeling. On the front step of number twenty-seven stood a tall man with short blonde hair. He was pounding on the door so hard it looked as if his right palm would smash through it like The Hulk.

"Jemel!" shouted the determined individual. "Jemel, just come to the door!"

Mr. Logan and Butch Gro sat in the Hummer nearby, watching the man intently.

"Who's that, Mr. Logan?" Butch asked.

"That'd be Michael Geller, one of Barreto's ranch hands and former Sergeant."

"He must be looking for Jemel, too."

"Yep, thanks for the insight, Butch," quipped Logan.

"Do you think he's in there?"

"He could be hiding like a rat inside, who knows. Eventually he'll turn up. Jemel will need his drugs. After this guy leaves, we'll go in there and scope the place out."

"How are we getting in? Bustin' a window or door, Mr. Logan?"

Logan took a breath. "I can pick the lock."

"You're a straight gangster, boss!"

Logan couldn't help but smirk at that remark, but still shook his head.

Mike gave up trying to get Jemel to answer the door. He walked back to his vehicle and drove out of the complex.

Logan wasted no time. "Come on, Butch. Let's do this."

He snorted a bump of cocaine off the cradle of his right hand and grabbed a small leather case wedged between the seats.

Jemel, however, wasn't home. He was sitting in a raggedy old 1993 Pontiac Duster across the street in the parking lot of an old combination mini-mart and package store. He was parked next to a dumpster, watching in horror as Logan and Butch infiltrated his crappy abode. He was trying to figure out his next move, but he felt trapped.

Do I turn myself into Logan and plead my case? he pondered. If I do that, he might make me go back to the ranch to murder my friend's girlfriend. Do I go on the run? With no money, no place to live, no access to painkillers or drugs. And if Logan catches me, I'll most certainly be killed for defying him.

Jemel was already starting to feen again and his leg was throbbing. He turned his head and looked at the four orange ceramic planters sitting in his backseat. He had been growing peyote plants as a backup. Unfortunately, most of the plants were still inside his apartment in the spare room. That's one of the main reasons he stopped home, but he also needed clothes. He had been wearing the same ones for days, and he was ripe.

Jemel wanted to run. He knew how Logan thought and they'd never let him out of the organization. It was a permanent membership; he was told that when he sold his soul and joined up with them.

He grabbed one planter and put it in his lap. He gently pulled one of the plants from the soil. On the root was a bulb that looked sort of like a radish without the red color. His eyes widened and he salivated just looking at it. Biting into it savagely, he sucked out the juice like a vampire. Once the bulb was bone dry, he nibbled on the vegetable. His eyeballs rolled as the serum took its psychedelic effect on his brain.

He no longer cared that Logan and Butch were inside his apartment. Jemel was transported back in time to a happier place. He was in Panama in 1989. Mike was at headquarters being debriefed after they had escaped from the Panama Defense Forces on their most recent mission. Poor Chuck, who had heroically saved the day out in the jungle, was being held in The Santo Tomas Hospital in Quarry Heights, Panama, waiting to be sent back to the United States.

Jemel, Mitch, Kirk, Will, and Burt had been allowed by their next level commander to visit Chuck briefly before they would be shipped off to the Gulf for their next mission. They were flirting with the nurses and asking them where to find Chuck.

A young lady dressed in an all white nurse's uniform said to the wise-cracking Burt who was leading the pack, "I think he's over in wing three."

The hospital was chaotic, swamped with injured patients. It was more than apparent that something major had taken place to leave so many wounded.

The boys walked the halls until they found the correct wing. There were fifty people, maybe more, lying in cots, and they had to scan slowly to find Chuck. Will spotted him first.

"Look, guys!" he pointed. They all laughed at Chuck who was sitting upright with a pillow behind his backside.

He was all the way at the other end of the dirty room. The grungy ceiling was low enough for Chuck to bounce a green tennis ball off of and catch it with his one good arm, obviously bored out of his mind. He saw his friends walking toward him, laughing, and placed the ball on a small table next to the bed.

Chuck smirked. "Hey, you guys here to get me out?"

They surrounded his bed, smiling, happy to see that he still was okay and acting like himself.

"Hey dude, you don't look too bad for the wear 'n tear! Is that your little nurse?" joked Jemel. "You gettin' summa dat?"

"Even if I could, Jem, I don't think I'm in much condition to perform at my best," said Chuck. The guys laughed. "I just wanna get the fuck outta here and get back out there with you guys. I'm fine, but these sons-of-bitches say I need surgery."

"They're sending you back to the states for that I heard, Rockstar," said Burt.

Chuck's face fell. "Yeah."

"Dude, get healed. There's no rush. We'll be waiting for ya in the hot, dusty desert."

"What's been happening anyway? It's mayhem in here," said Burt.

"A lot of injured here. And 21 dead American soldiers. Those motherfucking guerillas!"

"What happened?" asked Will.

"A General named Thurman said there was a rocket grenade attack on the Panamanian police. And Endara's Vice President, Calderon, survived an assassination attempt by snipers."

"Where was he, dude?" asked Jemel.

"In his car. He was leaving a national assembly building. Two of his aides were injured, I heard."

"Wow, that's impressive political intel, brother!" joked Kirk.

"Believe me, I am not political, just bored out of my mind sitting around here. I pick up on a lot since I have nothing to do but listen."

"Don't worry, Rockstar," said Kirk, "you'll be back in action in no time."

"That's right, my dude!" said Jemel.

The guys started saying their farewells to Chuck as present-day Jemel began to fade from memory to sleep.

"Hey fellas?" said Chuck.

They all stopped and turned to look at him.

"Never forget… we live together, we die alone!"

Chuck was playing hooky from working on the ranch with Gary, Uncle Armond, and Junior the day before the wedding. Their first stop was the movie theater in Wolford City. Afterwards, they were going across the way to pick up their tuxedos at Mr. Tux. The four of them were giddier than school kids sitting next to one another, each with their own large, overflowing bucket of popcorn.

Chuck and Gary both had their popcorn laden with extra butter. They each had a wad of napkins to keep their fingers clean, there was so much.

They were all excited about the movie, The Matrix Reloaded, but Junior even more so because he had just met Keanu Reeves in California. Gary was a little jealous about that, but his life was his life. He was committed to Lilly, for better or worse.

Junior was sitting at the end with Armond and Gary in between him and Chuck. He kept throwing kernels across at Chuck, who returned fire.

It did not impress Armond who was engrossed in watching Neo, Reeves' character, flying across the screen with his costar Carrie Ann Moss playing Trinity. As she was trying to fight villains, Armond was gorging on two large orders of nachos and plum-sized pretzel bites oozing with drizzling, hot cheese. He couldn't eat fast enough, almost taking his fingers off along with the food. As the cheese dripped onto his shirt, he tried to swipe it off with a napkin.

Though Gary had his phone on silent, he kept getting text messages from Lilly. She was wrapping up with the bridesmaids at the dress shop. Gary was trying to be inconspicuous as he read the messages.

Chuck was getting annoyed. "Everything okay, bro?"

"Yeah, yeah," Gary shrugged him off, though he was far from okay. Lilly was asking him if he had talked to Chuck about Gussy's Pitts, but he didn't want to talk about it in front of Armond and Junior.

He sent a message back to her. I am working on it.

"Lilly was just asking me about your buddy, Bob, and his band playing tomorrow at the wedding and the song list," Gary whispered to Chuck.

Damn, I forgot to find that song for Bob, Chuck thought to himself. I'll do it soon as I get back home tonight.

Chuck had a designated spot for all of his old tracks down in his basement with the band equipment that sat collecting dust.

His phone buzzed and he pulled it out of his pocket. A number from Washington DC was on the caller ID screen. Chuck couldn't help but be curious about the call, so he excused himself and went out into the lobby.

"Hello?" Chuck answered the call just before it went to voicemail.

"Hello, Chuck. This is Chip Karrington. Is this a convenient time?"

What in the hell does this asshole want? Chuck thought.

"The great Senator Karrington of Massachusetts! Congratulations on your win. What could I possibly do for you, Senator, after all you've done for me and my family," said Chuck sarcastically.

"Chuck, I know that you and your family are having major differences right now with the governor of Wolford City over the rights to Gussy's Pitts," said Chip. If Abby and Jed had come through in convincing Chuck and his family to concede with the governor's orders, Chip wouldn't be embarking on this regrettable conversation, but it was up to him.

"You mean the same differences you and I had last year when my ex-wife was trying to swindle me out of that land?"

"Chuck, I feel like all this legal jargon is getting blown way out of proportion. So before this goes any further, I'd like to take the opportunity to talk it through in layman's terms with you and your family before this gets any messier or costlier."

"Costlier?" said Chuck sharply.

"I'm referring to the city's lawyer, who is funded by hard-working taxpayers, and your attorney, who I'm sure doesn't come cheap either. The governor is doing what is best for the people, and they will not stop until the judge grants an easeway through your family's property so that the repairs on the city bridge can commence in a much more expedient fashion, Chuck. After the repairs are complete, we will pull out of your valley."

Karrington's voice was so sticky-sweet sounding it was giving Chuck a toothache. No matter what this guy promised, Chuck's mind was already made up.

"You know, Senator, the last time we had a conversation like this, a week later there was a failed attempt on my life. What are you gonna try now?"

"Chuck, that allegation has been disproved. I deal with all kinds of constituents in this line of work. My people had nothing to do with that and I've sent my apologies to you and your family for our mistake of receiving contributions from The Lonestar Group."

"OK, Senator, keep talking," said Chuck angrily, "but we'll see what Silus Kobol has to say about your actual connections to them in court."

"Chuck, I don't know the man personally. Maybe we met briefly at one of my campaign rallies." Chip was uncomfortable and loosened his neck tie. He felt his forehead getting sweaty, as Chuck had struck a nerve. He continued making his case. "Listen, Chuck, I just called to offer an olive branch and try to save your family from any further debt. More than likely, a decision will come down in favor of the people."

"You and your thugs will never set foot on my family's land. Never! Save it, Karrington. From now on, you got something to say to me, call my attorney. Good day, Hoss!"

Chuck hung up the phone. The bewildered Senator looked over at his campaign manager, Alicia Stone, sitting on the corner of his desk with a big white legal pad on her lap.

"That could've gone better," she said.

"What is it with this guy? He's got rocks for brains," the Senator said as he shook his head disgustedly.

"That's not all either, Chip. Blackwell is now slightly ahead in the average poll numbers this week."

"We have time, and with your help, Alicia, we're an unstoppable team. We will get our numbers back up there. And when we win the election again next year, my first order of business will be to fire Jed Ferrari and Abby Taylor."

"I'm not going to disagree with you on that one," she responded.

A few hours before dusk, Samantha pulled into Woodrow Cemetery. She had finished up with the girls, and her beautiful vintage dress was hanging in plastic in the backseat. She told Lilly, Stacey, and the other girls she had to cut out early to check on some horses back at the barn, but in reality, what Kelly had told her earlier in the day was gnawing at her.

Sam remembered where Chuck's fake burial had been. She shut her car off, got out, and after walking a short way on the well-groomed lawn in between various tombstones, she found the now empty spot where Chuck's gravestone had been. You could see where the land-scapers had grown new grass; it didn't match exactly with the rest of the lawn.

Right next to it stood a granite stone, two feet wide but not quite a foot off the ground. The front of the stone read "Armond Senior and Rita Lussier" with their birth dates, and in Armond Senior's case, the death date too. She recalled a time when Chuck and Armond had talked about Armond Senior being in World War II briefly on one occasion.

Sam looked to the next stone, which was for Mary Cavalier. Samantha recalled that she had died right after September 11, but she also remembered that Mrs. Cavelier had no husband because he had left her shortly after the family had immigrated to the United States, taking his younger son with him.

She continued looking around. Right behind Mr. and Mrs. Lussier's headstone was one that towered over it. The stone was black and shiny with silverfish stones inside the finish and beautiful, curved beveled edges. Sandblasted in the middle of the stone was the name "Shandi". Below her name was the quote, "Thou Lovers be Lost Love Shall not: And Death Shall Have no Dominion. Born 1969-1988."

Samantha repeated the words on the stone to herself aloud. Her heart sank and her blue eyes welled as she realized that Chuck must have chosen that sentiment.

What if my sister is right, and he somehow believes I am Shandi? she thought.

Tears ran down her cheeks.

"Oh Chuck!" she wailed.

CHAPTER 18

SHANDI'S SONG

MID-MAY 2003

CHUCK RUSHED HOME after the movie and the perturbing conversation he had with Senator Karrington. He truly didn't have time to worry about it and tried to push it from his mind. He had to focus on Garry's big day.

Chuck sat on an old, brown leather couch in the basement next to the band equipment. He kept the old cassette tapes, vinyl albums, and eight tracks in a cabinet to the left. He rummaged through it until he found an old, red shoebox. Chuck pulled it out carefully, as if he were handling a live creature rather than some cardboard, and blew the dust off the best he could. On the outside of the box was Shandi's handwriting. In faded black marker it read "1987-88, Shandi n The Boys".

Even her penmanship could make him yearn for her.

On the aged wooden coffee table in front of him, Chuck set the box down right next to the stack of yellow legal pads on which he was writing his manuscript. He gingerly lifted the lid off of the box to view its contents. Inside were a number of tapes of old recordings from when they were in the process of making the album with the great Bill Arkin. To his surprise, there was also a stack of old Polaroids held together with one of Shandi's pink hair ties. He gently took the tie off to look through the photos.

Chuck grew nostalgic looking through them. A lot of the photos were of them together in the studio, having fun. He took out the ones of just the two of them, holding and kissing each other, and placed them on the table with extra care. One by one, he sorted through the cassette tapes, reading Shandi's meticulously written labels detailing the session and studio name.

He took a pair of old headphones from a hook off the wall and plugged them into the ancient stereo system. He had a few box speakers wired to the system, but he didn't want anyone in the house to hear. He pushed the power button on the system. As it came alive, it made a thumping noise and a small green light came on.

Chuck picked out a random tape, numbered seven, popped it into the cassette tray, and pushed play. It began spooling through the stereo, and sounds he hadn't heard in a long time filled his ears.

Mr. Thorn was standing on the deck of his home overlooking the Wolford City River, drinking some very fine whiskey from a glass. The water below was calm, and his usual bodyguards stood to the left and right of him, far enough away so that his phone conversation was private. He waited a few seconds until Mr. Logan picked up the call.

"Good evening, Mr. Thorn," said Logan. "I was just getting ready to call and give you an update."

"Tell me some good news, son."

"Lots to tell, sir. Operation Kawaii is on point for tomorrow, as scheduled. Our mutual friend will join us for the festivities, as requested. Your yacht, The Swift, is all ready to go for your trip as well, sir."

"What about our two loose ends, Mr. Logan?" Mr. Thorn said coolly.

"We've temporarily lost one of them; he's off the grid. But I am certain, Mr. Thorn, it won't be long now. The other one will be handled by the morning light."

"Loose ends never end well, Mr. Logan. Look what happened to our mutual friend. He left loose ends unattended."

"We certainly won't make that mistake, sir. Speaking of him, Mr. Thorn, you'll be glad to hear I have the van in place, too."

"Excellent, Mr. Logan, excellent. Did you get the CB radios installed with the frequency I requested? Just in case."

"Yes, sir, we did that as well."

"Well then, Mr. Logan, I will let you get to it, and I will catch up with you tomorrow."

The phone call ended. Logan was sitting inside the Hummer with Butch in the passenger's seat. He took out a small glass jar and put a bump of cocaine on the crown of his right hand.

"How much longer do we have to sit here, Mr. Logan?" Butch asked before he could ingest it.

Logan gave him a dirty look, then snorted the mound of white powder into his right nostril.

Something still enthralled Chuck as he listened to the tapes in his basement. He had found the song he was looking for on tape number 12. When it came on, he couldn't believe how beautiful it sounded.

Shandi's unforgettable vocals washed over him like a wave. He listened to every syllable, picturing Shandi singing them in his mind like it was yesterday.

"I made you kneel before me/ It's sad that misery will love company/ I ruined everything, not you/ It's not your fault, I am not what you need."

The hair stood up on the back of Chuck's neck and he was startled when something gently touched his shoulder. He turned quickly, looked upwards, and saw Samantha smiling down at him. He clumsily jumped up, accidentally yanking the headphone cord from the stereo. He quickly took the earphones off and the music blared. Shandi's voice filled the room.

"Baby, angels like you can't go to hell like I can/ I am everything they told me I was/ Hmmm, hmmm, hmmm…."

Chuck was like a thief that just got caught with his hand in the cookie jar. He bent down and pushed the stop button.

What a day Samantha was having. She looked down and saw all the Polaroid photos of Chuck and Shandi on the coffee table. Her eyes welled up with tears. She stepped closer to Chuck, reached down, and picked up one photo, looking at it closely.

Chuck spoke quickly. "Sam, this is not what it looks like. The band playing–"

She interrupted him as tears poured down her cheeks. "You're living in the past, Chuck, and the only reason I am here is because I look like her. But I'm not her!"

" I-I-I know you're not," he stuttered, searching for the words to explain. "I told you that back when we started this thing between us. There's an explanation for this, really."

"I'm not sure I want to hear anymore," she spat, her sadness turning to anger. "I've tried so hard to understand, but I think it's a lost cause."

"Sam!" Chuck exclaimed.

"When were you going to tell me that the man that was responsible for kidnapping my sister was captured? When Chuck?"

"Sam, I was trying to keep you safe from all this stuff, but I was going to tell you everything. In fact–"

She interrupted him again as she put the picture in her hand back onto the table. "Chuck, I think you and I need a break. I can't think straight anymore. After this weekend, I'm going to get my own place." She turned slowly and walked over to the stairs.

"Sam, please, give me a chance to explain all of this. Please, Sam!" Chuck pleaded.

As she reached the top of the stairs, she turned. "Don't call me that anymore. My name is Shalon. It's time to stop playing pretend. I'll be your friend, Chuck, but that's all. I can't go on with these games anymore."

She disappeared through the doorway and Chuck put his head down in despair. He thought about chasing her up the stairs to try to make his case, but he figured it would just make matters worse. He sunk back down into the couch and stared at the pictures on the coffee table.

"Damn you, Chuck!" he yelled at himself. "You're a fucking idiot!"

After a few minutes went by, he grabbed the photos off the table, ejected the tape out of the stereo to give to Bob, picked up the yellow legal pads, and walked upstairs into the kitchen. He listened keenly for any movement upstairs, but it was quiet. Rupert was probably with her, and if Chuck knew anything about the little guy, it was that he could be very intuitive. The pup was likely consoling her. He'd give her some space, then in a few hours, try to go upstairs and make up with her somehow. Chuck knew one thing: he needed Shalon and didn't want to lose her over a grave misunderstanding.

He put the pictures and tape in a brown paper bag to give to Bob before the wedding. He figured Bob would probably appreciate the photos. Chuck didn't need them anymore. He wanted to move on from those days.

Chuck sat down at the breakfast bar to contemplate what to say later. He looked up and saw a fifth of Jack Daniels, still half full, on top of the kitchen cabinet. The fading light coming through the kitchen windows was hitting the bottle just right, illuminating the brown liquid so as to make it seem to glow.

He thought to himself, God, how I'd love to take that down and pour a nice, smooth glass right now. Realistically, though, it wouldn't help and Chuck enjoyed the sober side of himself. He hadn't touched alcohol since the last ferocious night he quarreled with Kelly in the kitchen.

A more positive idea popped into his head. I'll sit here in the kitchen, make some coffee, and finish this damn manuscript for Kenneth. The writing process always helped him to clear the cobwebs from his mind.

After a fresh cup of java, Chuck sat at the bar with his pads and a pen. Thoughts poured from his head and onto the yellow paper like he was possessed. He had been using the true story of what had happened to him and Jed last year with Lonestar, embellishing some of the facts to make it even more thrilling. He was almost finished with the finale, and he recalled that at this time last year, Chuck had been in hiding while Kelly and Lonestar thought they were free to do what they wanted with his family's land.

Chuck shook his head, still in disbelief at the twists and turns of his own life. His pen moved rapidly across the paper until his eyes grew heavy.

CHAPTER 19
FIVE MINUTES TO COUNT

MID-MAY 2003

IT WAS 9:00 p.m. and Elliot Birch was in his moonlit office in the Sky Tower, burning the midnight oil at his desk, engrossed in the messy paperwork spread out over his desk. He was punching the numbers on the big square keys of a calculator and recording the values on paper. Miss Ryder, his secretary, had just gone home for the evening. It had been a late night, but it was not unusual for an ambitious mogul like Elliot.

He loosened his necktie some. He had kept it on just in case any of his business associates rang, which they often did to invite him out for evening drinks in the city. Elliot liked to project a clean, business-like image at all times.

While he reviewed the finances of properties he built through-out the country, he noticed the small light was flashing on his desk phone. An unknown number registered on the caller ID. He was a little edgy recently as his right-hand man was still missing. He picked up the phone.

"Yes, Elliot Birch here." There was silence on the receiving end of the phone followed by heavy breathing. "Hello?"

"Elliot! It's me, Eddie!" said a voice.

Elliot jumped up off his plush leather chair. "Eddie! My God, I have been worried about you, man. Where are you?"

"I've been worried about me, too. I'm down in the parking garage a few rows behind your car."

"Why? Are you OK?"

"I've been better, believe me. Elliot, you're in trouble- the dangerous kind. I don't know if they've been following me. These guys are good."

"Who, Eddie? What happened when you went to the Cavalier Retirement Home?"

"Elliot, come down to the garage and get in my car. I'll explain everything. You've got to pull out of the casino hotel project before it's too late."

Elliot could not believe his ears. In all their years of friendship, he had never heard so much fear in his friend's voice. "OK, Eddie, I'm on my way. Just hang on."

"Watch your back, boss."

Elliot hung up and tapped the gun underneath his suit jacket to make sure it was there and ran out of his office, forgetting to shut the lights off. He quickly locked the outer door with his key as fast as he could, jogged to the elevators, and pushed all three buttons impatiently. The neon green numbers above the doors showed that they were all on the lower floors. Come on, come on, let's go! he thought to himself.

The middle elevator ended up reaching him first. As soon as the doors opened, he leapt inside and pressed the button for the garage. The doors closed and Elliot had an uneasy feeling. He watched intently as the numbers changed and he descended. The bell chimed, announcing he had arrived, and the doors opened up into the low-lit parking garage.

Elliot walked briskly towards his reserved parking spot as he looked around for Eddie. The pristine black automobile was parked, but Eddie wasn't anywhere in sight. Two rows behind his vehicle, his friend's Corolla sat with the engine off. As he looked through the window, he could see that something was undeniably wrong. Eddie's head leaned against the headrest, lifeless and caulked to the right of his shoulder. His mouth hung open and the interior of the vehicle was spattered with blood.

Elliot walked faster, his heart beating through his chest. He remained vigilant, but there was no further movement. Only the distant sounds of cars outside gave any sign of life nearby.

Elliot drew his weapon and held it down in a ready position, like Eddie had taught him, and opened the driver's door with his left hand

"Eddie!" Elliot said, his voice cracking. He reached inside and shook his friend's right shoulder. Eddie's head flopped around, lifeless.

Elliot pulled his hand from Eddie's shoulder and his palm was covered in fresh, warm blood. He then realized that Eddie's nose had been cut off, and it looked like there were several bullet holes in his burly chest.

Elliot quickly stepped back, the horror of the gore washing over him. He tried to scan the area for the culprit, but instead emptied the contents of his stomach onto the cement.

The next morning, roll call was being conducted at the Pocomtuc Prison while the prisoners were still locked in their cells. Most of them had still been sleeping and were less than enthusiastic about being woken.

Inside the specialized unit for protective custody convicts, Officer Henry Millinozzo had made his round. He called the numbers in for verification, and the captain on duty cleared the block to conduct business as usual. Officer Sue Marlo was working with Henry for their shift, as she did five days a week.

The overnight officer they relieved had worked alone, as the prisoners were locked in for the duration. It was his responsibility to do several counts before the end of shift.

Marlo turned on the lights inside the cells from the officers' podium so that Millinozzo could see the inmates clearly, living and breathing inside their assigned cells. Millinozzo was slogging his way down the tier, looking into each cell window and writing down his count in a small notebook. When he got to cell 33, he stopped for a few extra seconds before coming full circle back to the podium.

"Whatcha got, Henry?" Marlo asked with a heavy Boston accent. She was a tiny woman, but a feisty spitfire who didn't take crap from anyone.

"We have 14, Marlo," replied Millinozzo, sounding unsure.

"Fourteen? The overnight officer said we got 15."

"Yeah, I'm pretty sure the inmate in 33 is not in there. Did he go on a court or hospital trip last night or something?"

Marlo was frustrated. "I don't see anything written down about that. I'll just call it in and we'll see what they say." She picked up the phone, dialed the number, and waited for an answer on the other end.

"We got 14," she said to the man in the control room. You could tell by her expression that 14 was not the correct number. "OK, we'll redo the count!" She smashed the phone back into its cradle and gritted her teeth.

"That's not right, is it?" Millinozzo asked.

"No, no it's not. Probably that idiot on overnights! Just do the count over and I'll call the Sergeant just in case."

Henry had a bad feeling as he grabbed a flashlight. He remembered the previous year when his partner had missed a round and an inmate ended up deader than dead in cell block ZX. That partner, consequently, happened to be the same officer who had worked the overnight shift.

Inside the Captain's office, Lieutenant Loya was going through the schedule of events in the prison for the day, preparing to help the shift run as smoothly as possible in a maximum prison. He sat working at a computer diagonal from Captain Chapman, who leaned back with his feet up on his desk.

Chapman was carefully smearing a thick layer of cream cheese onto a plump, warm bagel. He took a huge bite. "Mmmm, yummy." He reached over and grabbed a Frankenstein mug full of piping-hot coffee. He slurped it loudly and then said, "Hey, Gabe, what's taking so long for the count to clear?"

Lieutenant Loya looked at his computer screen. "We're still waiting on block J-7 to clear. Kev, you got a little something on your nose."

The Captain wiped a glob of cream cheese off the tip of his nose with a napkin as he chewed. "It's getting late, Gabe. Call down to J-7 and see what the problem is."

Before he could pick up the phone to dial the block extension, it rang.

"Lieutenant Loya here," he answered.

It was the block Sergeant for J-7, Dennis Venkman.

"Lieutenant, we have a problem!" he said, panicked.

"Dennis, take a breath, and then tell me what's going on down there," said Loya. He listened for Venkman's explanation and then furrowed his brow.

"Gabe, what's happening down there?" Chapman asked impatiently.

"Hang on, Dennis," Loya said and put his hand over the receiver. "They're missing the inmate in cell 33, and there's no record of the inmate being out on any kind of trip."

"What?! Who's the inmate?"

"Silus Kobol."

"Who in the fuck worked that block on the overnight?"

"Take one guess, Kevin!"

"Rick Guardian."

Loya nodded his head. Chapman took his feet off the desk, and perhaps for the first time in his career, grabbed the bill of his backward uniform baseball cap and turned it to face the proper way.

"Gabe, call control. Have them lock down the prison 'til further notice while I inform the superintendent. Then get down to that block and find out what's going on and where that inmate is!"

"On it, Kev," Loya said as he dialed the number.

"Oh and Gabe, find that asshole, Guardian. Have the guys in control get him on the phone, now!"

CHAPTER 20

WHITE WEDDING

MID-MAY 2003

CHUCK WAS IN block ZX with Jed. Every morning, Chuck did the first inmate count of their shift and Jed would do the second one in the early afternoon. Jed turned on all the cell lights in the block so that his partner was able to see clearly inside them. Chuck began his count, stopping at every single cell door and looking in the windows carefully. There were two inmates inside almost every cell.

As he walked down the tiled floor that their runners kept nice and shiny, Chuck saw that a dirty pair of tattered Nike high-top sneakers sat on the floor next to the door of cell number 10. He grew angry because he had told the inmate in that cell repeatedly the prior week not to leave his shoes outside his door.

The inmate was a younger Hispanic man named Noel Figg who was extremely hard-headed. Chuck wanted to make an example out of him. He was ninety percent sure he could get Figg to come around, but today the young convict was not going to like him.

Chuck approached his cell door, purposely picking up the pace to gain enough momentum. He swung his right leg hard and fast, striking the pair of sneakers as if he were attempting a field goal. The shoes went sailing across the tier and hit the shower doors at the very end of the block.

"Damn you to hell, Figg! I told you not to leave your disgusting sneakers out on our nice, clean tier!"

Jed put his hand on his forehead and burst into laughter.

Chuck looked into the cell window to address Figg, but his view was obscured by inmate scrubs that had been cut and then tied around the light fixture built into the wall. He grabbed his long, black flashlight and beamed the light inside the cell as he kicked the bottom of the door.

"Figg!" Chuck called. "Figg! It's count time!"

At first, Chuck saw no one inside the cell. When he flashed the light over to the right of the confined space, he was startled to see a body hanging from one of the metal hooks welded into the wall that was intended for a coat. Peering more closely, he could see that a bedsheet had been tied up like a rope.

"Holy fuck!" Chuck shouted.

"What's wrong, Chuck?" Jed yelled back.

Chuck beamed the flashlight directly at the lifeless man's head. The man's eyes were bulging out of his skull and a bulbous tongue hung out of his purple face. It was at that moment that Chuck realized the man was not Noel Figg.

"Hey! It's not Figg," Chuck called. "It's Silus Kobol. He hung himself!"

Suddenly, Chuck woke from his dream to the smell emanating from the blue ceramic mug of freshly-brewed coffee Uncle Armond was holding under his nose.

"Good morning, Meathead," said Armond. "Did you forget we had a wedding to go to today?"

Chuck sat up slowly and took the cup of coffee from his uncle who was already proudly dressed in his tux. "Ah no, I must have fallen asleep on the couch last night. I was up late working on the new manuscript for Kenny."

"Is that what that is in the kitchen? I saw a package on the counter that looked like it was ready to be mailed out."

"That's it, Arm. It's finished," said Chuck. He looked at the clock in the living room. "Shit! I gotta get ready. Where's Sam?"

"She left already to meet the girls. She told me to wake you up. Everything OK with you two?"

Chuck walked into the kitchen to put his cup on the counter and saw Uncle Richard was also already dressed for the event.

"Yeah, everything's fine, Unc. I just wanted to finish this script, that's all."

Armond knew better, but he didn't press. "Okay."

"Do you want us to wait for you, Chuck? We can all drive together," said Uncle Richard.

"No, that's OK. You guys go on without me. I'll be right behind you. It shouldn't take me long to get ready." Chuck raced upstairs to the bedroom.

Jed was at Abby's townhouse, getting ready for Gary and Lilly's wedding. He walked out of the bathroom as Abby was getting the contents of her purse together. She looked over at him, a bit astonished.

"Whoa! You clean up nice, Mr. Ferrari," said Abby.

"You look amazing too, Abb."

"Do you think anyone will say anything about us showing up to the wedding together in the same vehicle?"

"I don't think so."

"How would it be if we danced together for a song or two?"

Jed paused. "I think that will still be fine. There should be nothing wrong with that."

"OK, I'm going to hold you to it."

Jed's cell phone rang from the nightstand next to the bed. She watched him as he walked over and picked it up. "I have to take this."

She nodded. In their line of work, there never was a true day off.

"Vince, what's going on pal?" Jed answered. It had to be important if he was calling him on a Saturday.

"Yeah, Jed, sorry to be calling you like this on a weekend, but I thought you'd want to know about this news right away."

"I was just getting ready to leave for a wedding, but what's going on?"

"I'm sorry. You know Mr. Birch, of course, and the missing person report he filed on his head security guy?"

"Yes, I remember that. Has there been a development?"

"You could say that. I am actually standing outside of Birch's office right now. Another detective is taking his statement."

"About what?" Jed asked, his curiosity piqued.

"He found the employee dead in his car, parked in the garage right in the SkyTower. He was shot several times in the chest and his nose was…removed."

"Great Caesar's ghost, Vincent! Do we know who it was?"

"No, but the shooting is akin to the killings done at Indians Leap and that of Detective Miller…with the exception of the nose injury, of course."

"Could that have been some kind of message?"

"That was my thought as well."

Abby was listening intently to the conversation and she had a bad feeling about it.

"How is Mr. Birch doing?" Jed asked. Abby's ears perked up when she heard his name, especially because he never called her back to tell her if he found anything out about the shareholders.

"He's pretty shaken up. Understandable, considering he is the one that found his pal. I should know more soon. There's no need for you to miss the wedding over this. I'm on top of it. But there is one other issue that I should tell you about."

"OK, what other issue, Vince?"

"This morning we got an alert that an inmate may have escaped from the Pocomtuc prison."

"What? Who?"

"All city lines are being manned, and it may be the inmate is still hiding somewhere inside the facility. My man and I are in constant contact and awaiting more details on this."

"Who's the inmate, Vince?"

"Silus Kobol."

Abby observed Jed's shocked expression as he held the phone to his ear in silence for a few seconds.

"Jed, are you still there?" asked Vince.

"This changes things immensely. The wedding is my best friend's brother's, but maybe I should meet up with you somewhere."

"Mr. Ferrari, there's nothing you can do that's not already being done. I'll stay in touch via text. I'll call if something crazy comes up."

Abby bounced on her heels with impatience as she waited for Jed to fill her in. She wanted a cigarette badly.

"OK, Vince. Be sure to send officers to Wolford City Harbor."

"Already done, Jed. I have people everywhere just in case this is a legitimate escape. This guy escaped once. It won't happen again."

"Do me a favor, Vince. Send one or two of your men to the area of the Starboard Yacht Club, too."

"Isn't that where the governor and Chip Karrington keep their boats?"

"It is. You never know. You can't be too careful."

"You're not worried if we get any blowback for doing that?"

"No, not at all. We have to cover all our bases, no matter what."

The young detective wondered if Jed thought that was how Kobol had escaped the previous year, but what politician in their right mind would harbor a fugitive and assist in an escape?

Jed hung up the phone, perplexed, and filled Abby in. He didn't want to ruin the Barreto family's day, but how could he keep this information from Chuck?

"Why would Kobol escape when he had a good chance of getting off in court tomorrow?" Abby wondered aloud.

"That's a great question, Abb. I cannot figure it out. None of it makes any sense to me."

"Jed, would you mind if I run to the Sky Tower to check in with Mr. Birch and then meet you at the reception? Elliot's a tight-lipped kind of guy, but I have a rapport with him. Maybe he would tell me something more than he has told others."

Jed couldn't help but be a little jealous, thinking that maybe she had a thing for Birch, but he didn't let on.

"No problem. Good idea, Abb. I will meet you at the church or reception, depending on how quickly you get done."

She thought he looked a bit annoyed.

"Hey, I've been looking forward to going to this wedding with you. You know, being out in public on a kind of a date, instead of the two of us sneaking around all the time."

She drew closer and wrapped her arms around Jed, kissing him sensually. "I'll be quick. Don't worry."

Chuck ran down the stairs in his tux, his hair tied neatly in a ponytail for the event. He was the best man, after all. He had to look as presentable as possible, having forgotten to get a haircut. He grabbed his speech off the counter from its place next to his manuscript. Sitting next to it was the locking mechanism for the Charger that he still hadn't installed. On the barstool hung his NASA jacket.

Damn, he thought, no time to mail out the manuscript. I'll do it tomorrow on the way to watch that piece of shit Kobol lose in court, and lose he will- royally!

His cell phone began to ring and he pulled it out of his pocket. "Hey, Ma!"

"Chuck, where are you?" she asked.

"I'm on my way. I'll be there before the ceremony. Don't worry, Mom."

She laughed. "You better be!"

"I gotta get moving. Anything you need before I get there?"

"Well… I felt a need to tell you this. I apologize for letting you know at the last minute. I received a phone call a few days ago from

Kelly and Samantha's father, Vic. He's here, visiting. He wants to sit down with you and Samantha, and I know the timing is bad, Chuck, but really, he is a nice man, I believe."

"OK, Mom, how could I say no?"

"I also invited him to the wedding, since he's in town, but he didn't tell me whether or not he'd come."

Boy, Chuck had his hands full now. Samantha was already upset and now this. When it rains it pours, he thought. What more could go wrong?

"Well, I won't keep you. I just wanted to let you know. I'll see you soon."

Chuck was about to head for the door when he heard Rupert bark from the living room. The dog's arthritis was getting worse, and he limped into the kitchen, his tail wagging and his bulging eyes pleading with him not to go.

Chuck crouched down and patted him on the head.

"It's okay, little man. I'll be back," Chuck told him. Rupert continued barking. "Okay, okay, buddy. Don't worry. The boys are here and they'll be in to feed you and take you out for a walk."

Chuck walked over to a shelf, reached into a large glass jar full of treats, and handed one to the pup. Rupert devoured it and Chuck pet him again, then grabbed the paper bag with the photos and music tapes and his best man speech, and walked to the front door.

On the front porch, Chuck spotted Mitch and Dave hooking a trailer to one of the four wheelers.

"Hey! Look at you, Rockstar," Mitch called out to him. They chuckled.

"You look like James Bond, dude!" said Dave.

"Very funny, Dave. Hey guys, can you keep checking on Rupee today? He seems a little out of sorts."

"Yeah, we will, dude. I'll have Candie take him to the barn with her."

"Perfect, thanks," said Chuck as he walked towards the Jeep.

"Hey, Rockstar, what about the blue beast? How cool would that be?" Mitch asked.

"Yeah, you know what? Why not, Mitchell, great idea."

"What about the passenger door?" Dave asked.

"Ah, it's fastened up pretty good with a bungee. It should be alright."

Abby rode the elevator to the top floor of the SkyTower to see Elliot Birch. The door opened and she stepped out and walked down the long hallway to Birch's main office door. Inside, the secretary was sitting at her desk on the phone. Abby sat down in one of the artsy chairs off to the right and checked her watch. She wanted to keep this short and get back to Jed.

The secretary finally hung up the phone and Abby stood.

"Yes, may I help you?" she asked.

"Hi, I'm Abby Taylor, the assistant attorney general."

"That's right, of course, Miss Taylor. What can I do for you?"

"I was hoping to speak with Mr Birch, if he's in."

The secretary was hesitant to answer. "Mmmm, let me see if he's taking visitors. He's had a hectic morning." She was unsure how much Abby knew about the morning's events, though she assumed she would be privy. "Mr. Birch, there's a Miss Taylor here to see you."

A long silence followed, then the speaker came on. "Send her in, Miss Ryder."

Abby noticed that he didn't sound like his usual cocky self.

Miss Ryder gestured for her to head in. Abby thanked her and walked into Birch's office. Elliot was slumped behind the desk without his suit jacket or tie, and a few buttons were undone on his crisp, white dress shirt. It was atypical for him to not be put together. On top of the desk sat a half-full bottle of bourbon. He swilled the crystal glass in his hand and then downed some of it and looked up at her.

"Why, Miss Taylor, you didn't need to get all dolled up like that just to come and see me," he said hoarsely. He was making an attempt at his usual charm, but it was like someone had sucked half the life out of him.

Abby decided it would be appropriate to change her planned approach with him under the circumstances and softened. "Oh, this? I'm actually on my way to a wedding. I heard what happened and wanted to stop by quickly."

"Oh. I'm fine, Miss Taylor. There was no need to stop by. Just another day at the office," he said as he poured himself another glass. "Would you like one? Get your party started early."

"No thanks, Elliott."

"Right, no drinking and driving for the squared-away AG's assistant."

"What happened, Elliot?" Abby asked, getting straight to the point.

"My one and only security man was following a lead he had on those shareholders you had inquired about. As you know, he disappeared for a bit, then showed up this morning in the garage. He was shot to death in his car."

"My God. What was he doing in the garage? And you need to get yourself some protection if he was your only security."

230

Strapped in a holster on Elliot's back was a small Glock. He carefully reached around, pulled it out, and placed it on the desk next to his bottle. "That's my security right there, Miss Taylor."

Father Goslin's thunderous vocals were bouncing off the high ceiling as Jed sat in a middle pew at Saint John the Baptist Church with a hundred other guests. He was lost deep in his thoughts about Silus Kobol's whereabouts when his phone buzzed in his pocket.

"Chuck, the ring, young man," said Father Goslin. Chuck had been momentarily distracted by watching Jed abruptly leave his seat, walk down the side aisle, and out of the door. He fumbled in his pocket, pulled out the sparkly diamond, and handed it over to Gary.

Outside, Jed stood in the sunshine on the cement steps overlooking a side-street lined with cars as he answered a call from Detective Giovanni. He had been impatiently waiting for an update about Kobol.

"Hey Vince," Jed said anxiously. "Please tell me you have some good news for me."

"Uhhh…," he hesitated. "Unfortunately, Mr Ferrari, it's not so good."

Jed's blood pressure rose and he could feel his face turning red. "What? Vince, what's wrong?"

"I don't want to ruin your day, sir. Just rest assured, we have men swarming the surrounding towns of the prison. There was another incident. A corrections officer that works the overnight shift in the J-7 block that Kobol was housed in…."

Jed took a deep breath, impatient with how long it was taking the detective to get to the point. "Yes?"

"He was found dead on the side of the road in a ditch inside his car on Route 3."

"You can't be serious."

"I'm afraid I am Mr. Ferrari."

"How?"

"Shot, the same way as the others. Same caliber as Miller and Chellis."

"I should probably come in."

"Jed, we're handling it. There's nothing more you can do. I'm down at the docks in the city right now with my men, and we're not going to miss a trick."

"Every boat, Vince. Check every single god-damned boat."

"Yes. Jed, I won't let this bastard slip away again."

"OK, Vince, keep me updated."

"Yes sir, will do."

Abby had a bad feeling about Elliot Birch after leaving his office. The man didn't trust her enough to share what his next move would be. She took the elevator down a few floors and walked briskly to Kelly Ann Texeira's office, hoping she wouldn't be there. It was the weekend so she thought it unlikely, but the lobby door was – to her surprise – unlocked.

Abby walked in and saw no one sitting at the secretary's desk.

"Hello? Anyone here?" she shouted.

"Yes, I'm back here. Come on in," Kelly responded. Abby followed her voice to an office. "Miss Taylor! What are you doing here on this bright Saturday?"

"You heard what happened to Elliot's man in the parking garage this morning?" Abby asked, skipping the courtesy of a greeting.

"I did," she said haughtily. "Don't tell me you think I had something to do with that, too."

"No, no, of course not. I was just wondering if you could go up-stairs and check on Mr. Birch before you leave today. He doesn't seem quite right, and he doesn't trust me enough to tell me."

"Hmmm, can you blame him for that?" Abby looked bashful enough for Kelly to tone down the sarcasm a bit. "Well now, you have a type, dontcha?"

Abby looked aghast. "Who, me? Oh no, it's not like that at all, I just–"

"Okie-dokie, Miss Taylor," Kelly held up her hands in faux surren-der. "I was just teasing, mostly. I love Elliot. He's a great guy. Actually I was just getting ready to go on up there to see how he was getting by."

"Thanks. Well, I should go then. I'm late for a wedding."

"Oh, isn't that nice. Anyone I know?" she asked pointedly.

"Gary Barreto, but I'm assuming you already knew that."

"Oh yeah, my sister's one of the bridesmaids."

"Oh… that's nice," said Abby. The conversation had quickly grown awkward and she was unsure of what to say.

Mr. Logan was with Butch Gro and two other associates in the Hummer, speeding through the back roads of Woodrow on their way to some undisclosed destination. Sir Lawrence and Tiny Felix were sitting in the back and Butch was riding shotgun. Logan had the pedal to the metal. His left hand was on the top of the steering wheel and he glanced at the clock.

"How we lookin' on time, Cowboy?" asked Felix, a short, stocky man.

"We are looking good, Tiny. Let's just pray those phone numbers Jemel gave me before he betrayed us are still good."

"Do you think he would have told anyone about us, Mr Logan?"

"I really doubt it. He's running scared out there somewhere. We'll catch up with him soon. Speaking of, keep it down boys. It's time to call Sergeant Gill." He grabbed a cell phone from the middle console, opened it, and pressed a number. He put the device to his right ear and it rang seven times. It was about to go to voicemail when the wounded veteran answered from a boat on the river in Wolford City.

"Goodday, Mr Logan," he said as he stood on the stern.

"How's Operation Kawaii, Gill?" asked Logan.

"I'm waiting on you. Just give me the word. And it better be soon because it's getting hairy out here."

"What do you mean by that, Gill?"

Gill looked out at the docks. "I can see cops scattered around, checking boats that are docked. There's also a police boat searching for an inmate that escaped Pocomtuc. Just our luck I guess. That's all the chatter I've heard on the scanner all morning."

"It won't be long now, Gill, hang in there. The word will be given soon," said Logan as he continued to speedily maneuver his way through the streets.

"Try to make it even sooner."

As they ended their conversation, Butch shouted, "Look out, Mr Logan!"

A red Jeep pulled out of a side road. Logan's lightning-fast reflexes kicked in and he steered around it, whizzing past as he honked his horn.

Inside the rented cherry-red Jeep was Vic Texeira and Chance.

"What a schmuck!" Vic said.

"Yep," said Chance, shaking his head. "Massholes, they call 'em. People are in such a rush to go nowhere out here."

234

"What's the next street?"

Chance was holding a piece of paper on which the desk clerk had written directions from the Holiday Inn.

"The next set of lights, Vic, take a right," said Chance.

They were on their way to Gary and Lilly Barreto's wedding reception.

A white Chevy van sat adjacent to the entrance to Gussy's Pitts. Large magnets on either side read, "O'Donnell's Dry Cleaning Service". Buddy, a large man in his twenties with a long red beard, sat in the driver's seat. In the vehicle's rear were two much more slender men of the same age, fully armed with weapons that were hot and ready to go. In the passenger seat, wearing a baggy brown t-shirt, jeans, a pair of old Reebok sneakers, and a pair of cheap, oversized sunglasses was none other than Silus Sin Kobol.

Even if they had guessed Silus' usual clothing size, the digs still would have been loose on him because of the weight he had lost in prison. He was certainly in no position to complain; he was just grateful to be out. He desperately wanted to get out of dodge before he was captured again. Silus had one more debt to pay before that was possible.

While he waited for an important phone call, he reminisced back to the day he first set foot on Gussy's Pitts. He had met up with Chip Karrington a year ago to try to persuade him to get Rita Barreto to sell the land that was gifted to Gary, Stacey, and Chuck. He still couldn't understand why his boss, Mr. Thorn, was so hell-bent on getting his hands on it.

A little red cell phone rang from a tray in the middle of the dashboard.

"Pick it up, Silus. That's for you," said Buddy.

Silus reached for the phone and saw that the caller ID read 'Unknown'.

"Hello," he answered, tentatively.

"Silus, my boy!" said Mr. Thorn laughing, putting Silus at ease. "So nice to hear your voice as a free man."

"Thank you for getting me out of that hell-hole, Mr. Thorn. I am grateful, sir."

"Silus…I know I was tough on you a few months ago, but that's only because I raised you like you were my own son. Today I ask you to complete one more task, and then you will live the highlife in the tropics."

Silus felt like crying. "Yes, sir." At this point, he'd do anything for the man.

"After this is over, my boy, you'll join me on my yacht. She's all ready to go."

"You're here, sir?"

"Indeed, I am. I am at the house right now. We'll sail to the Connecticut airport. I've had a fake passport made for you, and you will fly out with our man, Mr. McQueen, to the amazing Galápagos Islands."

"Are you going as well, sir?"

"No. After we drop you off, I'm sailing to Washington. Maybe in a month or so I'll drop in to see how you're doing."

"I can't thank you enough, Mr. Thorn. So why am I at Gussy's Pitts, sir? What is the final task?"

"Yes, I was just about to get to that. We are setting a trap for Chuck Barreto. You are going to lure him into Wolford City. Once he's there, our men will take over and you will be on your way to paradise."

"How am I going to do that, sir?"

"Do you see the CB radio inside the van?"

Silus had first noticed the device when he had been picked up on route three. "Yes, I see it, Mr. Thorn."

"When our men are ready, you are going to contact Mr. Barreto on it. He has one in his car."

Silus was starting to get a clearer picture of their plan. "Yes, I remember that, sir." That's something he didn't forget,as it was a unique method of communication for the times.

It was a gorgeous day, especially for a wedding. The church ceremony had wrapped up and the guests drove over to the magnificent Vanished Valley for the festivities. Large, round tables covered all but the dance floor and tall bouquets of flowers adorned each. White drapery hung from wall to wall creating a romantic atmosphere. Rita Barreto would have nothing but the best for her son.

Before they had announced the wedding party, Chuck had snuck over to the back entrance to say hello to his old bandmates, Bob, Harry and Dan. He also met the new lead singer, Madeline Star. She was a stunning young lady, but by no means measured up to Shandi as far as Chuck was concerned. He had given Bob the tape of the song he had asked for, as well as old photos of the band. Bob thanked him, and then Chuck ran to the back of the hall to be announced with the rest of the wedding party.

Jed saw Abby walking in and he immediately got up to talk with her off to the side, even though Chuck was in the middle of giving his best man speech to the attentive crowd. He didn't feel right about keeping all this information from Chuck, but Abby reassured him that he was making the right choice. She told him that there was no need for them to leave as of yet, unless something more serious developed.

Jed reluctantly trusted her instincts for the time being, and their conversation concluded just as Chuck was wrapping up.

"Here's to my little brother and a great guy, and his beautiful new wife, Lilly, who will live out their days as one!"

Everyone stood and applauded the speech, some dinging their dinner glasses for Gary and Lilly to kiss, which they obliged. The cheering and applause continued, and Chuck felt guilty because all he wanted to do was leave his table to try to talk with Samantha. The applause concluded and Bob took over the microphone.

As the band was getting started, Chuck thought to himself, The hell with it! I am going to talk with her now. He got up from his chair and noticed Samantha was gone from her seat. As he looked urgently around the room, it reminded him of the first time he thought he saw her at Chip Karrington's campaign rally. Chuck calmed down a little when he saw her by the bar. He headed towards her but was stopped by one of Gary's best friends, Larry Ellis. Chuck had known him since they were kids.

"Hey Chuck, fantastic speech! You killed it. Must be because you're a writer now, huh?" said Larry.

"Too kind. Thanks, Larry," Chuck said briefly, keeping his eyes on Samantha. He thought his clipped answer would keep the conversation short, but Larry continued talking as the band began playing and people headed out onto the dance floor. Chuck was happy for Bob and the boys; they deserved another run at success.

The band played an old classic tune and Madeline's vocals were commanding.

"Talk about the high cost of lovin'/ I think I hear freedom drummin' and it seems/ Give me your heart and I'll give you the stars/ Yeah right, maybe in your dreams," she sang.

While Chuck was trying to figure out how he was going to escape from Larry, he was also thinking about how the first song they had ever played with Shandi at the old skating rink was a David Lee Roth tune.

"Mmm-mmm! They're really good, Chuck, huh?" said Larry, breaking Chuck's thoughts. Chuck nodded in agreement and then Larry continued. "Man, I really love the television show based on your book, especially the main character."

Chuck was having a hard time paying attention as the band played on.

"Yeah, heat wave blast, kids are screaming/ Pavements hot, sidewalks steaming…"

Chuck looked at Larry. "Oh, yeah thanks, Larry."

"Was some of that character based on you?"

"Aaaah…."

Gary walked up to the two of them at that moment and Larry gave his friend a hug of congratulations. Chuck watched Samantha, who had left the bar and was talking with some of the other guests near the wedding cake.

"Hey Gary, shouldn't you be with your new wifey?" Larry asked.

Chuck heard the comment and chimed in. "Yeah, the band is probably going to have you two up for a dance soon."

"Yeah, I will," said Gary. "Larry, I just wanted to steal my brother for a minute, if you don't mind."

"No, not at all. I'll see you in a bit," said Larry. He shook Gary's hand before walking over to the bar.

The band then finished the song and Bob said, "Well alright, folks! Not your typical wedding song but we wanted to kick this off right." The crowd cheered.

"Thank you, thank you!" said Madeline. "Let's get this party started. Here's a little one I think everyone knows!"

The music started up again and more guests made their way to the dance floor.

"Don't go breaking my heart," Bob sang.

"I couldn't if I tried," Madeline replied.

"Oh, honey, if I get restless…"

"Baby, you're not that kind."

"Don't go breaking my heart."

"Wow bro," said Gary. "I forgot how good they were!"

"Yep, I gotta hand it to Bob. They can still play!"

"No doubt."

Chuck knew his brother didn't want to talk to him privately about the band. He saw him biting his nails and twitching. "What's up, bro? Everything OK?"

"Yeah, everything's fine. I just wanted to tell you what an impressive speech you gave. Thank you for that and everything else. The band, the open bar, this place…." Gary's eyes started to tear up.

"Yeah, yeah, you got it, brother. It's all good."

Gary wiped his eyes. "Ah, not everything."

"What do you mean?" Chuck asked.

"I feel awful asking you this."

"It's OK, Gary. You know you can ask me anything."

"Me and Lilly, well… we were just wondering if you could just buy us out of our portion of land at Gussy's Pitts."

Chuck paused. "What? Why?"

"Well…"

Before Gary could answer, Stacey joined them, smiling. "Hey, brothers! I am still the best looking one out of all of us."

Chuck replied wisely. "Hands down, sis!"

She hugged Gary and then Bob announced it was time for Gary and Lilly to come out onto the dance floor for their song. Chuck was left baffled by Gary's question.

Gary walked to the dance floor and met Lilly in the middle. They embraced and the song began.

"My love/ There's only you in my life/ The only thing that's bright/ My first love/ You're every breath that I make/ and I/ I-I-I-I…"

Stacey looked at Chuck, wondering how he felt about the singer taking Shandi's place in the band.

Chuck met her eyes. "She's good, Stace. No Shandi, but really damn good."

"I'm glad you said it first. Listen, I don't like butting into your personal relationships, but…"

"Sure you do!" Chuck smiled at her.

Stacey made a face. "Listen, I'm a little worried about Samantha. Did you two have a fight or something?"

"Yeah, I screwed up."

"Chuck, whatever happened, I'm sure you can fix it. I haven't seen you this happy in a long time. And, my God, Chuck- everyone just loves her… even our mother!"

"Even you?"

"Especially me! I'll admit I was skeptical because of the way you got together. But let me tell ya, the jury is in and so is she when it comes to our family's circle of trust."

"Message received, Stace. I'll see what I can do."

"That's a good brother," she smiled and patted his shoulder. "So what was that all about with Gary?"

Silus and his new associates were still sitting in the van awaiting further instructions from Mr. Logan. Silus was growing more anxious about how the scenario would actually play out for him.

"Excuse me," he said to Buddy. "What if we run into a roadblock going into the city?"

"The Cowboy assured me that's already been handled. He had obtained a detailed list of checkpoints from a CO."

Silus had a feeling he knew who that could be. "Was it Guardian?"

"Yeah, I think that's the pig."

"Are you boys sure that he'd be a reliable source?"

"I don't know, man," said Buddy, irritated. "Ask your boy Logan!"

"Don't you work for him, too?" Silus asked.

"Nah, man. We were hired out, just for this specific job, but after this goes according to plan, we'll be given the option to join up full time. Ya know what I mean, jelly bean?" he said cockily.

"Sure," said Silus.

He was not so sure.

At the far end of the mighty bridge that crossed over the river that flowed into Wolford City sat an unmarked, dark blue Ford with "Department of Corrections" lettering on the sides. It had seen better days. A couple of wooden horses blocked the lane leading out of Woodrow. Two of Pocomtuc Prison's finest officers, Chris Wayne and Betty Mills, were at the checkpoint that had been set up to look for Kobol.

Betty was checking the vehicles, then giving Chris the okay to move the roadblock for them to cross over the bridge and into the city. Thankfully for the officers, the traffic was light that day. No one was in a rush and there were more vehicles on the other side coming in than going out.

Chris walked over to Betty. "Hey, I just got a call from the Woodrow Police Department. Officer Niel Reeves told me they're gonna send one of their officers to give us a hand."

"Cool. I guess there must not be much happening over there, today. I doubt this Kobol guy would try getting through here, though. That would be moronic."

"Yeah, he's probably hiding out in the woods somewhere off the highway near where they found Guardian in his car, like a rat."

"What about that guy?" said Betty, disgusted. "You think Rick helped Kobol escape, or what?"

"If you do the math… I think the conclusion is yes, definitely."

"Then the question is, who shot Rick and left him for dead?"

He shrugged. "I don't know about that one, Betty."

They continued talking and a car pulled up. They looked to see who it was.

"Hey, that's not a police cruiser," said Betty.

"No," said Chris. "It looks like one of ours."

"Why would they send a replacement here this early? We're not due to be relieved until 3:30."

"I don't know. Maybe they found the inmate," Chris suggested.

"No, they would have called us over the radio if they did."

Two corrections officers got out of the car. The driver was short and stocky with a head of blond hair. Veins bulged from underneath his uniformed collar.

"Hey there! I'm officer Souza. We came from the medium prison next door to you guys to relieve you. Your Captain wants you both to go back to your prison right away," he said energetically.

Betty was confused. "Captain Chapman?"

"Yep, that's the one."

"Did he say why? Did someone find the escaped inmate?"

"We have heard nothing about him being found and your captain didn't tell us why. We were just sent here to relieve you both."

"OK, Chris, I guess we're going back then," said Betty. "Oh, fellas, before we go. The Woodrow Police are sending another cruiser here to help out."

"We'll keep an eye out for them," said Souza as the two baffled officers walked towards their vehicle. "Oh, I almost forgot, guys. I need your equipment. We only have temporary cubits from your facility to exchange with."

Though Betty and Chris were not used to exchanging from the prison facility next-door to them, that was the ordinary procedure for the officers at Pocomtuc. They figured it must be legit because of the unusual circumstances.

Chris handed them his small nickel-plated, rectangular pieces of metal that were used to bring back to the control room to account for their equipment. Souza and his partner, Carlton, fastened their security equipment to their utility belts as a couple of vehicles pulled up to the bridge.

"I almost forgot, you boys will need this," said Betty. She handed Officer Souza Silus Kobol's photograph for reference. "Have a good one and stay safe."

After Betty and Chris' vehicle was out of sight and Souza was finished looking inside the vehicles, Carlton walked over to him. "OK Matt, let's get the hell out of here!"

Officer Souza was really Matt Helfer, and his partner, Carlton, was really known in Thorn's organization as Wilson.

"We were all set until those CO's told us a policeman could be coming here. Now we have to stay put!" said Helfer.

"What happens if they do end up sending someone? And how long do you think it will take before they find out we're not real COs?"

"It will take them a half hour to get back… I figure maybe another fifteen to twenty minutes to find out that the prison next door never sent anyone to have them relieved. Then they'll call the local PD to send someone here to see who the fuck we are. So, I'd say there's forty-five minutes to an hour for The Cowboy and Kobol to execute their plans. And if a cop shows up before then…" Helfer mimed a slit across the neck.

CHAPTER 21
THE HOUR OF SILUS SIN ROBOL

MID-MAY 2003

THE BAND HAD finished the traditional wedding party songs and was getting everyone else out onto the floor to join in. Most of the tunes were from the eighties and Chuck was bobbing his head along, intermittently interrupted by old friends and relatives who wanted to discuss his successes in writing.

"Come on all you lovebirds!" Bob called out. "Here's one for ya!"

"We're running with shadows of the night/ So baby, take my hand, it'll be alright/ Surrender all your dreams to me tonight!" Madeline crooned. Harry hit the drums just as Chuck remembered, and then couples rushed out onto the floor and embraced.

Everyone, that is, except for Chuck and Samantha. He was really feeling like shit.

Chuck couldn't believe it when he saw Jed and Abby in the crowd that swayed to the beat slowly as the strobe lights washed over them. As he continued scanning the dance floor, he noticed Stacey was with a tall, slender blond. Chuck had never seen him before and wondered who he could be. As if she could feel his eyes, Stacey turned around and nodded her head towards Samantha.

Chuck had lost sight of her when he was talking to everyone, but he spotted her over at her assigned table talking with his mother. He took a breath of courage and began walking over to them, unsure of how Samantha would receive his presence and wondering when Vic would arrive. There was no way that man would blend into a crowd, and there had been no sign of him as of yet.

Chuck reached the table and smiled.

"There's my son!" exclaimed Rita. "Isn't everything just great today, Chuck?"

"Everything's perfect, Mom. It couldn't be better, really."

"Come here, you two," she said to Chuck and Samantha. She stood and hugged them both. "Now go get out there on the dance floor!"

Samantha gently took Chuck's hand into hers. "Okay, Rita."

Chuck didn't think he'd ever been so thankful to his mother. It was a relief to feel the touch of Samantha's delicate fingers again.

They found an open area on the floor and embraced, which felt even better, but also awkward at the same time. His heart melted as he looked into her light-blue eyes.

She broke the silence. "What?"

"Nothing, I'm sorry. I have to confess, I actually was coming over to ask you for one last dance. I mean friends can still dance, right?" he said in an attempt to lighten the mood.

"It's fine," she said shortly.

He tried to think of something more to say. "Did you know that Vic might be stopping by the reception?"

"I knew he was in town. Your mom just told me that he had called her a while ago and she gave him an invitation. Vic's here for the weekend to see my sister."

Chuck was contemplating how to tell her that he didn't want it to end between them.

"What do we tell Vic about us?"

"I'm not sure, Chuck," she said, shaking her head slightly.

He remembered a reference that was told to him not so long ago. "You know, Shalon, the Chinese have a saying."

"Oh yeah?" she said dryly. "What's that?"

"I saved your life last year, so…. I'm responsible for you forever."

Her demeanor finally shifted as they continued dancing. "I think I actually have Rupert to thank. And you must have gotten that saying from my dear sister, didn't ya?" The look on his face told her the answer. "We heard those old sayings from Vic growing up."

It was now or never; he needed a more direct approach. "I'm crazy about you and I don't want to lose you."

"Well, for now you will be."

Even though he had tried to prepare himself for the worst, his heart sank. "Why, Sam?"

"Because the band wants you up on stage right now." Chuck had been so consumed with talking to her that he didn't even hear Bob calling him.

"Chuck Barreto, I ask again. Can you please come up on stage?" said Bob.

Chuck was frozen. He couldn't believe Bob was doing this to him. Everyone was cheering for him to cooperate.

Shalon broke his trance. "Chuck! Go ahead, go up. We'll talk after."

That seemed reassuring and gave him some hope that he had a second chance with her.

Chuck had pep in his step as he wandered up on stage, everyone still clapping and hollering at him. It felt strange being on a stage with his old buddies after more than a decade..

Bob covered the microphone with the palm of his hand so no one else could hear them. "Come on, buddy, play a song with us for old times sake?"

"I don't know if I can remember how, Bob."

Bob smiled. "Like riding a bike broheim! Gene, give this man a guitar!"

Chuck had met the new guitar player earlier. "I'm not so sure I'm in your class."

"That's not what I heard, Chuck," Gene replied.

He had an extra guitar next to the amplifier that was ready to go. Chuck swung the strap over his shoulder and dawned the guitar. He had to admit it felt damn good, but it was bittersweet.

Madeline Star was wearing an eighties-inspired dress. She had a beauty mark on her cheek and a mop of curly orange hair. She smiled widely at the crowd. "Hey, everyone knows this guy!"

The crowd cheered and Harry hit the bass drum. Bob, Gene, and Chuck plucked the strings on their guitars.

Chuck knew the song and played like he had never taken a hiatus from the stage. His guitar pic came down deftly on the strings, and he moved his fingers along the neck, surprising those that had never seen him play before with his talent.

"Holy cow! Jed, when did Chuck learn how to play like that?" said Abby.

"He once told me briefly about being in a band when he was younger. They had started to record an album. I can't believe it either though, Abb. The guy never ceases to amaze me!"

Madeline started swaying to the song and Chuck couldn't help but wonder if Bob had coached her to mimic Shandi's style.

"Here we stand/ Worlds apart, hearts broken two, two, two/ Sleepless nights/ Losing ground, I am reaching for you, you, you, you/ No, no!" Madeline sang.

The hairs on the back of Chuck's neck stood as he was reminded of when Shandi sang the song.

Shalon watched. Chuck's guitar playing gave her chills. This was a part of his past that he had buried and subdued. How can I compete with it? Maybe I can't, she thought.

"Someday love will find you/ So we touched and went our separate ways... NO! NO!" Madeline continued as Harry smashed on the drums.

Shalon heard her cell phone ringing in her tiny white purse. She took it out and stepped backwards into a narrow, carpeted hallway to answer it. She didn't recognize the phone number as she flipped open the phone.

"Hello?" she answered.

"Yes, hello, is this Samantha Dixon?" said a male voice.

"Yes..."

"Miss Dixon, this is Detective Lindell. I am so sorry to bother you like this. I got your number from Jemel Landau. He works for you?"

She was certainly surprised to hear that name, since he had gone missing. "Well yes, he has worked on Chuck Barreto's ranch. Is everything OK? We haven't seen him in a few days now."

"He's not in a good way, ma'am. I know this is a strange request, but we're actually out in the parking lot of Vanished Valley. Are you inside there now?"

"Yes, I am. Why?"

"Is there any way you could come out here in the parking lot? We have Jemel in our custody and I just have to ask you a few quick questions."

"Mmmm, maybe I should go get Chuck. He's here too."

"No, no, that will not be necessary, ma'am. That would just put a damper on his day. Plus, ma'am, Jemel specifically said to ask for you. It won't take long, I promise you"

She thought about it for a moment. "Okay, I'll be out." She hung up the phone and started walking down the dimly-lit hallway thinking to herself, What kind of trouble could Jemel have gotten himself into?

She passed an elbow off the hallway that led to the men's and ladies' bathrooms. Ahead of her she saw a tall man dressed in a black suit. As the man got closer to her, he smiled. Before she could return the gesture, an enormous arm came up and wrapped around her neck.

Shalon's instincts took over and she reached behind with her left hand, grabbing the person's hair. She lurched forward, bending her knee slightly, and used the assailant's own weight against him by pivoting and flipping the individual right over her shoulders. The attacker hit the floor with a thud, and he grunted in pain and disbelief that such a small woman could take him down.

This man in the suit dashed forward to grab her. She surprised the hell out of him by jumping and kicking him in the sternum with her right leg. She moved with astounding agility in a dress. The man stumbled backwards and fell onto the ground.

Shalon had learned some self-defense from Chuck after the events of the last year, but she was raised tough by Vic and Chance, too.

She now knew that the phone call was a set up and turned to run back into the reception, but when she did, a large, bald man wearing dark-green overalls was right behind her. He grabbed the back of her head and covered her face with a cloth doused in an agent that caused unconsciousness.

Shalon passed out in Butch Gro's arms. As he held her up, he said to his embarrassed associates, "Come on, guys, get up and help me with her!"

Chuck and the band finished the song to resounding applause from the crowd, but Chuck was eager to get back to his conversation with Shalon, hoping to patch things up with her. He took the strap off to place the guitar back on the stand.

"Wow! How about another one, Chuck?" Madeline said into the microphone.

"Sorry guys, maybe another time," Chuck said, torn having been put on the spot. He shook Gene's hand and turned to Madeline. "You're fantastic. I am so happy for you and my old bandmates. You'll do well."

"I'll talk to you after," Bob smiled.

Chuck nodded and exited the stage. He had seen Samantha head off towards the bathrooms while he was performing. The band started up again.

"Tonight, I want to give it all to you/ In the darkness, there's so much I want to do/ And tonight, I want to lay at your feet/ Cause boy, I was made for you, and boy, you were made for me..."

Chuck looked around, thinking maybe the song they had played hit a little too close to home for Shalon. He walked toward the hallway where he had seen her last, but he was stopped many times in the short distance by people praising him for his performance.

Aunt Joanne, his cousin Dawn, and another aunt, Ellie, rushed up to him.

"Chuck, wow! Amazing!" said Aunt Joanne.

"Your mom told us you used to be in this band back in the day, too," said Dawn.

"Yeah, a long time ago, Dawn."

"Have you been practicing? Because you played like you owned the stage!" said Aunt Ellie.

"Ah, I don't know about that," said Chuck humbly. He felt a presence behind him and then someone touched his shoulder. He turned around to see two men wearing spiffy leisure suits and oversized cowboy hats. Vic and Chance.

"You're a pretty busy fella! You play guitar too, Mr. Chuck?" said Vic.

"Not really anymore, Mr. Teixeira," he said nervously.

"You can call me Vic, you know. For now anyway, young man."

Ellie, Joanne, and Dawn sensed some tension with the Texans.

"Nice to see you again, Vic and Chance. We'll talk to you later, Chuck," said Aunt Joanne.

Chuck kept a happy facade for his relatives and then turned back to Vic and Chance. Chance had his arms folded across his chest as he gave Chuck a stony look. Vic was less obvious.

"Now. It's nice to finally see ya in person because, ya know, we missed you at your funeral, and then your amazing resurrection, and then your annulment to my little girl. And then I find out my other little girl is working on your ranch and you two are together now! Wooooo-wee! Chuck, my boy," Vic said, still smiling.

What a tangled mess I'm in, Chuck thought to himself.

"Ah, Mr Teixeira…."

"Call me Vic, I said. Chuck, I darn well know that my girls are no angels, especially Kelly Ann, but what in all tarnation is going on out here? I think someone owes me one hell of an explanation." His raised voice was drawing the attention of people nearby.

Chuck calmly swallowed his pride. "Absolutely, Vic, you do. Why don't we go sit at one of the unoccupied tables and I will do my best to make sense of it all, sir."

Vic smiled. "Well, alright then. But, not without a drink first. And is my little Shalon here, son?"

"Yes sir, I think she went to use the bathroom."

"OK, do me a favor, Chuck. Go and fetch her and I'll get us all some drinks. Whatcha havin'? Still drinking them Jack and Cokes?"

"Yes sir. I mean, Vic."

"OK, me and Chance will meet ya at that table over yonder," said Vic pointing to a table in the far left corner.

Chance still looked pretty angry as Chuck acknowledged Vic and walked off to find Shalon.

Vic glanced at Chance as they watched him go. "Relax, partner. I get it. Good cop, bad cop. Let's give them the chance to explain."

Chuck reached the bathrooms and waited outside for a few minutes for Shalon to come out. Eventually a young lady came out that he did not know. She must have been someone from Lilly's side of the family.

"Excuse me, miss, is there anyone else in there?"

"I didn't see anyone. Would you like me to go back inside to check for you?

"That's alright. Thank you anyway."

The woman walked back to the party. Chuck waited another thirty seconds and then walked to the lobby to look outside. Shalon's Pontiac Sunfire was still in the parking lot right next to Stacey's car, but she certainly wasn't out there.

He yanked his cell phone out of the pocket of his tuxedo jacket and looked at the screen. One unread message.

Chuck flipped open the phone to read it. His eyes widened and his head began to spin. He walked over to the cement wall of the building and punched it.

"FUCK!" he yelled.

He reopened his phone and hit a programmed number.

Jed was at the bar getting a drink for Abby while she mingled with some of the other guests. Jed felt his phone ringing in his pocket, pulled it out, and saw that it was Chuck calling him. He politely excused himself and walked a few yards away.

"Hey bud, where are you? That was unbelievable guitar-playing," said Jed.

"Jed! Don't ask me any questions right now, but we have a fucking situation. Don't say anything to anyone. Just meet me out front at my car, right now. I'm parked in the second row."

"On my way," said Jed. He closed his phone and hustled across the room. Making direct eye contact with Abby, he held up his index finger indicating that he needed a minute.

Vic and Chance were waiting for Chuck to return with Samantha when Vic saw Jed head down the same hallway where Chuck had gone.

"Hey Chance, isn't that Chuck's pal? The attorney general who perpetrated the hoax of the fake funeral last year?" said Vic.

Chance looked. "Why, I believe so. Where do ya think he's off to in a hurry?"

"I don't rightly know, but I don't believe in coincidences."

"Me neither."

Jed was on the wide front steps looking for the blue Charger. He found Chuck standing by the driver's door in a frantic state. He must have found out about Silus's escape, he thought to himself. He hurried down the cement steps and across the parking lot over to Chuck. He saw that his friend was most definitely in a bad way. He held his cell phone in a hand with bloodied knuckles.

"What happened?" Jed asked, gesturing to his hand.

"Nevermind that!" said Chuck. He handed Jed his phone with the message pulled up on the screen. Jed squinted and read.

A picture showed Shalon with a black handkerchief tied across her mouth. Underneath the picture was a text message that read, Chuck, go to your car and wait for further instructions. Bring Jed Ferarri with you. DO NOT TELL ANYONE ELSE OR CALL THE POLICE, OR SHE IS DEAD!

Chuck's car was running and the driver's door was wide open. Jed handed the phone back.

"Listen buddy, try to calm down. We'll get her back."

"That's easier said than done! Could you be calm if you were me?" Chuck was so angry his chest heaved. He turned away from Jed, hunched over, grabbing the roof of his car.

"GODDAMMIT!" Chucked shouted. "THESE MOTHER-FUCKERS!"

Jed didn't know what to do. He was going to attempt to comfort him, but then the CB radio started sputtering static. Chuck stood at attention.

"Capricorn Chuck! Capricorn Chuck, come in!" said a voice.

Chuck knew the game. He lowered himself into the car and sat on the edge of the seat, reached over, and unclipped the receiver.

"This is Chuck, over!" he responded, gritting his teeth.

"Capricorn Chuck," the voice said. "This is Freebird, come in."

Chuck immediately knew who it was and couldn't believe it. Jed winced.

"Chuck–" Jed began.

Chuck cut him off. "Kobol."

"That's a big ten-four. There's no flies on you. Your mama raised no dummy."

"Chuck, let me talk to him," Jed said evenly.

Chuck shot him a look. "No! I got this, Jed."

"Chuck! Are you still with me?" Silus taunted.

"Oh yeah, I am Kobol. It's your move. What's next?" Chuck replied angrily.

"I'll tell you what's next, Capricorn Chuck. Is Ferrari with you like I asked?"

"He's with me, Kobol."

"Good boy, Chuck. Now both of you get in your magnificent car and meet me and your pretty little blondie at the entrance of your papa's land. You have 10 minutes max, and if I see or hear the police, Chuck, you will never see her again. We're in a white van. You can't miss us. Over and out!"

The radio went silent.

Chuck had no time to get into it with Jed about how Kobol escaped or to come up with a plan.

"You coming or what? We got 10 minutes. No time to think," Chuck called to Jed.

"Is that even a question? Of course I'm coming!"

Jed was now, more than ever, regretting his decision to attend the wedding instead of joining the search for Kobol. He ran around the nose of the car.

"No, no, you gotta get in on my side. The passenger door is broken!" said Chuck. He moved out of the way so Jed could slide across the leather bench seat to the passenger side.

Jed observed the big bungee cord holding the door shut from the inside and thought, Great, this is going to be a fun ride.

Chuck, full of anger and fury, took his suit jacket off and flung it over the seat. He sat and slammed the door, shifted into reverse, and pulled out of the parking spot. He hit the gas pedal. The rear tires spun and smoked as the Charger thrust forward like a rocket. Jed had never been in Chuck's Charger before, and if they weren't in the middle of an emergency, he'd be having the time of his life.

Jed couldn't hold on to the door for any kind of support because it was fairly unstable, so he held on tight to the roll bar over his head that Gus had installed when Chuck was a teenager. They sailed out onto the main road.

"You going all the way down Atkins Road?" asked Jed, alarmed.

"Yep, then cutting through on a couple of back roads I know. We'll make it in plenty of time."

CHAPTER 22

SHOUT AT THE DEVIL

MID-MAY 2003

VIC, CHANCE, RITA, and Abby left the hall to look for Chuck, Samantha, and Jed outside.

"Well, there's your daughter's car, Vic," said Rita, motioning to Shalon's vehicle.

"And Jed's car is here, too," said Abby.

"Me and Chance saw Chuck's parked over there when we came in," Vic said as he pointed to an empty spot. "But it ain't there no more."

Rita pursed her lips and took out her phone.

Chuck was flying down the road, zipping around cars that got in his way. Jed was trying to strategize when Chuck's phone rang. He pulled it out and handed it to Jed.

Jed looked at the caller ID. "It says 'the boss.'"

"Shit, don't answer it. That's my mother."

Jed's phone rang next. "Agh, it's Abby."

Chuck glanced at Jed as they came up quickly on a tractor trailer. "Don't answer that, Jethro! We're playing by Kobol's rules for now."

Jed wasn't going to argue, especially as he was too busy worrying about the ass end of the trailer they were about to crash into. At least when they were flying in the helicopter, he didn't have to worry about nearby vehicles.

Jed gripped the roll bar above his head even tighter. The nose of the car was only a few feet away now.

"Chuuuuuck!" Jed yelled.

His left hand on the top of the steering wheel, Chuck bore slightly left into the wrong lane to go around the truck. An oncoming vehicle began blaring the horn. Chuck veered onto the shoulder, spitting up dirt, and the car passed by with only a split hair between them. He pivoted back into the lane until they passed the truck's cab, and then he maneuvered back into the correct lane in front of it.

Jed's grip loosened slightly. He had a feeling he was in for a really rough evening.

The Woodrow Credit Union, only sixty yards from the bridge that went over the river into Wolford City, was to the right of the road and surrounded by woods. On the left side, a steep hill led down to the river running past it. Logan and his cronies pulled into the bank parking lot. He circled around until he found a spot where he was able to see the bridge clearly.

"Yeah, this will do nicely," he said to Butch as he backed into the spot. He took out a walkie talkie and did a bump of cocaine.

"Is that Helfer and Wilson over there, Mr. Logan?" Butch asked.

Logan sniffed. "Yep, we're just waiting to hear from Buddy."

Before he could finish his words, the walkie talkie sounded. "Cowboy! Are you there?"

Logan clicked the button on the side of the device. "I'm here, Buddy, and in position. How we lookin'?"

"We are looking good. They're on their way to us now. Do you have your scanner on?"

Logan looked at the scanner that was installed just below the glove box by Butch's knees. "I do. There have been no police alerted to your location, but don't take anything for granted, keep your eyes peeled and let me know when they get there."

"As soon as these mothers arrive, you will know!"

Logan switched the channel on the walkie and spoke into it again. "Matt, come in. Come in!"

Helfer and Wilson, disguised as corrections officers, were in Logan's sight at the bridge.

Helfer pulled out his walkie. "Matt here, Cowboy."

"Matt, we are in position. You boys can get out of there now and meet us down at the harbor. We'll take it from here."

"We might have a problem with that, Cowboy. There could be a local on his way here to assist us."

"Shit," Logan said to himself aloud. "This is unexpected." He spoke into the walkie. "OK, you guys stay put for now then. If anyone shows up, you know what has to be done."

* * *

Chuck and Jed crossed over the border into Woodrow, flying through a stop sign and banging a right onto Miller Street. Vehicles in the opposite lane passed by in a blur.

"Chuck, I'm sorry I didn't tell you about Kobol's escape. I only learned of it myself this morning during your brother's ceremony. I never thought things would go down like this," Jed said apologetically.

"This time, pal, believe it or not, it's my fault. I couldn't let it go and I went after him, but I should have thrown that asshole out of the helicopter when I had the chance. This is my damn fault, and this is the price Sam pays for being with a cursed guy like me."

Jed admired the humble side of his friend. "Hey, it's all going to turn out in our favor, Chuck. We'll get her back unharmed. It's what we do."

"Damn right, we will, and after we do, I'm going to let her go so this never happens again."

The double yellow lines streamed by as they continued down Miller Street. Chuck maintained control as he went around a bend, hugging the curb. They passed by a mobile home settlement called "The Hillside" and hit another sharp curve before the road straightened out again.

Chuck grew more anxious as they closed in on their destination. It was familiar to him; they passed Gus' auto shop. Directly across the street from it was Chester Farm that Stacey had worked at every day after school. At the end of the road was a four-way intersection, and Jed was curious if Chuck was even going to stop.

Chuck glanced quickly, and yes, there was another vehicle coming down East Street. He hit the gas and made it past in time. They whizzed by a pizza place and a country store called "Uncle Bob's" where Gus used to stop in his old tow truck to get lottery tickets and cigarettes. After that was finally the entrance to Gussy's Pitts.

Chuck and Jed saw the white van parked in the far corner of the entrance, its grill facing out toward the main road.

The rear windows of the van were tinted. Inside the van, one of the two men in the back looked out the window with binoculars. "Oh, fuck! Buddy, this guy is driving like he's Mario Andretti."

Buddy tapped the gas pedal and pulled out onto East Street. "OK, Silus, do your thing."

"If that's them, they're leaving," said Jed.

"I see that. I'm on them," replied Chuck as he sped up.

"Freebird to Capricorn Chuck. Is that you behind us?" Silus said through the CB.

Jed handed Chuck the receiver. "Where are you going?"

"To a more quiet, secluded place, Chuck. Someone wants to meet you very much."

"Who?"

"I think you know. Who were you asking about when you and your sidekick came to visit me at the prison?"

Jed and Chuck looked at one another. "Thorn."

"Chuck, there's no way. He's baiting us," said Jed.

"I'm aware, but as long as he's got Sam, I have no choice but to see this through."

"Buddy, he's right on our ass now," said Jarrett, one of the men in the back of the van.

"Give him some warning shots. That'll give them a hint," said the driver.

"Are you sure that's a good idea?" asked Silus.

"Shut the fuck up," said Buddy angrily. "This is my operation until we reach the city. You just do your part on the CB when I tell you!"

The back window of the van opened up slightly and a gun turret stuck out.

"Chuck, look out!" Jed yelled.

Bullets ricocheted off the hood of the Charger, one hitting the windshield in the upper right corner, causing a crack straight across. Jed ducked down as Chuck swerved into the oncoming lane and tapped the brake a little. He drove back into their own lane and the bullets stopped. Jed sat up and grabbed the gun strapped to his ankle. He was about to return fire when Chuck held out a hand to stop him.

"Jed, no! You could hit her!"

"I was going to try to hit a tire."

"She could still get hurt or killed!"

Jed brought his weapon back inside the vehicle and spoke into the CB receiver. "What the hell was that?"

"Attorney General?" Silus said. "Mr. Ferrari, tell your buddy not to drive so close to us, but do keep up."

"You could have just said that in the first place."

At this point, Chuck was preparing for battle. He pointed at the radio. "You mind?" he asked.

"Go for it," said Jed, knowing that music helped Chuck focus. He pressed the power button and music began playing as they reached another four-way intersection and took a sharp right onto Chapin Street.

"Sometimes I'm good for nothing/ Sometimes the best you've ever had/ Sometimes I need your lovin'/ Sometimes I stab you in the back/ I found meaning/ Just what I needed/ Cut on the bathroom wall."

Logan heard local dispatch announce that there was gunfire heard coming from East Street, just past the highway overpass. All cars in the area were to respond.

"Buddy! What the fuck is going on?" Logan said into the walkie. "Is that you assholes firing weapons?" There was no answer. "Buddy, did you hear me?"

"Yes sir, it's all under control now. That dumbass rancher was following us way too close so we had to give him a warning, that's all. We're all good now. He's following us at an acceptable distance," said Buddy.

"Well, fucknuts, the local PD just dispatched police in that direction. You guys better not start any shit."

"We won't. A few cruisers with their lights on just went past us. We'll be at your location shortly, Cowboy."

"OK. No more shooting unless I say so."

Buddy agreed and Logan let go of the walkie.

"Goddamn idiots," he muttered to himself. He changed the channel on the walkie and pressed the key again. "Matt, are you guys all set? Get out of there and meet us at the rendezvous. All the local police have been dispatched to another part of town."

"See you soon, Cowboy," Matt responded. Logan put his walkie on top of the dashboard and stared out the window, frustrated.

Dave and Mitch were feeding Rupert in the house at the ranch when they heard the "shots fired" announcement come through the scanner.

"Dave, you hear that? You rarely hear stuff like that in this town."

"Yeah, unless Jed and Chuck are getting into trouble," said Dave dryly.

"Well, they're both at a wedding today, so it can't be them."

The Charger drove by the town hall, the entrance to the highway department, and Woodrow High School while music still played through the speakers. "Midnight reflection/ Craving attention/ Under the disco ball/ Night crawling, sky falling/ Gotta listen when the devil's calling."

After another quarter mile, they reached yet another four-way intersection where the fire station was located. The van cruised through with Jed and Chuck following behind. Jed was thinking hard, trying to figure out where they were headed, while Chuck just focused on the music.

"Can't shake it, I'll taste it/ When it's yelling out my name, I chase it/ Come on, come on/ Night crawling."

Continuing down Chapin Street, they passed the retirement community and the cemetery where Chuck had been falsely buried last year. They ultimately reached – yes – another four-way intersection controlled by stop signs only. The van, without using its blinker, took a left onto Reynolds Street. Chuck whipped the Charger to the left, barely looking the other way to see if a car was coming. Jed held on tight.

"Sometimes my thoughts are violent/ Sometimes they bring me to the light/ Sometimes I sit in silence/ Sometimes I'm running for my life/ I found a meaning."

Jed felt the need to call someone. Abby had left several messages of concern, but he knew Chuck would freak out if he tried to answer. Recalling the trap that was set for them last year with the bomb inside the vehicle at the Holiday Inn, his instinct was telling him that this was more of the same and he needed to remain vigilant. A hippo would never paint stripes on itself to try and be a zebra.

The Charger passed a shopping plaza, a middle school, and another big condominium complex. Then they went through another underpass and by a bar until they reached the end of the road. At that point there were only two ways to go: left or right.

"Night crawling, sky falling/ Gotta listen when the Devil's calling/ Can't shake it, I'll taste it/ When it's yelling out my name, I chase it."

The van took another unindicated, sudden left. Chuck followed. Jed sucked in a breath; thankfully the cars coming towards them were far enough away so as not to collide.

The road they were on was only a quarter-mile long, and if they took a left, they'd be going back where they came from, essentially.

If they bore right, they would be headed to Wolford City. Jed held a breath, anticipating which direction the van would go.

The van took a right.

"Chuck, they're headed to the bridge!"

The word 'bridge' reverberated in Chuck's mind.

He saw a blinding white flash before his eyes, just like the time the chiropractor first cracked his neck. Instead of the music that had been playing inside the Charger, he heard something else familiar. It was a Credence song that had played in the waiting room of the doctor's office.

"Whoa, though it was a nightmare/ Lord it was so true/ They told me don't go walking slow/ The devil's on the loose/ Better run through the jungle…"

Chuck looked down at his clothes, which had turned white. He was no longer driving in his car with Jed. Instead, he was walking through that familiar white cloud tunnel he had seen so many times in the past. It compelled him, for some unknown reason, to walk forward. His insatiable curiosity caused him to abide.

The walk was not far this time. He saw a white room at the end. In an operating room, female medical professionals surrounded a table with a patient lying on top. The patient was hooked up to tubes and unconscious, ready for some type of operation. Chuck moved closer to the beautiful women and tapped one of them on the shoulder.

"Yes?" answered an attractive Asian woman.

"What's going on? What happened?"

"He's an officer in a prison. An inmate assaulted him and he has a serious hernia."

"Oh, okay, thanks."

He looked more closely at the patient and saw that he was looking at himself. Chuck was envisioning his own operation, when he had dreamed of his father. Gus had told him to look out for the bridge.

It startled Chuck when a middle-aged surgeon tapped his shoulder. She pulled down her mask to speak more clearly. She looks a lot like the actress Nichelle Nichols, Chuck thought to himself.

"Excuse me, young man. What ails you?" she asked.

Chuck was baffled. "I'm sorry, ma'am?"

"You look thirsty, if you don't mind me saying so. Would you like a drink?"

He hadn't realized how parched he was. "Yes, please."

She turned and reached for something on the shiny, silver surgical table where her tools waited. Her fingers wrapped around a small, tarnished gold goblet and lifted it off the table.

"Here. Drink, young man," she said, lifting it up to him.

He didn't hesitate. He took it out of her hands carefully. It had an assortment of colorful stones embedded in it. "Thank you so much, ma'am."

The doctor smiled at him and he took a refreshing gulp. When he pulled the cup away from his face, the operating room and surgical staff had disappeared. He was now sitting on a bar stool in his old house. Someone on his left nudged him sharply with an elbow.

"Hey! Stop your grinnin' and drop your linen, bro! You watching the movie or what?"

Mike Geller sat next to him wearing white and drinking a beer with Mitch.

"Why are you guys dressed in white?"

Mitch chuckled. "What are you talking about, Rockstar? Look at yourself, with your white dress pants, shirt, and shoes."

"Yeah, I can't figure that one either, Mitchell."

Mike nudged Chuck again. "Check it out- our favorite scene is coming up."

They turned their attention to the television. Playing was the movie, A Bridge too Far. The character in the scene was Brigadier General Gavin, played by the actor Ryan O'Neal.

"What's the best way to take a bridge?" he asked Robert Redford's character.

"Both ends at once!"

"I'm sending two companies across the river. I need a man with very special qualities to lead."

Mike and Mitch laughed out loud at the line.

"I know just the man!" said Mike.

"Who, Mike?"

"Sergeant Gill Selleck!"

Chuck was confused and looked at Mike. "What?"

He heard familiar sounds coming from behind him: keyboard notes being played and a soft humming. My Lord, he thought. It was Shandi, working on the song he had given to Bob at the wedding. The very same song that put a roadblock between him and Samantha.

Mike saw the look on Chuck's face. "Go on, get out of here! You're no use to us. Go on and see her."

Chuck blushed. "Thanks, guys."

He got off his stool and walked over to the door that led into the basement studio. Shandi was sitting at her keyboard looking at her sheet music, playing and humming along. She was stunning as ever and dressed in white like everyone else, tapping her foot along with the song. Chuck could go on watching her forever, but she looked up, sensing someone else in the room. Her face brightened upon seeing Chuck.

"Hey there, sweetheart! I didn't hear you come in."

"I was just listening. Didn't want to interrupt your song," said Chuck, smiling sadly.

Shandi got up from behind the keyboard and strolled over to him. "What's wrong, Chucky, my love? You don't look quite like yourself today."

He hesitated to answer. "Ahh, this is really hard to say, Shandi."

She held his face in her hands. He had forgotten the softness of her touch. It was so wonderful, which made it even harder for him.

"We always tell each other everything, you and I. No matter what. It'll always be OK between us," she said.

Chuck felt a little relieved by her response. "Shandi, this is probably the toughest thing I've ever had to tell you."

"It's OK, babe," she reassured him.

"I think maybe I'm falling for someone else."

She leaned in gently and brought her lips to his ear. "Chuck if you ever want to see Samantha again, you better not try to go over that bridge!"

Another light flashed and Chuck heard the music playing in the Charger again.

"Just what I needed/ Cut on the bathroom wall/ Midnight reflection/ Craving attention/ Under the disco ball."

Chuck startled when he felt Jed's hand shaking his right shoulder. "Chuck, did you hear me? The van is headed over the bridge into the city."

The episode he just had, oddly enough, only lasted a moment in time and he was about to take a right turn to follow the van. He suddenly realized that in every other dream-like experience he had like that, someone had warned him about a bridge.

Right before the stop sign, there was a steep, grassy knoll that ended in a dried-up gully just off to the right of the road.

"I heard ya, Jethro!" Chuck said as he veered the Charger off into the grass and slammed on the brakes. The tires screeched and the car stopped so that it was leaning at a steep angle.

Jed couldn't believe Chuck was giving up the pursuit, but before he could question what was happening, Chuck took hold of the hook that was attached to the bungee cord rigged to the dashboard and the passenger door came loose. He swung his legs up and pushed Jed in the chest with his feet. The passenger door catapulted open as Chuck's strength was assisted by gravity, and Jed went barreling out of the Charger and rolled down the hill.

Chuck snatched the end of the loose bungee cord and pulled with all his might until the door closed again. He snapped the hook back into place to keep the door shut.

Jed brushed himself off and started running up the hill. "Chuck! What the hell? Are you crazy?!"

Chuck hit the gas pedal. At first, the Charger had some difficulty taking off at a slant, but the blue beast eventually made it back onto the road.

"I'm sorry!" Chuck yelled out the window. "We live together, we die alone, brother!"

Jed reached the top of the hill and watched in frustration as Chuck turned right.

"Chuck! Darnit, have you lost your mind?" Jed shouted. But it was too late.

Jed ran into the middle of the road, waving his arms frantically, trying to flag down the next vehicle. Three vehicles drove around him before a teenager driving an old Toyota Tacoma pulled up alongside him with his window rolled down. Jed's hair was drenched in sweat and he was gasping for air as he engaged the boy.

"I'm the Attorney General, law enforcement," he panted and showed the kid his badge. "I need a ride. It's an emergency!"

"Shit," said the kid. "Yeah, get in, dude."

Jed jumped into the passenger seat and slammed the door shut. "Thanks, kid. Can you head for the bridge going into the city?"

"Yes sir! Where are we headed after that?"

"I'm not sure yet. I'll let you know in a minute."

As they drove, Jed took out his cell phone and tried calling Chuck, but it rang until it went to voicemail. Jed shook his head. "Great Caesar's ghost!"

The kid looked at him curiously. Jed called Abby and told her to call in the cavalry.

Chuck had to make up some speed. After passing a few vehicles, he was catching up to the white van. His CB clicked and he turned down the music to hear it better.

"There you are. We thought we lost you," said Silus.

Chuck took a hold of the mic. "Not a chance. Listen to me, Kobol. I'll meet you anywhere and do anything you ask, but I'm not going over that bridge." There was silence on the other end. "Kobol, did you hear me? Do not go over the bridge."

"You're a funny guy! You know that, Capricorn Chuck?" Silus said loudly.

The vehicles passed the Woodrow Credit Union at high speed.

"Silus, for fuck's sake! It's a setup, a trap!" yelled Chuck.

"Well then," Silus replied, laughing. "See you on the other side."

Buddy changed channels and grabbed hold of the mic. "Cowboy, we're passing you now. Chuck and the AG are right behind us."

The vehicles ascended the loop that led up onto the bridge. Across from it was the old Woodrow Memorial Library and an open park with cobblestone sidewalks, picnic tables, and a large, white gazebo in the middle. People were out and about, walking their dogs and relaxing on what was –for them– an ordinary day.

"Copy that. We see you," Logan said to Buddy, smiling. He switched channels. "Gill, are you ready?"

"Give the word," Gill responded.

The white van hit the ramp of the bridge with Chuck's Charger hard on its heels. He steered the car into the far right lane and sped up alongside the van. At this point, there was nothing to lose.

Chuck looked over to his left and saw Silus looking back at him from the passenger's seat. He smiled and took off his sunglasses to make direct eye contact with Chuck.

"Silus, don't be a fool," Chuck shouted into the receiver, "Or we'll all be shouting at the devil tonight!"

A strange transmission came through the CB speaker.

"And I heard, as it were, the noise of thunder! One of the four beasts saying, 'come and see'. And I saw, behold, a white horse!"

Both Chuck and Silus were perplexed, but then Silus finally believed what Chuck was saying. He realized that his boss had set him up.

"Mr. Thorn, I am the huckleberry?" Silus asked into the mic. He looked at Buddy and yelled, "Get off the bridge! Turn around!"

"Get fucked, Kobol, it's too late for that. Relax, will ya?"

Logan sat calmly in the Hummer and waited. He turned his head towards the rear seat. Shalon Dixon was sitting between the two henchmen in black suits. She had a handkerchief tied around her mouth.

"Say goodbye to your boyfriend!" he said coldly. He keyed the button on his walkie. "Gill, release the kraken."

Tears streamed down Samantha's face and she kicked her feet, desperately trying to get out of the ropes that were tied around her ankles, but the two men held her back tight against the seat.

Gill and his men were down below on the river sitting in their black and white Intrepid 407 boat. Some men were half dressed in diving suits, though Gill did not know why. He sat on the stern, looking at the bridge from a distance.

"Here it comes," Gill said into the walkie.

Gill had attached a silver metal box with an antenna to each of the four enormous cement columns that supported the bridge. At the bottom, just below the waterline, a ferocious set of explosions sounded. It echoed for miles, shaking structures in surrounding towns, including buildings in the city. As the bridge was about to crumble, it made a noise that sounded like a dinosaur had a stomach ache.

People enjoying the day in their sailboats were in awe and shock and pointed to the bridge. Those that were going about their day in the park stopped doing what they were doing. The young kid driving Jed came flying around the corner to the scene. He was so excited to be assisting in what he perceived was a crime that he hadn't noticed the bridge was out.

"Stop…stop!" Jed yelled.

The kid realized the infrastructure was crumbling and slammed on the brake until it hit the floor. The truck zigzagged all over the road, tires squealing. The rear churned up smoke, and then the vehicle finally came to a stop.

The kid took his Red Sox cap off a wild head of hair. "That was mad dope!"

Jed could not argue with that assessment. He, too, was in disbelief. "Chuck…how did you know?" he whispered to himself.

Pieces of the bridge crumbled and dropped into the rapidly flowing river. The nose of the white van pitched forward. The henchmen in the back dropped their weapons and rolled into the metal grate behind the front seats.

Silus knew their fate was sealed. It would only be moments until he and his companions would meet their watery demise. The look on Buddy's face was one of regret for not having heeded Silus' belated warning. The force of the fall threw Silus out of his seat; his face smashed into the windshield. His odd rabbit-like eyes appeared to pop out of his skull.

He opened his mouth wide, and screamed.

The Charger looked like a sparkling blue bullet as it dove toward the river alongside the other vehicles that had been on the bridge. For the first time in his life, Chuck grabbed the seatbelt strap from behind him, pulled it over his chest, and clicked the buckle securely, preparing for the ride of his life.

I failed to save Shandi and now, Samantha. I got this coming to me. "I'm sorry Sam!" he said aloud. He turned up the radio.

"Night crawling, sky falling/ Gotta listen when the Devil's calling/ Can't shake it, I'll taste it/ When it's yelling out my name, I chase it."

The nose of the Charger pierced the surface of the dark river.

In the SkyTower, Elliot Birch was hard at work drowning his sorrows in a crystal glass of bourbon and swallowing it down like a Viking. His long hair was in disarray, and he wore no suit jacket or necktie. His dress shirt was untucked and some of the buttons were undone. Kelly Ann was sitting across from him. She had come in only moments ago and was trying to engage in a conversation with him about their old age community project when the entire building shook like an earthquake was in progress.

Kelly jumped up out of her chair and looked out the window at the city below. "What in tarnation…"

Elliot, curiosity piqued, stood and joined her. He put his arm around her as they watched the spectacle in awe.

Mr. Thorn watched the scene, elated. He had a small table set up on the glorious wrap around porch at his Longmeadow home overlooking the bank of the river, laden with crackers, cheese, vintage wine, and an old CB radio.

"Operation Kawaii, success," he smiled to himself. "Mr. Logan, you are the man!" He turned to his bodyguards and gestured to the table. "Boys, would you like some? It's delicious!"

They declined, and Thorn told them to prepare the car to bring him down to the harbor.

Mitch and Dave were listening to calls about the bridge come in over the scanner.

Mike walked into the house. "Hey, you two! How long does it take to feed a little dog?"

"Mike, the bridge down in the center of town going into Wolford City just collapsed. There were some major explosions."

"OK, alls you had to do is ask for the day off, Mitch."

"No, Mike. It's true, he's not kidding!"

"Well, shit. I'll call Candie and Amy on the walkie and have them hold down the fort here. C'mon guys, we'll go down there in my car."

Ten hours later, barricades had been set up around the Woodrow Library and the park. A crowd of people stood behind them. Some of the people behind the barricades were family members of those that had not returned home after the catastrophe. The flashing lights from the helicopters, news crews, and search lights rendered them seemingly oblivious of the late hour. The police, paramedics, and rescue boats were scattered about, trying to find survivors. Nobody in the sleepy town had imagined something so horrific could happen in their humble orbit.

Mike, Mitch, and Dave were somewhere down at the river helping with the search for survivors, including their comrade. Vic and
Chance had also joined the efforts. Vic was a mess thinking about
the loss of Shalon. Jack Bufford had called Jed and told him he would
come to Woodrow within the week to assist him in the investigation
into the crime.

After the incident had occurred, Jed had to explain to Chuck's
family and friends what happened. Rita was somewhere inside the
park barracks making phone calls. Gary and Lilly's honeymoon was
on hold; she looked none the happier about it. Stacey, Uncle Richard,
and Uncle Armond were inside the library helping to coordinate information for family members of others who had been on the bridge.

One of the command centers was set up across from where the
bridge used to be. Jed, who was not a patient man, was waiting there
to hear word of Chuck.

Detective Giovanni was out on one of the boats when a significant
discovery was made. He said over the radio, "They found the white
van, Mr. Ferrari."

"Did you find the girl?" Jed asked, knowing that if he did, the
outcome would not be a positive one.

"There were no females inside, only four males. The van was
crushed like a beer can. Mr. Ferrari, are you sure she was in that van?"

"I thought so, but I'm not sure, Vince. What about Kobol?"

"I'm sending you a pic now. You tell me. Just please delete it after
you see it."

Jed's phone pinged and he opened up the message to see a mangled
face on his device. He looked closer. Even with the disfigurement of
the dead man, there was absolutely no denying it.

"That's him. Tell your men."

"Yes, sir. There are a lot of casualties. It's awful."

Jed felt like the detective was avoiding his most anticipated question. "What about the Charger, Vince? Has it been found?"

Vince hesitated. "Yeah…they found the car. It was also mangled pretty badly, but it had a roll cage inside, like a stock racecar."

"Vince, did you get Chuck Barreto out of the car?"

There was another pause. "Uh…no, Mr. Ferrari."

"Why? Why not?"

"Well, he wasn't in the car. He must've jumped out or the current dragged him down river somewhere."

Jed's head was pounding. "OK, Vince. Keep me posted. I'm not going anywhere."

Jed put the radio into the holder attached to his belt and told the officers next to him he'd be back shortly.

Feeling defeated, he trudged across the street to the spot where the bridge had broken off from the road. Abby was talking to one of the officers watching the area, but she excused herself when she saw him. He relayed what he had learned, and if they were not in the midst of tragedy, it would appear a romantic moment under the stars. Abby didn't know how to console him, so she took his hand into hers and held it tenderly as they looked out over the river.

"C'mon, Chuck, don't do this to us again," Jed said aloud, but to himself. A song popped into his head.

"Voices, a thousand, thousand voices/ Whispering, the time has passed for choices/ Golden days are passing over, yeah/ I can't seem to see you/ Although my eyes are open wide/ But I know I'll see you once more/ When I see you, I'll see you on the other side/ Yes, I'll see you, I'll see you on the other side."

EPILOGUE

THREE WEEKS HAD passed since the bridge collapsed. There were no survivors. The search continued for the missing, but there had been no sign of Chuck or Samantha.

Rita, Kelly, Vic, and Chance stood by a grave in Woodrow Cemetery. Kelly looked ravishing in black, her long red hair tied neatly into a bun. They stood with heavy hearts by the Barreto family plot. They had been standing silently for a while now. The new stone read, SHALON DIXON, June 7th 1973 - May 30th 2003. An enormous heart of gold, a timeless beauty.

Vic stood next to Rita stoically. "Thank you, Rita, for letting us have this plot for my little girl. There'll be another down in Texas when we eventually return, but I just needed this done. Thank you, ma'am."

Rita put a hand on his shoulder. "That's not necessary, Vic. She was very special to all of us, especially my son."

Kelly shot Rita a look that thankfully she did not see.

"Thank you for saying that. I know this is none of my business, and if I'm out of line... But what about putting your son to rest?"

Rita surprisingly gave him a warm smile. "We tried that once before, Vic. If I know my Chucky – and I do – he's out there somewhere right now." Rita couldn't imagine her son would have let anything happen to Shalon, either, but she wasn't going to share that at the moment.

Vic returned a pat on Rita's shoulder.

You're dreaming, Rita, Kelly thought to herself.

"So, what happens now? You're not returning to Texas?" Rita asked Vic.

Vic looked at Chance. "No. Now, Rita, we go to war. I want to know everything about this LoneStar Group. Who took over for them with the casino in Wolford City? And why would this Kobol who kidnapped Kelly be on that bridge when it exploded?"

Kelly interjected. "Daddy, LoneStar has been bought, and the new shareholders hired The Birch Group. His name is Elliot. He's an honest man. He wouldn't be involved in anything like that, and he doesn't care about going into Gussy's Pitts for any kind of development."

Rita glanced skeptically at Kelly. "Vic, our attorney has been doing a great job to prevent the governor from getting his mitts on my children's land, but now that the main bridge is completely gone, I'm not so sure how long she can fight them off in court."

Vic stared hard at Rita. "Ladies, could I have a moment alone with Chance? I'll meet y'all back at the car momentarily."

"Certainly," said Rita.

"Yes, Daddy," said Kelly.

As the two women started walking back to the vehicle, Rita surprisingly put her arm around Kelly.

"Call Stitch," Vic said to Chance. "Let him know he's going to be running things down there for a while."

"Can do, Vic. Anything else?"

"Yes. I want all our best attorneys flown into Wolford ASAP. We're going to flush these fuckers out. No one's getting into Gussy's Pitts. And lastly, Chance, I want you to find out everything about this Elliot Birch character. Everything."

A boat named The Swift, the size of a small house, had been designed by a team of three: a naval architect, an exterior designer, and an interior designer. It had the capacity for ten guests and seven crew members. The suave vessel was currently docked in National Harbor, just outside of Maryland. Security vigilantly walked the upper deck. Inside, there was a luxurious wrap-around bar across from a fireplace and plush couches.

Mr. Thorn looked spiffy as usual, sitting at the middle of the bar on a cushy, white swivel chair having a drink. To the left of him was a doctor employed by the organization, Doctor Brunnel. He was frail-looking– beyond retirement age – with thinning grays. He had lost his license for being under the influence during an unsuccessful operation, and Thorn's recruiter had scooped him up. On the other side sat Matt Helfer and Mr. Logan. They were engaged in a conversation about an interesting dilemma involving the onboard doctor.

"You sure, Doc, about a drink?" asked Thorn.

"No, Mr. Thorn. I'm fine for now."

"So then, tell me about our guest today. How is he?"

"Do you mind?" the doctor asked as he pulled out a pack of cigarettes from his worn, white coat.

"No, not at all."

The doctor's hands were shaking as he lit his cigarette. He took a puff. "Well, he's coming-to. He was in and out of it last night. He's a remarkable healer, but… it seems the diagnosis I gave you earlier is still status quo."

Thorn sipped his drink. "Status quo? Will he remain this way? Will the damage be permanent, Doctor?"

Matt and Logan listened intently.

"There's no telling, Mr Thorn. There were a significant number of contusions. I don't have enough advanced medical equipment here to really be sure, but what I did find is that he likely had damage earlier on in his life that contributed to the severity of his current injuries."

They all looked at each other and Thorn grit his teeth. "So, if you were a betting man Doc…what would you say his odds are?"

He puffed more deeply on the cigarette and blew out the smoke. "Well…while it's possible he makes a recovery, I would bet that he will not. I think it's a permanent diagnosis."

Matt interjected. "Mr. Thorn, why chance it? Let's just off them now, be done with them!"

The boss smiled. "Mmmm no, Mr. Helfer. I like to play with things like this for a while," he chuckled and looked at Logan. "If the Doc is wrong, you know what to do."

Logan nodded. "Yes, sir."

"Where's the girl right now, Mr. Logan?"

"She's up on the deck with security."

"Bring her down, please, Mr. Logan, and then we will go and visit our patient with the doctor. You wait here, Matt."

A nurse in her early thirties was tending to the unconscious patient in the bed of a cabin on the boat. An IV was hooked up to the patient's right arm and a thick beige bandage was wrapped around his head, partially covering his eyes. She sat in a chair next to him reading a book while he rested. There was a knock on the cabin door and then it opened slowly. The doctor entered and she put the book down and greeted him. He walked further into the room, and a young lady, Thorn, and Logan followed.

The young lady was dressed in comfortable cream-colored slacks and an oversized navy blue shirt. She looked scared and confused.

"Did you take him off the drip?" Doctor Brunnel asked the nurse.

"Yes, doctor. He's just waking up now."

"Good, good."

Doctor Brunnel leaned over the patient. "Young man, can you hear me?"

The patient was groggy, but rested. "I…I can hear you, but I can't see." He picked up his arm and felt the cloth covering his eyes.

"We're going to remove your bandage now," said the doctor.

Thorn looked at Logan, and Logan reached for the Glock on his hip. He pulled the gun out and took the safety off.

"Nurse Martin, if you please."

The nurse turned to the patient. "Just stay still." She gently un-raveled the bandage, one hand under his head lifting it slightly off the pillow.

The patient's head was throbbing and his vision was blurred. All he could make out was the vague shapes of the people around his bed.

The doctor leaned over him with a small penlight, flashing it in his eyes, which seemed to only aggravate his visibility issue. The patient groaned and shut his eyes.

"Sorry about that." Doctor Brunnel shut the light off.

The people around the bed gained definition.

"How about now?" Brunnel asked the patient.

"Yeah, yeah, it's getting better. Where am I? And who are you all?"

Doctor Brunnel turned his head and looked at Mr. Thorn. Thorn moved closer to the bed.

"My name is Thorn. You work for me and you were in a terrible accident. Do you remember any of this, son?"

The patient looked around for a moment. "Nope, I don't have a clue who you are."

Thorn turned around and gestured to the young lady to come closer. Her eyes were watery. Thorn smiled. "Do you know this pretty lady?"

The patient looked carefully at her beautiful long brown hair and sad blue eyes. He felt comforted by her presence but couldn't put a finger on why. "Mmmm...no. Sorry ma'am, who are you?"

Thorn nodded for her to respond. You could hear the hoarseness in her voice. "Um...My name is Shandi, Shandi Dunn."

The patient smiled at her. "Well, it's nice to meet you, Shandi. Do I know you?"

Thorn interrupted. "You're good friends, son, and you both work for our organization."

"I'm sorry, I don't remember any of you. What is it that I do for work?"

"Various things...we'll get to that. We hoped that Shandi here would jog your memory, but we'll take it slow. You've been through quite the ordeal. Mr. Logan will get you reacquainted with your life again." Thorn looked at the doctor.

"Do you remember anything at all about your life?" the doctor asked.

The young man looked around intensely. "Sure, I do remember one thing."

"You do?" the doctor glanced nervously at Thorn. "What's that?"

"I remember my name!"

"What's your name? Who are you?"

Logan tightened the grip on his gun.

"M-m-my name is…Steve Burnett."

Shalon Dixon, now Shandi Dunn, was stunned by his answer.

Thorn smiled at Logan. "Yes, son. That is your name. Well done."

ABOUT THE AUTHOR

Born 1967, in the sleepy little town of Ludlow Massachusetts and now having completed my second novel. Yes this is the sequel to Capricorn Chuck's cruel world. Still not retired from the department of corrections yet, but I think we're getting there soon. The third book to Capricorn Chuck's world of pain should be out within the year, stay tuned! I love writing about all these intriguing and interesting characters. I hope all will enjoy the stories and relationships in them. Have a great read and thank you to everyone for following Chuck's world.

ACKNOWLEDGEMENTS

Thank you to Palmetto publishing (Kristin, Nicole, and the Palmetto Team), as usual a stupendous job in helping bring Chuck's world to the readers in a very classy, sexy way.

I would like to thank my interior artist Deb Nicholson, who worked on some last minute illustrations for me at an accelerated pace to get them done me. She was fantastic to work with and I am hoping to have her back for the next book and who knows…maybe other ideas and projects I have rolling around in my head. She did an exceptional job in this last hour on capturing my characters, structures and events in the final chapter of this book.

Briana Buffone: My editor and chief who keeps my words real and where they need to be! I feel like Mark Twain working with her, LOL! Without her I would not have learned all that I have so far and she has worked extremely hard on these two novels for me. I am truly grateful to her patience, generosity and professionalism. I can't thank you enough for believing in this!

To my mom and dad that taught me self-reliance, how to love, fight, work, and be kind to those that are to you in life. They gave me great insight on what life can be if you want it. They were the original Bonnie and Clyde!

I am lucky to know Paulo and Bill from Family Chiropractor in Wilbraham and Ludlow, who keep my back straight, helping me get right with the world! And what would my weekly or more visits be without a little Creedence, Rock on fella's!

My two siblings that I love very much, Gary my little brother who we both talk about life everyday. My sister a guardian angel! I was sitting in a diner a lifetime ago and it was late at night, snowing everywhere and I was drinking some coffee not knowing where my life was headed as I looked out into the cold night. I felt something, turned my head and looked up and saw my little sister Stacey with a heartfelt smile looking down at me.

All my love to Jess, Paige, Candie, Aub and Neco!

Thank You to Linda Chapman-Collette, one of my biggest supporters and promoters on this new endeavor of mine.

Always grateful to all my partners over the decades in the department, Arty, Mack, Scott, Jack, Emma, Dennis, Laury, Mike L, Chap, Dave, Richard, Paul, B Wood, Matty,Gus, Jake, Mikey G, Mitch,Joe, Jamie, Craig, Tod, Harlan , etc…On and on all my brother and sister officers who have had my back for over 25 years now.

And of course, finally to my partner in crime who's worked hard over the decades to keep me honest Mr. Teddy Beriau, we are back in action my friend and the adventure continues!

Follow Author Steve Pendelton on:

Facebook-Steve Sevivas
Twitter-chuckheston007
Twitter-@stevesevivas
Tiktok-@omegaman027
Instagramomegaman006
Truth social-Chuck Barreto@Chuckheston007
You Tube-steve sevivas@TheSteve141
Amazon-Amazon.com/author/capricornchuck
Email-st3v3007@hotmail.com

STAY TUNED….CAPRICORN CHUCK WILL RETURN IN:

THE TWO WORLDS'S OF CAPRICORN CHUCK!

Printed in the USA
CPSIA information can be obtained
at www.ICGtesting.com
CBHW071140240624
10562CB00009B/864